ESCAPE FROM OTHERWORLD ISLAND

Escape from OtherWorld Island

The Adventures of Rae & Danae

SAGE ROOKER

Tree-Lion Press

Tree-Lion Press
Purveyors of Particularly Audacious Ideas

This is a work of fiction. Names, places, characters and incidents
are products of the author's imagination or are used fictitiously
and are not to be construed as real. Any resemblance to actual
events, locales, organizations or persons, living or dead,
is entirely coincidental.

Cover art and design by Kiply Travis

Library of Congress Control Number: 2024915072

ISBN (paperback): 979-8-9886993-0-9
ISBN (e-book):   979-8-9886993-1-6
ISBN (hardback library edition): 979-8-9886993-2-3

For the real Team Rugged Stuff sisters
and all of their real cousins.
And, as always, for IAK.

Contents

Dedication v

DANAE'S LOG: PROLOGUE (MISPLACED PAGES)

1   DANAE'S LOG 1: Hello Everybody, My Name's Danae, What's Yours? 6

2   DANAE'S LOG 2: Trapped in Paradise 19

3   NOAH & LEVI'S JOURNAL 1: "Into the Adventure!" 32

4   DANAE'S LOG 3: New Discoveries 42

5   DANAE'S LOG 4: Food for Thought 56

6   NOAH AND LEVI'S JOURNAL 2: "Into the Tunnel!" 67

7   DANAE'S LOG 5: Challenges and Opportunities 72

8   DANAE'S LOG 6: Something Shocking 78

9   NOAH AND LEVI'S JOURNAL 3: "Into the Bowels of the Research Facility!" 96

10   DANAE'S LOG 7: Back to the Beach 108

11   DANAE'S LOG 8: Home Again and Home Again 116

12   DANAE'S LOG 9: Another Day, Another Trap 124

13 DANAE'S LOG 10: Busting Out   134

14 NOAH AND LEVI'S JOURNAL 4: "Into the Ops Center!"   143

15 DANAE'S LOG 11: Colin Null Goes Too Far   146

16 DANAE'S LOG INTERLUDE 1: Nessa Null Profile   151

17 NOAH AND LEVI'S JOURNAL 5: "Into NYC!"   155

18 DANAE'S LOG 12: Tea with Nessa   161

19 DANAE'S LOG INTERLUDE 2: Nessa Null Transcription   167

20 DANAE'S LOG 13: Colin's Plan, Revealed   172

21 DANAE'S LOG 14: War Council   183

22 DANAE'S LOG 15: Under the Null Corp Building   202

23 NOAH AND LEVI'S JOURNAL 6: "Into New Jersey!"   208

24 DANAE'S LOG 16: Behind Enemy Lines   230

25 DANAE'S LOG 17: Onward and Upward   240

26 DANAE'S LOG 18: Friends and Enemies   249

27 DANAE'S LOG 19: Looks Like It's Time for Plan D   261

28 DANAE'S LOG 20: Lights, Camera, Action!   271

29 DANAE'S LOG 21: Just Us, and Justice   287

30 DANAE'S LOG 22: Cut it, Print it, That's a Wrap!   294

Acknowledgements   307
About The Author   309

DANAE'S LOG:
Prologue
(Misplaced Pages)

BOOM!

I looked toward the huge explosion up near the peak of the volcano. Red-hot lava was pouring over the lip of the crater. It was flowing down the face of the mountainside with the speed of a proverbial freight train. And not just any proverbial freight train but a proverbial freight train made of deadly magma and consuming anything unlucky enough to get caught in its path!

"Oh, dagnabbit," I muttered under my breath. Okay, maybe that's not exactly what I said, but hey, I'm trying to keep my memoirs G-rated here. Let's just agree that what I said wasn't very nice. Then I turned my attention back to the set of wires I was working on. I fiddled with them and then glanced at the computer monitor. Nothing. Well, nothing good, anyway. There *was* a slight crackle and the stink of burnt ozone, but the monitor just continued to flash its red low-battery symbol. Huh. The small power source in the computer was still putting out a trickle of juice, but nothing was coming through from the other platform.

Double dagnabbit.

I frowned, kneeled down as best I could on my left leg, with my stiff right leg stretched out beside me, and got back to work on the connections.

"DUH-NAAAAAAAAY!"

Hearing my name being shouted, I jerked my head up and looked toward the treeline.

Rae busted out of the jungle and onto the beach, directly between me and the volcano. She was running full-tilt across the hundred or so meters of sand, right toward me and the platforms. She yelled, "I got them! I GOT THEM! The time has come for us to vacate the premises! That means go go go GO GOOOOOOO!" And that girl's got a set of lungs on her, so when I say she yelled, I mean she YELLED!

"Argh! It's not ready yet!" I hollered back.

"Well, it needs to GET ready at this point in time, or the window of opportunity is likely to be closed forever. In other words, it's now or never, Sis!" Rae finally reached our OtherWorld Portal equipment and jumped up on the platform to stand next to me. Her bulging canvas rucksack hung from one shoulder.

I looked past her and saw the glowing wall of lava burbling its way toward us, swallowing up the trees right where she had emerged from the jungle just less than a minute ago. It went something like this: Tree. Then lava. Then *pffft* into ash and smoke. Tree. Then lava. Then *pffft!* Then— well, you get the idea. A massive flow of painful molten death. Heading straight for us. I gulped, trying to push my heart down from my throat and back into my chest where it belonged, and said (as casually as I could), "Hmmm. I see what you mean."

Fingers shaking, I tried another combination of the wire strands. And felt a glimmer of hope because there was a slight tingle of electricity between my fingers! From the corner of my eye, I saw the computer screen brighten and begin to flash with the green "Battery A-OK" icon. From where I knelt, I looked down at the small panel door that was open at the base of the stand. Three fist-sized glowing spheres of energy stared out at me. I spoke to them in a trembling voice. "Okay guys! Now's the time. Fire it up and give it all you've got!" In response, they began to glow brighter. And brighter and brighter. I gave them a quick thumbs-up and closed the panel.

Then I pulled myself to a standing position and turned my attention to the black little lump at the center of the metal tube around the top of the stand. (It's called a toroid, by the way, just in case you were wondering. The metal tube, that is, and not the lump. You already know that the lump was called Rocky.) Speaking of Rocky—who was the same size and shape as its three counterparts who were *inside* the toroid stand—well, Rocky gazed at me with such a look of confidence that I started to feel as if this might really work, after all. Right on time and according to plan, the silver patterns that criss-crossed over the surface of Rocky's black body started to glow and spark. Electricity began to flow into the little guy, electricity provided by its companions who were wired into the stand below. I quickly closed the lid over the top of the snug metal nest and fastened it tight.

Fingers of lightning snaked out from the Tesla-coil equipment and began to encircle the whole platform, including me and Rae and our gear. As it made a complete plasma globe of sparks centered around us and the coil, I looked at Rae and squeezed her hand. "See you on the other side, Sis!" My voice was confident and brave. I mean, the voice coming out of my mouth, *that* one was brave. But my inner voice, the one bouncing around inside my head, *that* voice quavered as I mentally added, "...I hope!"

A brilliant white light engulfed the center of the toroid and almost instantly swelled large enough to fill up the entire plasma globe. It washed over us with a barely audible little snap, like when your bubblegum pops. At the same time, I could see the first ropy tendrils of lava approach the edge of our platform. They began to melt everything they touched, but before they could reach us, the world disappeared in a blinding flash.

Hey, Little Sis!

The previous pages took unauthorized
leave of their companions whilst
I was perusing your literary
endeavor, and they will require
re-insertion to their proper
location should you ever embark
on a publishing career.

I mean to say, this section fell
out of your journal when I was
reading it and we'll need to put it
back in the right order when you get
around to having it printed up!

-Rachel

Chapter 1

DANAE'S LOG 1: Hello Everybody, My Name's Danae, What's Yours?

Rae and I were working in the lab when the door opened with a loud click. Dr. Mike Kane stepped into the room, started toward us, and then stopped in his tracks. With his customary military precision, he performed a crisp about-face, stepped back out of the laboratory and shut the door. Rae and I looked at each other with eyebrows raised.

I didn't have to be any more of a science nerd than I already am in order to figure out what his problem was. He had seen Rae working on her computer, fingers tapping out a steady rhythm on the keyboard. And he had seen me, the 15-year-old younger half of Team Rugged Stuff, standing in the center of the lab, performing a series of random gestures and actions—raising my left hand up into the air, shaking my shoulders, twirling my walking stick like a parade baton. And he had probably seen the *other* me, standing over in the corner of the room. And the *other* me was also raising my/her hand over my/her head, also shaking my/her shoulders and also twirling my/her walking stick.

Right on cue, Mike stepped back into the lab for another look. "Hmmm-hmmph," he cleared his throat. "Ah, good afternoon, Rachel and Danae. And... Danae?" He raised one eyebrow in the direction of me and my double. "Am I to take it, then, that the big secret project that you've been working on for the past year—your, um, side project other than the OtherWorld Portal venture, that is—is a... cloning experiment?"

Rae grinned while I laughed out loud. But before I could explain what my project really involved, Rae started discussing how a cloning experiment couldn't, in actuality, make a real-time duplicate of a person. "It's a common misconception, really, fostered by a misunderstanding of cloning that is perpetuated in popular culture. But a clone of any living being wouldn't age any quicker than normal. Therefore, the only way that a clone of Danae would be an exact duplicate of her would be if cells were taken from her and incubated when she was a newborn. Even then, environmental influences would likely result in some small differences in appearance..."

I'm, like, mad-scientist smart, but I *work* at it. My big sister is, in all honesty, even more of a Brainiac than I am, but it all comes naturally to her with hardly any effort at all. She usually reins herself in and keeps her conversations on-point, but sometimes she gets so wrapped up in an idea that she sidetracks herself.

So I interrupted her. "Yeah, yeah, yeah, we get it! A real clone probably might look something like me, but not exactly." Then I turned toward Mike. "Even though a cloning project might be on my to-do list (and would be super cool!), what I'm working on right now is holography and empathy feedback!" I pointed at a small piece of hardware sitting on the lab table in front of me. It was a dirt-bike helmet that I had modified with high-definition optic sensors and projectors and a batch of cybernetic tech hardware. The other Danae in the corner duplicated my actions. "I developed a cutting-edge video projection system a while ago. Now my new software can figure out what the subject of any optical input would look like from all angles and then it compensates and uses my projection hardware to create a perfect three-dimensional image of the subject, with details and definition no matter what direction you look at it from."

"Danae has had the hardware perfected for quite a while. As a matter of fact, the entirety of the equipment specifications upon which we have worked during the past year or so have this new projection technology of Danae's incorporated into its structure," my big sister piped up, not at all put out by my interruption. "So we didn't even have to engage in a retrofitting procedure for any of our gear or equipment when she had the software ready!"

She was right—everything I've designed over the past 18 months, all the exploration and adventure gear has this technology buried in it, and now that my coding upgrades are ready, the hardware doesn't have to be replaced in order to use the new software; I just pushed a digital improvement out over the internet. Poof!...any Team Rugged Stuff physical gadgets that are out in the field and connected to the interwebs are able to utilize my latest and greatest improvements immediately and *right now*. And without the need to physically adjust the equipment! Yeah, pretty cool, right? What can I say, I'm kind of a genius that way.

Michael walked over near my holographic double in the corner, folded his arms and cupped his chin in his hand. "Well, I must say, this is very impressive. It doesn't look like any hologram I've ever seen. There is, ah, no shimmer, the projection is absolutely opaque and solid, and there is no de-resolution at the edge of the image." He walked around the duplicate image of me, checking it out from all angles. "And as you say, it is perfectly three-dimensional. Based solely upon visual inspection, this, ah, version of you is as real as I am."

As a matter of fact, I was pretty darned proud of how this research and development was coming along. "The 360-degree holography is a refinement of my existing technology, compatible with the hardware specs for the whole line of existing Team Rugged Stuff lab and field gear. But what I've also got planned for this baby," I tapped the high-tech dirt-bike helmet on my head, "is to eventually use the theta-wave sensors that I've installed in it to help the AI make the holographic image even MORE lifelike!" Theta waves are a function of the brain that taps into our emotional under-standing of other people...it's a fact, look it up! I dare you!

Mike shook his head, straightened his spine and glared at us. "As fascinating as this hologram is, and as innovative as your empathy research may be, I believe that it will need to, um, be put aside for the moment." He activated the lab's smartboard, the one that was set into one wall of the room and then he logged into the Team Rugged Stuff network. "This is security footage from the room where we have been running the OtherWorld Portal project."

The smartboard screen came to life and showed one of our labs, full of cool technology. Computer terminals, electronic equipment and several men and women in white laboratory coats were visible, and in the center of the room, a small raised platform that was composed of two different-sized circles. It stood with its pair of floors at perhaps a meter above the laboratory floor, with the larger circle being four or five meters in diameter and the smaller one about half that size.

A Tesla coil (that's Tesla as in *Nikola* Tesla, not *electric car* Tesla, BTW, LOL) stood a meter tall on the large half, the loop on the left, while a small computer station took up much of the center of the smaller loop on the right. (I always think the whole thing looks like someone put two small circus platforms side by side, one slightly larger than the other, with a metal mushroom growing out of the big half and a computer terminal growing out of the smaller half.) A time stamp in the upper right-hand corner of the screen showed the footage to have been taken three weeks earlier.

"This part, we are all, uh, familiar with," said Mike, as he fast-forwarded through images of a robot probe and drone —along with the floor, stand and the Tesla coil—disappearing in a flash of plasma, replaced with an identical floor, stand and coil, but no robotic gear. As the video progressed at high speed, there was another flash and all of the original components, with probe and drone, reappeared. This was all footage of the preliminary survey we had done on the OtherWorld, when we had sent remote equipment over to sample the environment, and we had all watched it over and over, probably two or three dozen times.

This was followed by a scene dated just one week ago, the footage of Rae and me in environment suits. Just like the probe and drone earlier, we also disappeared from the platform along with the coil and then reappeared, this time with the suit helmets unfastened and held by our sides.

"That locale is absolutely sublime!" said my sis in a dreamy voice.

"If by that you mean that you love that place, then yeah! Me too! I can't wait for the data analysis to be completed," I agreed. "I've got the portal scheduled for the day after tomorrow for our next expedition." This was the biggest discovery of our adventure-scientist careers. My tech developments had made it possible for us to build a gateway to— well, to *somewhere*. To somewhere *else*. To somewhere else with a *beautiful tropical island*. And we were only just in the very preliminary stages of sorting through all the data that we had collected about this strange, new (to us) world.

Mike scowled and waved his hands in a 'slow down' gesture. "Wait until you see what comes next. You may have to change your agenda," he warned. The security footage advanced through several more hours at high speed, and then he turned off the fast-forward, finally letting the image move at normal speed. "This, as you can see from the time stamp, is, ah, yesterday afternoon, when the portal lab was shut down and offline, pending the results of your data analysis. Or, I should say, we, hmmm, we *thought* it was offline."

The screen showed the OtherWorld Portal lab, with everything appearing exactly as it should have, given that the room was closed and quiet at the time. Machinery was powered down, overhead lights were turned off. Everything was murky and dim.

Then the door at the end of the room opened! Three figures entered, wearing environment suits—helmets and all—and carrying large crates. I couldn't believe my eyes, because even in the low light, the insignia of the Null Corporation—a red circle with a slash through it, like an old-school computer-code zero—was visible on the right-hand shoulder of each of the figures.

"Whaaaaat!?" Rae and I yelled simultaneously.

Then I followed that up by screeching, "Null Rats?" (Null Rats, that's what we call the Null Corp minions, the people who work for our arch-enemy.)

My older sister gritted her teeth and growled to Kane, "How could this circumstance possibly have taken place? There are three separate and distinct levels of security protocols that should have put a halt to this egregious invasion before they could get through that door! In other words, how in the world did this happen!?"

"I know, I know," Mike said glumly, "or rather, I, um, I *don't* know. We'll figure it out sooner or later, and I take full responsibility, but this next scene is where my focus is and where, um, yours should be as well right now." He pointed to the screen as it showed the Null Corp agents move to the platforms. We watched as two of them took their cargo onto the Tesla-coil platform, while a third went to the computer platform, to the control panel—to *my* control panel!

Rae studied the movements of the figure at the computer station. "This is an extremely serious matter," she said thoughtfully. "There is no hesitation in his actions. He knows exactly what he's doing and how to work the controls. We have a very serious security problem here."

"He *or she*," I corrected Rae. "There's no way for us to tell who's who, under those helmets."

"True. But given Colin's disdain for females, there is a statistical probability that he has employed only males for this particular endeavor. In other words, he doesn't think very highly of girls or women and probably wouldn't trust them to get the job done."

I had to admit, she was right on the nose in this case. That Colin is a certifiable jerk.

"Now watch the platform," said Kane, as the two agents uncrated their equipment. Tossing the packing material off to the side, the men were left with a large box of some sort, as well as various wiring and electronics. They nodded to the agent at the control panel. The people and material on the large side of the platform disappeared. Mike jabbed a finger at the action taking place on the smartboard video play-back. "Remote monitoring equipment, I'm sure of it. Null Corp is trying to steal your research on the OtherWorld!"

During the next five minutes, the footage revealed nothing more exciting than the remaining Null Corp agent trying to scratch an itchy nose that they couldn't get to through the environment suit's faceplate. (The lab environment is sterile, the loser could have easily opened up the helmet to scratch that itch, but I guess they didn't know that. I hope it drove them *crazy!*) Then a blinking light on the control panel caught the agent's attention and the platform area was suddenly occupied again; two figures in environment suits, the floor, the stand and the Tesla coil, but no equipment.

"See?" Kane pointed at the newly-returned platform. "They're back, but the, hrmmm, monitoring equipment isn't. They've installed it at the OtherWorld Point to record all of your progress there and report it back to their boss." The remaining coverage of the security breach was uneventful.

The three Null Rats shut down the lab equipment, removed any sign of their presence and left through the same door at the end of the room.

"When I get my hands on that Colin..." I snarled and clenched my walking stick tight enough to make it creak in my grip. (I'm just exercising a little literary license here—There's no way I could ever really damage my walking stick even if I wanted to, my Mom designed it and constructed it out of airplane-grade metal alloy, it's light as a feather and strong, strong, strong...like indestructible strong!)

I could see Rae give a little involuntary wince. "When you say it like that, I can almost dredge up a feeling of sympathy for him." Colin Null is the founder and owner of the Null Corporation, the guy who everyone considered to be the best young scientist adventurer in the world until the current iteration of Team Rugged Stuff came along (that is to say, me and my sis—Danae and Rachel Rugg—carrying on the family business). "But then I contemplate what we've just observed," Rae frowned, "and I think that perhaps whatever punishment you can manage to inflict on him is probably justified. That is to say, I hope you can get a chance to really let him have it."

"Erm, actually..." Kane hesitantly interrupted us.

"Yeah?" I grunted, while Rae said, "Yes?" with her trademark perky attitude.

"Actually, hmmm, I have what I think is a better idea." He looked at us with eyebrows raised. "If we could take control of the monitoring equipment, then, ah, not only would Colin Null and the Null Corporation *not* be able to steal your data and research, but you could actually feed him some false information. You could put him totally and, hmm, absolutely onto the wrong track!"

"We're listening…" said Sis.

"Yeah, do you have a plan?"

"Well, we could power up the portal, the two of you could slip through to the OtherWorld Point, and it would be a piece of, ahem, cake to re-wire their equipment. We could backtrack their signal and input false data." We nodded in agreement and he rushed on to the next step in his plan. "I'd go myself to carry out the, hmmm, modifications, but I strongly feel that we have a very short window of opportunity in which to accomplish this. The two of you—and only the two of you—are already somewhat acclimated to the OtherWorld Point environment, due to your, hmm, initial expedition there. So instead of waiting for several hours for myself or someone else to go through the preparation protocols, we could send you through immediately. It should take five minutes at the most to modify the, ah, remote monitors, that is, to subvert them to our own use. Then Bob's your uncle, you return back here to the Rugg labs, and the tables, as they say, will have been turned!"

I gave Rae a look. *Bob's your uncle, R?* Me and my sis have worked together so close for so long, we can sometimes practically read each other's mind.

She shrugged back with an expression on her face that seemed to say, *Mike's tendency toward using British-type idioms manifests when he's under stress, D.* Meaning, he pops off with funny English sayings when he's worried. To Kane, she nodded. "Hmmm. It all seems to make sense, I guess." But there was some hesitancy in her voice.

"Yeah!" I piped up, overriding my sister's note of caution. "Easy-peasy, right, Mike?" I knew he felt bad about the security breach and I wanted to cheer him up, so I decided to go along with his plan as enthusiastically as I could and throw in another funny English phrase as my way of making him feel better.

"Precisely! Aha! Lemon-squeezy!" Kane's face showed enormous relief as we accepted his proposal and he headed for the door.

"Mike really wants this to work, Sis," I muttered to Rachel. "I think he feels guilty about the breakdown in security. It's like if we can do a quick fix, we can turn the tables on Null and then this mistake won't be hanging over Mike. It'll be like it never happened, no harm and no foul."

"Okay, let's engage and get it accomplished... in other words, let's do it!" she replied quietly in a whisper that only I could hear. We each grabbed our custom-made canvas shoulder duffel bags from the table and rifled the supply closet for likely tools and gadgets for the task ahead.

From the doorway, Mike looked on anxiously as Rae downloaded several megs of schematics and electronic data onto her computer tablet and as I swept my arm across my worktable, dumping a bunch of gear, circuits, electronic *tchotchkes*, wiring, and even the hologram helmet, as well as my goggles and a field chemistry kit, all willy-nilly into my duffel. He stammered, "I, I don't think you'll need any of that—the monitoring equipment that those scoundrels put there has already been in place for, for nearly a day—a small basic tool kit should be sufficient—time, time is of the essence—"

I'd never seen him so fidgety. He was seriously stressed to the max.

"It's okay, Mike. We're ready," Rae reassured him.

I just rolled my eyes. Now that we had a handle on the situation, this would be a straight-forward operation, not much different than any of dozens of other missions that me and my sis had undertaken in the past. I felt bad for him and I didn't want him to beat himself up over the security breach, but since when had our operations advisor gotten so jittery?

We double-timed it out of the workroom, with Rae jogging and me keeping up with my own particular hop-skip lope because of my stiff leg, down several corridors and into the portal lab as Mike brought up the rear. He took his place at the control panel while Rae jumped up and I used my walking stick to help me clamber onto the Tesla platform. We adjusted our grips on our shoulder bags and were ready to go.

"Hit it, Mike!" I yelled.

"We will have returned before five minutes pass," asserted Rae.

At the computer platform terminal, Mike tapped the keyboard and engaged the portal. We heard him call out, "Good, ah, lu—" and then he was gone.

Or more accurately, *we* were gone.

From the viewpoint of anyone watching from within the lab, it would have looked as if a globe of plasma enveloped us and our platform and that everything within that sparking bubble just flashed out of existence. From our side of things, however, it was the lab that disappeared, and it was replaced by tropical island scenery. Beneath our feet, we felt the floor settle into the rounded base of the platform that had been constructed on the beach on this side of the portal and the transfer was complete. One microsecond, we were in our lab; in the next microsecond, after a flash of white light, we were on a golden stretch of sand, framed on one side by an ocean and on the other by a jungle. We stood on a Tesla-coil platform identical to the one back home, adjoining a computer terminal platform, also identical to the one back home, the one where Mike was operating the keyboard. All of this was just as it should be.

Except...

There was one unexpected difference, one that made me gasp out loud. On the platform alongside us here on the beach, sitting right next to the computer console, was a large black treasure chest. It had a small red blinking diode, about the size and shape of a grape, positioned just above the keyhole on the clasp lock. It was sounding off a slow and steady *bip——bip——bip,* in perfect time with the pulsating light.

We were familiar with the tropical scenery—we had already seen it up close and personal, when we had discovered it just a few days ago. The black box, however, was something for which we were not prepared. I had expected to have to search quite a bit in order to find the Null Corp remote monitoring equipment. After all, what good is a secret transmitter if it isn't secret, right? But against all expectations, this gear was just sitting right out in plain sight!

Sis and I gave each other questioning looks—*What's all this appear to be then, R?* my glance asked her.

The look on her face replied, *Dunno, D, but p'raps we'd best be on our toes*—and then the beeping and flashing got faster and faster. *bip——bip——bip—bip—bip—bip-bip-bip—bipbipbipbpbpbpbpbpeeeeeeeeeeeeeeeeeee.* I had just enough time to recognize it as a countdown timer before the Tesla coil at the center of our platform burst into a pillar of fire! *FOOM!*

Chapter 2

DANAE'S LOG 2:
Trapped in Paradise

Yup, that's right. FOOM.

And then, *pufff-hisssss.* The flame died down and disappeared just as suddenly as it had begun.

"Are you okay, Danae? I mean, did you sustain any injuries?" Rachel is a really cool big sis, but she always acts like she's got to look out for me, ever since the car wreck that messed up my leg.

"I'm fine! Just fine!" I snapped. Then I reconsidered and said wryly, "But I do feel as if I got an instant sunburn!" It turned out that both of us were pretty much unharmed, along with all of our gear and the Tesla coil framework. The black treasure chest and computer station on the adjoining platform were hunky-dory, too.

But when I looked a little bit closer at the equipment, I saw that my chunk of Widmanstätten meteorite—that's the tennis-ball-sized heart and soul of my transport system that normally sits right in the center of the whole contraption—

well, that meteorite was melted down into a tiny slag heap. Checking inside the metal column that held it all up, I could see that my special super-charged battery pack was also *kaput.* Dead. Fried to a crisp. There was nothing left of it but a pile of black, gritty ash. The whole pyrotechnic show had apparently been designed to damage some very specific—and very vital—components of my tech. The plan, it seemed, had been to incinerate them into nothingness and leave everything else on the platform, including me and my big sis, relatively untouched. And the plan had worked.

"You gotta be kidding me!" I howled, looking at the ruins of my baby, my beloved OtherWorld Portal equipment. "I hate to have to tell you this, Rae, but our way home is now a bunch of burnt dust and a puddle of melted circuits!"

"It does appear as if my assertion that we would return within five minutes might have been a bit... premature," Rae agreed. Her attention wandered over toward the black chest that the Null Rats had left on the platform. "Any suppositions as to the purpose of that particular object? Meaning, what do you think this is all about?"

"There's only one way to find out." I tried to sound more confident than I actually felt. "Move back a bit." I stepped over to the box to examine it. Dark, glossy and solid-looking, the body was made out of wood, accessorized with brass and iron bindings, hinges and latch. There was just no doubt about it, this thing was designed to look exactly like the iconic concept of a pirate chest. I bent over and flipped open the clasp that held the lid down. All the while, I couldn't help but hum a tune from one of my favorite classic video games. You know, the one where the hero opens up a treasure chest and receives a reward?

"Yes, well, just you be careful, Link," Rae muttered as I pulled the lid up. *What do you know*, I thought, *I didn't realize she knew much of anything about gaming.* Classic films, television, books and that sort of stuff are really more her cup of tea, while I'm interested in more interactive hobbies. So it kind of surprised me for her to say something like that.

She peered over my shoulder as I opened the box. The chest seemed empty, but when the lid flipped all the way back, a tiny figure suddenly appeared to be standing inside, and we recognized him instantaneously. "Colin!" we both yelled in unison. Then I added, in a voice full of outrage, "It's a hologram!"

The image in the box began to speak, sounding exactly like a circus ringmaster presenting to an adoring crowd. "Good afternoooon, Team Slugged Rough! What a pleasure to see you in such an unfortunate situation!" Yup, that was Colin Null all right, looking chic and fit as ever, and jumping at the opportunity to make fun of our name. The projection captured him perfectly, in a two-foot scale image. There was his strategically rumpled bright red hair, there was his Italian camel-hair blazer over a black Peruvian-cotton turtleneck, (oh, he's a sharp dresser, make no mistake about that!) and there was the light dusting of freckles across his nose. Our rival looks more like a rich rugby player than he does a conniving and ruthless researcher, but there you go, just more proof that stereotypes can be a bunch of hooey.

Colin—or more accurately, the holographic image of Colin—chuckled. "Oh, no, I can't actually *see* you. This is just a recordin', prepared in advance for your viewing pleasure!" (Coming from anyone else, his Irish brogue would be pretty cool, but knowing what a creep Colin is, his accent is just annoying...) "But I can certainly imagine how the two of you look, stunned and confused and bewildered by the fact of me outwittin' you yet again, and you bein' stranded high and dry with a pile of banjaxed gear!"

"Banjaxed. Huh." I heard Rae mutter to herself. "Well, I don't know what that word means, but I can guess, given the context."

While Rae was pondering Colin's word choice, I was assessing the technical aspects of the image and mumbling under my own breath. "That's some great hologram, the projector and speakers wired into, actually embedded in the framework of the box, I couldn't do much better myself..."

"As you know, I'm a stickler for proper form," Null's image kept chattering, "So please consider this to be the obligatory braggart villain monologue. First of all, congratulations on your incredible scientific discovery! Your OtherWorld Project is truly a quantum leap in the history of technological advancement! And many thanks as well! It was a very cost-effective process to have *you* spend the brain power and resources to develop the portal technology for *me*. Not that Null Corp couldn't have accomplished this, but it's just so much more efficient to have you do the work and have me reap the benefits."

Rae and I glanced at one another.

This is bad, D.

I nodded. *Bad, bad, baddity-bad, R.*

"That havin' been said, now that the OtherWorld Point has been established, and the related technology has been developed—by you—I'll be more than happy to present the research to the world as my own achievement. At this point in time that my hologram is addressin' the pair of you," he pulled his sports coat sleeve up in order to examine the watch on his wrist—a Rolex, naturally, he loves to show off how rich he is— "I am sendin' out an announcement to the world's top journalists and scientists, arrangin' a press conference to be held at Null Corp. Four days from riiiiiiiiight *NOW*," he tapped his timepiece, "I'll be presentin' to the world in general—and to the scientific community in particular—*my* discovery of the OtherWorld technology, while the two of you are cooling your heels there at the Other-World, building sand castles an' cavortin' on the beach an' such."

The image gave a smug little chuckle. "Why, you could even sit around and write your memoirs, for all I care! Because you are goin' to be stuck there for a wee bit, at least until after I've solidified my reputation as the developer of the OtherWorld Portal tech!"

Rae and I both grimaced—it was actually a pretty effective plan. Evil, rotten, mean, and seriously messed up, but effective.

In the time we've been scientist adventurers, we've had enough experience with the politics of it to realize that if things went as Colin was describing, there would be no way we could set things straight. Rachel calls it the 'Rush to Publish' syndrome of the scientific community and says that it's based in the very real fact that the first one to go public with a scientific development or advancement is the one who ends up being credited with it. Even if we could later show that it was *us*, Team Rugged Stuff, instead of *him*, Null Corp, who had discovered the OtherWorld point and developed the portal technology, very few people would believe us.

And even fewer would at all care what the actual truth was. People can be pretty stupid. Or as Rae might say, 'willfully ignorant'.

"But don't stress your cute little brain cells about it too much," the holographic Colin continued.

Both of us growled. He has a knack for choosing the most obnoxious words and phrases.

"Once I've established Null Corp in the public eye as the OtherWorld developer, I'll send the proper circuitry and a new battery through that will allow you to repair the comeback portal and to return to your lab. After all, since your equipment seems to have met with... hmmm, shall we call it a *wee mishap?...*" I glanced over toward the Tesla coil and surveyed the melted remains of the black rock that had once sat in the middle of the toploader. Another smooth, smug chuckle drew my attention back to Colin. "I'm afraid that Null Corp benevolence, that is to say, *my* benevolence, is your only way to get home again!"

The hologram of Colin Null faded away, as our nemesis gave his best villain's laugh. "BWAH-ha-ha-HA-ha-HA-ha...!"

"What a grandstander," I grumbled, and then I got busy examining the chest. I flipped it over and used some of the tools from my shoulder pack to deconstruct the bottom of the casing. "There's a beacon point wired in here, so it looks as if he was at least telling the truth about the comeback tech." Then I yelped. "No wonder the hologram was so good! That's MY design!" I was so frustrated by what I had discovered that I couldn't even spit. All I could do was just stand there and shake my fist at the box.

"Pfft! Our security leak is much more extreme than we had, pfft, initially believed!" Even Rae was sputtering in anger. "Not only did he pilfer your hologram technology, but it appears as if he's going to be successful at plundering our OtherWorld Portal discovery as well!"

I opened the panel in the base of the Tesla coil column and confirmed what I had seen earlier. "And he wasn't kidding about the battery either. It's totally burnt beyond all recognition, along with my meteorite. That 'treasure chest' must have sent a command through the computer terminal for the power cell to unload its entire charge all at once into the circuit, destroying both the battery and the circuit in the process. So we've got no power, and even if we *did* have power, with my Widmanstätten meteorite destroyed, we've got no circuits for the power to flow through in order to make the whole thing work. In a word, we've got—as Mom likes to say—we've got *bupkis*."

Just then, the entire beach shook like crazy. It knocked my sister to her knees, and I lost my grip on my walking stick and went down smack on my rear end. After two or three seconds, the rumbling stopped. I growled from my sitting position, "What's that? Another little present from Null?" Rae stood up and reached down to help me, but I ignored her. I grabbed my walking stick from where it lay and used it to brace myself and get back to my feet.

My big sis ignored me ignoring her. She answered my question even though it had been halfway rhetorical. "I don't think so. It has the attributes of being too large and too widespread to be something he could manage to arrange. It seemed to be more of a naturally occurring seismic phenomenon. The drone footage showed a volcano here on the island, maybe it's more active than we realized."

"Hmph. That's just what we need right now, a natural disaster to go along with the *un*-natural one that Colin arranged for us." I put my hand up to my forehead to shade my eyes and peered at the horizon. "It looks like the sun is on its way down. Even if we can think of a plan that will get us home in time to stop Colin's press conference, we're not going to get much done in the dark. Let's gather some firewood and make a quick recon at the edge of the jungle and see if we can find anything to eat, like fruits or berries or something. Then maybe in the morning, we can figure something out."

We divvied up the chores and it didn't take too long for me to get a driftwood campfire roaring on the beach. The flames were awfully pretty as they burned yellow, blue and green, the colors a result of the salt residue left behind on the wood from the ocean water. While I got the fire going, Rae scouted out the area where the beach met the ocean and returned with fresh water from a stream and some bananas—or at least something that was a pretty good banana substitute—that she had found on a nearby tree.

"Well, it looks as if we have all four food groups covered for dinner tonight," Rae said. I didn't know what she was talking about and my puzzlement showed on my face, until she continued, "You know... raw bananas, fried bananas, broiled bananas and baked bananas!" Coming from anyone else, I wouldn't think it was a very funny joke, but for Rae, it was pretty hilarious. I laughed out loud.

"Don't forget bananas on a stick and Louisiana-style blackened bananas!" I replied and that cracked her up. It was good to find something to laugh about, given how rotten our situation was.

The climate was so perfect that we really didn't even need the fire and the makeshift lean-to that we put together next to the Tesla platforms, but it was still nice and comforting to have the light and heat and shelter. As we ate our dinner—bananas *hors d'oeuvres*, bananas salad, bananas entrée and for dessert, mashed bananas (yes, I'm running the banana joke into the ground and yes, I used my chem kit to run a quick analysis on the food to make sure it wasn't poisonous before we ate it, what do you think, I'm stupid or something?)—a pair of moons rose over the horizon. (Yup. A *pair* of moons.) They came up from over the water, opposite of where the sun had set below the island trees and mountains, so this helped give us some directions to label as east and west, and that meant we were on the eastern shore. The first of the moons was a faint pastel blue color, while the other, which followed about five minutes later, was slightly larger and tinted pink.

"Well, this is one way to speed up our exploration process," Rae said, as we settled into our cozy little spots next to the fire. "Total immersion, just like learning a new language. That is, we have no choice but to do or to die."

"Yeah, I guess so. And there's a lot of exploring to do. What a place!" I pointed at the sky. "Two moons! Or I should say, *at least* two moons, because there might be others that we haven't seen yet. And check out those constellations. There is nothing out there that I can even remotely identify."

We spent the next hour or so discussing our different theories about the nature of the OtherWorld. My own personal line of thought is that my portal creates a tiny wormhole and that our OtherWorld tech opened up a gateway onto a far-away Earth-like planet. This planet might be within the Milky Way or possibly even in another galaxy, but still somewhere within our chartable and navigable space. "It all makes sense this way, Rae. Why else would a chunk of meteorite be the key to the whole process?"

[So, sidebar time, I guess. I'd better explain the whole bit about the meteorite. Back at the labs, we've got a meteorite about the size of an elephant. Back before either Rae or I were even born, our grandparents, who were the original Team Rugged Stuff, discovered the huge space rock while they were adventuring in the Himalayas. They were trying to either confirm or disprove the existence of the so-called Abominable Snowman.

Their results were inconclusive so far as the Yeti was concerned, but during their search, they did run across a spectacular specimen of meteorite, half-buried in the side of a windswept cliff of ice. Excavating the big extraterrestrial boulder and arranging for its transport back home to their base of operations near San Francisco was one of the last projects they ever accomplished. Soon after the rock was put aboard a steamer in the Bay of Bengal for the long cruise toward America, both our Grandma and Grandpa Rugg were caught up in a huge avalanche in the mountains north of Nepal and they were never seen or heard from again.

The meteorite became a part of the Team Rugged Stuff corporate holdings, and when me and my sister Rae decided to revive the family business, one of the first jobs we had (after getting approval from our folks) was to dig through the big warehouse to analyze and catalogue all the decades' worth of gear and records and artifacts that were stored there, including the jumbo-sized meteorite. I was particularly excited about it, because I could see that it had a well-defined Widmanstätten pattern, and I had some ideas about that specific attribute that I wanted to explore.

[Sidebar to the sidebar: A Widmanstätten pattern is a not-uncommon characteristic of certain iron-rich meteors and meteorites. It's a criss-cross decoration of lines thought to be nickel-iron crystals and the effect has been noted and recorded by scientists since the beginning of the 1800s. It's a fact, look it up. I dare you. But to me, those patterns always looked like they were actually some sort of positronic circuitry. Whether they were naturally occurring or had been developed by some unknown extraterrestrial intelligence, well, that has yet to be determined. End of the sidebar to the sidebar.]

It was through my experiments with this circuitry from outer space that led me to develop the equipment that allowed us to discover the OtherWorld site. I found that when a specific array of Tesla-generated electrical impulses is fed through the Widmanstätten pattern, it can open up a gate to... *someplace*. In this case, this someplace was the beach where we found ourselves at this moment.

Different arrays of power through different meteorite patterns can (hypothetically, at least) open gates to *different someplaces*, so that's why we decided to name the whole thing the "OtherWorld Project."

My transport platform used a tiny piece of the meteorite, a stone about the size of my fist. But I always like to think of it as being about the same size as a human heart. (And people say I've got no romance in my soul!)

Anyway, that's the whole bit about the meteorite and my OtherWorld tech. End of the sidebar!]

And that's why I made the argument that this beach, this place, is somewhere *in* our galaxy or universe, because of the extra-terrestrial nature of what could be thought of as our blueprints. I maintain that this OtherWorld site is someplace far, far away from our home Earth, yes, but still within the same physical framework of our solar system, galaxy and universe.

My sister, on the other hand, held tight to a theory that our OtherWorld project opened a door into another dimension, or another plane of existence. "I don't dispute your line of reasoning," she said, "but I just have a feeling that I can't ignore. I have the sense that no matter how far a person were to travel from Earth, the only way to reach *this* place is via some sort of cross-dimensional portal."

"And you don't have any sort of evidence for this, right?"

"I'm afraid not, Little Sis. I just 'feel' as if we are more 'out of phase' with our home, rather than being 'far away' from our home."

Well, I didn't agree with her. I mean, maybe my theory didn't have enough solid science yet to back it up, but her theory was so wildly unscientific as to be an outright fairy tale! And yet, there was no way I was going to just dismiss her theory out of hand. It might not be something you can measure and analyze, but I've had enough experience with her 'feelings' to know that they turn out to be right on the nose more often than not. I'm techy and to-the-point, while Big Sis is dreamy and brilliant. I handle the hard sciences like electronics and computers, she takes care of the arts and soft sciences like linguistics and dramatics and such, and between the two of us, we're a pretty rocking team, if I do say so myself.

We'd hashed this whole discussion out countless times back home in the lab over the past few weeks, and unfortunately, nothing we could see here up close, on site and in person was much of a help in proving matters either way. We'd about exhausted the subject again. The moons had set in the 'west' over the jungle and the fire had burned down to just glowing coals when Rae nudged me. "Hey Danae, pick up that piece of driftwood that's by your leg and toss it to me, will you?" She spoke real nonchalant and calm-like and I couldn't figure out what was on her mind.

I grabbed the wood and handed it over to her. It was about the size and shape of a baseball bat. "Are you cold? Do you want me to build the fire back up?"

"No, that's not it at all. It's just that *you've* already got your walking stick with you and I have developed a sudden desire to have something in my possession that can also inflict a blow. That is, I want to be holding something that can pack a wallop. Take a look inland, just beyond the perimeter of the campfire light, in the darkness of the vegetation."

I stared out toward where she had indicated, and what I saw did, indeed, make me tighten my grip on the handle of my walking stick. Something was glowing out there in the gloom. Something that looked an awful lot like a pair of eyes!

Chapter 3

NOAH & LEVI'S JOURNAL 1: "Into the Adventure!"

Hey Cousin Danae! I wrote up some of my notes like you asked me to, but I wasn't sure where you wanted them, so I kind of stuck them in among your pages where it seemed like they would fit into the proper chronology. These are my verbal recollections as typed up by the transcription app on my computer! It's a new prototype that I'm testing out, it's supposed to allow for 100 percent hands-free document production, so let me know what you think of the final outcome. Plus, I'm afraid my brother Levi wandered by as I was dictating this, so there's some strange comments from him scattered here and there throughout the text...(you'll know 'em when you see 'em!) Don't forget, now you owe me a triple veggie-burger and big pile of sustainable and locally sourced fries, in exchange for these notes, just like you promised!
—Cousin Noah

"AAAAARGH!" I flinched as my twin brother, Levi Rugg, howled in disgust. He's not very smart, and as a result, he is easily frustrated.

Just keep it up bro, and my fists will teach you a lesson about which of us is not very smart...!

And now he's looking over my shoulder and threatening to punch me in the back of the head if I don't stop making him look bad in this report. Just goes to show that a low I.Q. often accompanies a tendency toward violence.

That's it, you asked for it!

Ouch! Hey, knock it off, I'm doing something for Danae here. Okay, okay, I do solemnly swear to provide a fair and honest account (mostly) of our recent adventure with our younger cousins, the sisters of Team Rugged Stuff.

That's better! But just remember, bro, I've got my eyes on you...

Yeah, right. So let's start again.

"Argh!" My twin brother, Levi Rugg, howled in disgust. We were in the rec room at our family cabin located on the coast of Alaska. We had just gotten back from a week-long hike into the wilderness and my bro was catching up on the business news from while we'd been off to the interior.

"What's up with you?" I asked, "The price of ground beef going up?" (We're fraternal twins, but look so much alike that we might as well be identical, for all intents and purposes. If it weren't for the different ways we have our hair—my shaggy long hair vs. his crew-cut—no one would ever be able to tell us apart. But we have very different tastes; for example, I'm a strict vegetarian, while Levi is a voracious carnivore.)

"No, something worse! And I didn't think *anything* could ever be worse than a hamburger costing even more than it does now!"

I joined him at the computer screen. He had a business news site up, and the lead story was blaring something about a Null Corp press conference scheduled to take place next week. The corporation's young CEO, Colin Null, had promised to deliver an announcement that would "change our understanding of the world as we know it!" I checked the dateline and saw that this story had hit the wires about three days ago. "Oh. *That* twerp. I wonder what the cousins think of this." We stay in pretty close contact with Rae and Danae and have even been on a science-adventure or two with them.

"Yeah," said Levi, "and I wonder what Nessa thinks of it."

(Like I said, there's a lot of differences between me and my brother, above and beyond our choice of diet and our hair. Levi's all about basketball, football and long-distance running, while I couldn't even hardly tell you what sport season it is at any given time of the year. Levi is wild about cowboys and his hero is our great-great-grandfather who was a bucking bronco.rider in Buffalo Bill's Wild West Show. Meanwhile, I'm more into studying the applications of folk remedies, herbs and medicines that have been handed down from our Native ancestors on another side of the family. He enjoys following the stock market in his spare time. I like nothing better than to lock myself away with a big book of poetry. (I mean, who doesn't like a good poem by Joy Harjo or William Carlos Williams, you know what I mean?)

Personality-wise, we are about the most un-twin-ish twins you've ever seen. But there *is* one thing we very much agree on that we are both crazy about, and that one thing is a person. And that person is a girl. And that girl is not just any girl, but is Nessa Null. And Nessa just happens to be the older sister of Colin Null. See how things can get very complicated, very quickly?)

"Hmmmm," I pondered, "knowing her, it's probably making her pretty upset." Levi and I both compete against each other for dates with Nessa, but our sibling rivalry doesn't hold a candle to the all-out war that Nessa has declared on her brother. She runs her own research consulting company pretty much on the up and up, but whenever she sees a chance to gain an advantage over Colin, I don't think she would hesitate to play fast and loose, not only with ethics and research protocols, but even with the law itself. "I think I'll get ahold of Rae and Danae," I decided, "I'll see what's happening with them, ask them if they've got a handle on what that annoying boy-wonder is up to."

"And I'll give Nessa a holler. She probably has the inside scoop. And I'll ask her if she wants to go out for a burger while I'm at it." Levi just barely dodged a punch from me. It was a playful punch. Mostly.

In a half an hour, we met back up in the rec room, with big picture windows overlooking the rocky windswept Alaskan coastline. Mom's a wildlife biologist with the university up here and our dad, one of the Rugg brothers (yes, *those* Rugg brothers) works with Alaska's division of forestry, all of which makes the location of our family cabin a perfect spot for both of their jobs. It's a pretty cool place for me and my bro to spend a lot of our time, too. "Alright, brother. Report. Who goes first?"

Levi said, "How 'bout me, since mine is short and sweet?" I nodded, and he continued. "Nessa says she doesn't know anything. Not nothin', no how, and no way. And that bothers her; puts her right proper in a tizzy, you might say. She's rarely seen Colin be so confident about an upcoming deal, and she says she's *never* seen him keep such a tight lid on information about a project. It's a complete news blackout. She said she would 'very much appreciate it' if we would let her know if and/or when we find out anything." Then he grinned. "And she said she'd love to have dinner with me. I'm going to meet her in New York on Saturday night and take her out to this new little authentic burger spot on 42nd street that I found out about, the chef is an ol' trail hand from Texas and he grills the burgers on an open flame using real mesquite wood that he has shipped in each week from the Lone Star State!"

'Cuz who can resist a big juicy hamburger, am I right or am I right?

His grin faded when I didn't rise to the bait and respond to his teasing about taking Colin's sister out to dinner and he groaned, "Ohhhhh, boy. When you don't have a come-back for me about going out with Nessa, things must be bad. I mean real bad, as bad as a ten-gallon cowboy hat on a two-gallon head. What's the news from the cousins?"

"There IS no news, and that's got me worried." I ticked bullet points off on my fingers. "First off, Team Rugged Stuff is entirely incommunicado. No messages going in or out. The computer network is down, there's nothing being broadcast other than a steady stream of static. Even with our special Team Rugged Stuff access code, there's nothing there... it's all just quiet. As silent as Robert Frost's lovely, dark and deep woods, one might say." If Levi's going to use his corny cowboy lingo, I feel totally justified in making a poetry reference or three.

I saw Levi's shoulders slump. He could recognize that this was all very disturbing. And the rest of my report was even worse. "Secondly, Aunt Ariel doesn't have much info beyond that, either. When I talked to her, she said that the girls had been making good progress on a new project. She's not sure just what it is, because she and Uncle Rick have been gone overseas for a couple of weeks on that Helsinki project. She said that Mike Kane—"

"Who?" (Levi doesn't have a great memory.)

Ouch. Okay, okay, I take it back, no need to punch me, bro. He has a good memory, but he still said, "Who?" And then he said..."Oh, yeah, the Team Rugged Stuff head of operations. British guy, right? *Dr.* Kane? As he so briskly—and brusquely—reminded me that one time."

"Yeah, that's him. Remember, we worked with him when we helped Rae and Danae on that job in South America?" I confirmed. "Anyway, three days ago, Kane sent Aunt Ariel a message that the cousins were going to be out of communication for a week or two, because of their current research. She said she might've been concerned except for the fact that Kane said everything was well in hand. But when I told her that the TRS network is down..."

"Wait, don't tell me. She asked if we might mosey on over and just see how things are going with our favorite team of scientist-adventurer cousins?"

"Right in one guess."

Levi cracked his knuckles. "Let's clear it with the folks, but I don't see any reason why we can't take a little trip down the coast to visit family. A bit of a vacation at Tahoe sounds like a great little getaway, just so long as I get out to the East Coast in time for my dinner date with Nessa!"

"And, of course, she also asked if we might have some free time in December and if we—you, me, Mom and Dad—might get to visit them during Chanukah this year."

Levi's reply was to grin, lick his lips, rub his stomach and make a 'yum-yum-yummy' sound. At home during Chanukah, we do all the usual stuff; we play dreidel for chocolate gelt (spinning a little four-sided top with Hebrew letters on it to win milk-chocolate in the shape of coins) and light the chanukiah and everything. Yup, just like Emily Bowen Cohen, we're a Two-Tribe family, Native and Jewish.

But let's face it, no one in me and Levi's household are great cooks or anything (Sorry, Mom and Dad...the truth hurts!) On the other hand, when we spend the holiday with our cousins, we get to gorge ourselves on a never-ending supply of potato pancakes smothered in applesauce and sour cream. Aunt Ariel makes the absolute best potato latkes in the world; she got the recipe from her Great-Uncle Julie (as in 'Julius') who was a cook in the Army and made them for the troops in World War II. My mouth started to water, just thinking about the holiday.

We got up bright and early the next morning and it was a fairly quick flight into the Reno-Tahoe International Airport in Nevada. After a brief text to our parents to let them know we had landed safe and sound, we took a cab to the Team Rugged Stuff laboratory complex. The taxi dropped us off at the front gate to the property, several hundred acres located in the Galena foothills between the Biggest Little City in the World and the second-deepest lake in the USA. Levi punched his TRS code into the keypad. The gate opened, we stepped through and then on up to the lab complex lobby. I pulled on the handle of the big glass door and nothing happened. I looked at Levi.

"Yeah, that's not good," he said. And he was right. Mid-afternoon on a weekday, there should have been someone staffing the front office. Levi cupped his hands up against the glass and peered in. No one at the desk, no lights on anywhere. "This doesn't look good at all, bro. I think this is going to end up being a working vacation after all."

"Right. Let's go suit up."

We turned around and followed a faint trail to a little house set back in the woods. Aunt Ariel and Uncle Rick and the cousins live here in a cabin set apart a little ways from the actual research facility itself. Our passcode got us through the front door. No one was home, but that's what we had expected, given that our aunt and uncle were currently out of the country and both Rachel and Danae seemed to be missing. Up the stairs and down the hall to the left and we opened the door to the guest room that Aunt Ariel and Uncle Rick have set aside for us to use when we visit. Each of us opened up our bag and got ready for work.

When we left our room, I'm ashamed to say that we each looked like a Hollywood version of some sort of super spy.

Be ashamed all you want, bro. But our work suits ROCK! While I normally prefer cowboy boots, a Stetson and some good ol' blue jeans, when it comes time to get down to business, our kind of business, there are worse uniforms that we could wear than what we had on when we stepped out into the hallway!

Yes. Believe it or not, we had on black long-sleeve shirts and hoods with masks that were, at the time, pulled back from our faces and hanging down from the backs of our necks. Black paratrooper pants tucked into black tabi boots, and small pouches slung crossbody from shoulder to hip completed the outfit. (Levi once joked that our possibles pouches hold such an array of gizmos and gadgets that they are to us what the utility belt is to a certain bat-themed superhero.) Our outfits look absolutely hokey and horrid, but the thing is, they get the job done.

Yeah, because back in the olden days, the mountain men who explored the wilderness and traded furs and stuff would often carry a bag with all of their necessary gear like a knife, flint and steel, gunpowder, that kind of thing. It was so that they could deal with all possible obstacles or challenges of life in the wilderness, and it came to be known as their "possibles bag." So we applied that to our spy suit pouches! Cool, huh?

Thank you, Mr. History. Can I get back to my story now?

So anyway, once we double-checked the house to make sure no one was home—and that no one was snooping on us while we were trying to snoop on them—we went downstairs to the basement and stood in front of a bookshelf that covered one entire wall of the room. Levi and I are one of just a handful of people who know that this bookshelf is actually a secret entrance to an underground passageway into the Team Rugged Stuff labs.

If by 'handful' you mean, 'anyone who happens to read this report,' then yeah, I guess so...

Oh. Oh! Right. Oh well, I'm sure Danae will edit this kind of sensitive info out before anyone else sees it.

Anyway, as we stepped up to the bookshelf, I laughed. "I still can't get over how corny our cousins are! I mean, our spy suits are one thing, as funny-looking as they are, but Rae and Danae's secret passageway...it's just crazy hilarious!"

Levi laughed too, but said, "Yeah, but if this turns out to be a real problem, if the cousins have really gone missing and this is the only way to check it out, then I guess the joke is on us. Rae always said that we might need to have a way to get into the labs that no one but family knew about."

Yes, you're quoting me accurately, and I was quoting Rachel accurately. A way that No. One. But. Family. Knew. About. Do you ever even listen to yourself? Have you ever looked up the definition of 'secret'? That was me talking to you in private, and here you are, setting the conversation down for posterity!

Pipe down, bro. I'm the one telling the story. And at the risk of getting ahead of myself and giving spoilers, you're not really one to talk about giving away family secrets, are you? Not after what you ended up doing later in this story?

Oh. Yeah. That. Well. I guess you do have a point there.

Uh-huh, that's what I thought. So, to continue with my astounding tale, I reached to the back of my neck and pulled my mask up over my head and then down to cover my face. Levi followed suit, but with his short hair, the hood fit a little bit more snugly on his head. Eyeholes positioned to give us maximum visibility, we nodded to each other and my brother reached out to the shelf and pulled out a very specific book, triggering the secret entrance that opened to the passage. Despite the seriousness of the situation, I still had to chuckle at Rae's choice of book to be the hidden lever. *Hardy Boys #25: The Secret Panel.*

Chapter 4

DANAE'S LOG 3:
New Discoveries

Well, I'll tell you what, we didn't get a whole lot of sleep during the remainder of that night. Before too long, a second set of eyes showed up. Both pair kept watch on us, never blinking, and always just outside the ring of firelight, so we couldn't make out any shapes or bodies to go with the eyeballs.

As the hours went by, it didn't seem as if they were too interested in coming any closer, so we took turns dozing lightly by the fire. It felt as if I had just finally fallen into a nice snooze when Rae nudged my shoulder. She motioned toward the horizon over the water where the sky was taking on a pre-dawn glow. "I regret interrupting your slumber, but I want to have you alert during the coming day's illumination. That is, sorry to wake you, but we'll both need to pay attention while it gets light."

I didn't even have to stop to think about it to know what she had in mind. "You're hoping we can catch sight of whatever is attached to those eyes."

"Affirmative. Even if they are nocturnal creatures, which seems likely given the behavior that we've observed, we may be able to ascertain something of their physical makeup before they retire for the day."

I was on board with that. If we could see what they looked like, it would help us to determine what kind of threat-level we should assign to them. "Right. I'm no scaredy-cat, but I'm kind of hoping they turn out to be curious herbivores, rather than hungry carnivores."

"It *would* be rather more pleasant if we didn't find it necessary to establish a serious defense perimeter today on top of everything else," Rae agreed.

The sky continued to lighten, shifting through the spectrum from black to purple, then almost green and yellow, finally into a beautiful blue. All around us, the darkness slowly faded and the scenery became visible in the morning light. The eyes were still there, still looking at us from out there at the edge of the jungle, but neither of us could make out any sort of bodies to go with them.

Finally, as the sun actually began to peek over the edge of the world and rays of light touched us, I thought I could see some sort of smudge or spot right where the eyes were still shining in the golden glow of dawn. "Rae, is there something there? Not a body, but…"

"Yes, I see it! It looks as if the ocular organs are situated upon a small globe of some sort that is levitating. Meaning, the eyes are attached to nothing but a floating orb!"

Both sets of eyes seemed to be set on spherical lumps about the size of a tennis ball and were hovering at a height of about a meter and a half above the sand... about eye-level to Rae, or chin-level to me. (My sister might be a couple of years older than me, but I've got a few inches on her!) We slowly made our way toward the strange sight, and as the sun shone fully on them, we could see that one of the *things* was colored a golden tan with gentle blue splotches splashed all over it. Looking closer, we could see faint blue and gold wisps about a half a foot long, trailing behind it like a delicate tail. Its companion had the same shape, but its coloration was a vibrant red and green, with those hues also duplicated in its tail. They looked almost as if they were exotic sea creatures floating along in a gentle current, but instead of ocean water, their environment was the tangy tropical air.

"Oh. My. Gosh!" Rachel breathed beside me.

"That's. For. Sure!"

"They're adorable!"

"Super cute!"

We finally turned from the sight in front of us to look at each other. Rae said to me, "This is—*they* are—incredible! And I say that in the very literal sense!"

"Absolutely! Scientifically speaking, those creatures are practically unbelievable!"

Yes, it's true, although it embarrasses me to say it. Both of us—we who were seasoned explorers and veterans of all kinds of adventures—we stood there and gushed over these floating little critters. It was like we were just little kindergarteners or something. It was all so sweet it would almost make you gag, but we just couldn't help ourselves.

And as if in response to our exclamations of delight, the *whatevers* began to drift closer to us. They didn't have wings or any other visible way to be flying like they were. I said it before and I'll say it again, they looked almost exactly as if they were undersea creatures, but swimming in the air instead of in water. When they got within a few meters of us, we could hear small, faint chirps and burbles from them. But that raised even more questions because they didn't seem to have any mouths. Each of them was just a beautiful little fluffball with a pair of glowing eyes and a fuzzy tail wafting out behind it.

My sister extended her hand and called out to them. "Come on little fella," she crooned, "I'm not gonna hurt you, I just wanna pet you…"

Wait a minute, I thought, *that sounded familiar.* I turned and looked at her with my eyebrows raised. "Um, *Swiss Family Robinson*? Disney movie from the midcentury 1900s?"

Rae was astounded. "That's right! I wasn't aware that you had a command of that sort of cinematic trivia!"

Huh. Serves her right. If she can pop off and surprise me by knowing about video games, well, then I can come back and give her a shock by knowing about the old movies that she likes so much! But I guess memories of that particular old film were bubbling up in both of our brains. It's about some people who get stranded on an unexplored jungle island with no way to get home. Unfortunately, our current situation couldn't be solved as easily as getting picked up by a passing ship.

"You know this is a little bit crazy, right?" Rae said to me. "These are wild, unknown animals. I will surmise that they have never before been seen by humans. We have not one bit of data as to whether they are dangerous or aggressive. For all we know, they are happy to see us in the same way that we would be happy to see a dish of ice cream or a slice of pie. That is, they could very well be predators regarding us as potential prey. And yet...and yet, we are acting as if they are just the cutest, friendliest li'l puffs of fluff that we ever did see."

"You're right," I said, "and I'm not exactly sure why we're behaving like this."

I scrunched up my eyes and actually focused some brain power on this mystery of why these little guys were so appealing. "Huh. Unless. Just one second..." A thought came to me, and if I were in an old-timey comic strip or funny book, there would have been a lightbulb over my head. I grabbed my rucksack from the ground near the campfire and pulled out my hologram empathy helmet and my little tool kit and did a little fiddling. "Hmmmm. Reverse this wire here, shift this connection over a bit, modulate the input vector, lower the power pulse there..." I grabbed a short USB cord and hooked the helmet to my tablet. "Upload the data from the drone's fly-over footage, and... Aha! Let's just see about this now!"

I engaged one of the switches on the helmet and set it on my head. A hologram appeared in the air in front of me, but instead of showing a duplicate Danae, it projected a 3D topographical map image of the island. Near one edge of the map were four blinking lights clustered together.

"Very impressive, D! What a great idea, using the holographic capabilities of the helmet to tap into and display our survey data." Rae studied the layout. "Yes, there's that volcano. And judging by the geographic positioning of the terrain, those dots represent you and me... and the two cryptozoological specimens here?"

I told you my sis has a big brain. She figured most of it out in the first try. "It's no big deal to convert the info from the drone recordings and have the projector create a map of the area. But I also added input from the empathy circuits to overlay info about any theta waves that my helmet can detect. Instead of just reading the waves from *inside* the helmet, it's now working as a short-range *external* empathy detector, and is subsequently displaying the sources of those waves on the map. But now for the really cool part. I also put my helmet's AI protocols to work on collecting data from the theta waves of these guys. Instead of then using this to create a hologram duplicate, I just had the software analyze the waves. And it explains why we took a liking to them so quickly... these fuzzballs are actually broadcasting friendly feelings!" I pointed to the fuzzballs in question. "At the risk of sounding absolutely unscientific and touchy-feely, these guys are giving off good vibes!"

Both of the creatures started chirping like crazy and began to flit around our heads in a display of pure and unadulterated happiness.

"They're natural empath transmitters AND receivers!" I took off my helmet and set it on my bag.

Rae stared wonderingly at the show they were putting on. "So what you are telling me is that your equipment has determined that they project their feelings or emotions to us and can, in turn, sense our feelings or emotions?"

"Yup! They like us, and we like them, and that makes them like us even more, and so on and so on! A closed-system empathy feedback loop!"

Rae sighed. "Well, I'll trust your science on this." She held her hand out to the nearest of the mystery animals. "Hi there! May I make an observation via enhanced proximity? That is to say, can I take a closer look at you?" The creature in question was the sandy-colored orb with bands of deep blue across what would probably be called its back, and a fluffy tail that was equal parts gold and turquoise. It chirped out a cheery *"bbbba!"* and landed gracefully on her outstretched palm. Rae petted it and it began to emit a low-level vibrating *"bbbzzz."* Sis glanced at me. "I think it's purring!"

We both looked more closely at the orb-lump-creature-animal-whatever. I held my hand out, and its partner landed there and started nuzzling me. "No mouth. No arms, legs, ears, nose, hands, fingers, toes, teeth, fins or feathers. And despite the fact that it flies through the air, it has no wings. It's just a colorful little beanbag with eyes and a tail. A beautiful, *beautiful* tail." I was flat-out astounded.

"I think it's time for us to name this discovery," Rae announced. Yup, she's a big-picture kind of girl, while I take care of the nitty-gritty stuff. "I don't want to keep thinking of them as just lumps or some such. I'd almost enjoy naming them Tribbles, but I think we can do without a copyright infringement lawsuit, thank you very much. Besides, as cute as the Tribbles were, the crew of the USS *Enterprise* had quite a bit of trouble with them, and I'd rather not jinx our relationship with these little guys right off the bat."

There she was again, referring back to classic movies and television shows. But I definitely knew what she was talking about this time, and she *knew* that I knew, because one of the main people involved in making the props and special effects—including the Tribbles!—for the old *Star Trek* television show was a Rugg. Look it up, it's a fact. I dare you.

"Yeah, okay," I said. I thought she was using an awful lot of brainpower thinking about what we *shouldn't* name them. "But there's something that keeps popping into my head as I look at them. The phrase, 'Bright-eyed and bushy-tailed.' But I can't think of what it's from..."

"'Bright-eyed and bushy-tailed'," she repeated after me. "Huh. That's something Auntie Bea used to say when we got up in the morning and she was at the kitchen table drinking coffee with Mom and Dad. 'My, my, my, aren't we all bright-eyed and bushy-tailed.'"

Auntie Bea isn't really our aunt. She's not a sister of either of our parents, but she's a friend of theirs from back when they were all in college together. A real crazy artist, she would sometimes stay with us for weeks at a time, and then be off traveling the world again. Probably the most un-scientifically oriented person I've ever met in my life, but tons of fun. "That's right! I always got the feeling it was some sort of expression she had picked up from living in the United Kingdom or something."

"Well, it sure does describe these fellows!" Rae addressed the little animal in her hand, "How about it, buddy? Are you a Bright-Eyed Bushy Tail?"

It burbled as if to say *"Yes!"* I looked down at the one that was purring on my palm. "You too?" The purring got louder, and I swear it murmured, *"mmmm-hmm!"* in agreement.

Then Rae frowned. "History, however, makes it abundantly clear that society prefers to truncate lengthy nomenclature. In other words, that name is way too long for everyday use. I propose using the term *BrightEyes*."

When Big Sis is right, she's right. "Sounds good!" I said. I transferred my 'BrightEyes' friend from my hand to my shoulder, and Rae followed my lead. While the little creatures perched there like pirate parrots, chirping and burbling, Rae and I each spit in our palms ("ptooey!") and then shook hands to seal the deal.

We spent the next couple of hours playing with our new friends and studying them. My favorite was the red and green one, but in examining it more closely, I could see that the red color also featured orange and maroon highlights, and the green was made up of many different shades. The eyes were a bright green but had flecks of red in the depths of the iris, and the tail had both red and green strands that were delicately feathered and fanned out lazily behind my little friend. Rae's buddy, on the other hand, the first one of the pair that had come to inspect us, was a blue and golden-tan fuzzball with a turquoise and yellow tail, and the colorations were a perfect representation of the sandy beach and tropical waters that made up our surroundings.

We had a midday meal of even more of the bananas, and we were getting so sick of the same food over and over that we gave up making jokes about the different ways to prepare it. "This diet, while probably sufficient for our short-term nutritional requirements, is most definitely lacking in variety. In other words, these things will probably keep us alive, but the food is going to get awfully boring," announced Rae.

"You're not kidding about that, Sis." When my research is going well, I usually treat myself with a chocolate bar and I figured that today's scientific advancement was worth at least two or three of 'em. "So I'm thinking it's time to come up with a plan of action and get home to throw a monkey wrench into Colin's big scheme."

As we sat and ate and pondered, the BrightEyes floated and flitted around our heads, swooping down now and then to nuzzle our ears or hide in our hair, then buzzing off again to play aerial tag with each other. Rae pondered, "Okay, the simplest option first. What, in your estimation, do you consider to be the chances that Mike will be able to mount a recovery expedition and retrieve us from the OtherWorld in time to prevent our nemesis from absconding with our discovery and stealing it from us on the world stage? In other words, can Mike get us out of here in time to stop Colin?"

I gulped down my mouthful of banana, shook my head and frowned. "I think we both know the answer to that. The chances are slim to none. Colin didn't get around our tight security and lure us here into this trap just to have our ops manager flip a switch and bring us home." I took another bite and continued talking around a mouthful of yellow mush. "He'll have put something into place back at the lab to prevent anyone on that side of things from rescuing us before he holds his press conference." Swallow. There was still quite of bit of the bland, vegetable-like food left, but I just couldn't stomach any more. "Blech! I want chocolate!"

"Your assessment of the situation is an identical match with mine. Both the determination of Colin's strategy, and your expression of desire for dessert. So that indicates that we'll have to develop an alternative tactic in order to return in time to set things right."

I stood up and brushed sand off my rear end. "Okay. Let's do this by the numbers. In any project, the first step is to figure out the final desired outcome, the goal. And our goal is to get back home and stop Colin."

"Check."

"Second step is always to take stock of your resources. So let's see what all we've got. I'm glad we didn't listen to Mike when he said we wouldn't need to bring along our rucksacks full of gear."

"Right! I mostly brought reference material downloaded onto a tablet, but it looked like you were loading up with quite a bit of hardware. I'll go through my files while you inventory your belongings."

I already had my chem kit out (remember, I used it to check out the "bananas"), so I started digging through my bag to see what else I had tossed in there. Big tool kit for big stuff, little tool kit for little stuff, extra wire, soldering kit, and—Oh! I smacked myself on the forehead, calling myself three kinds of forgetful. There at the bottom of the bag was my set of Ruggoggles. It was a pair of goggles modified to my own design and included adaptations for binoculars, rangefinder, microscope... and night vision. "*Now* I remember putting these in my bag, but I should've thought of them last night when we were trying to see what belonged to the eyes out there in the dark." But at least I could use them now to help analyze the full extent of the damage to the Tesla coil and platform components.

I put the Ruggoggles on my head and adjusted the lenses over my eyes to look at the remains of the battery and the meteor. My little bright-eyed buddy seemed fascinated by my work and kept moving in between my hands and the electronics, as if it wanted to study the technology for itself. I finally gave up and laughed. "Okay, okay, if you keep blocking my view, I'm going to look at you instead!" But when I aimed the optics at the fuzzball, I wasn't laughing for long. I might have even let out a gasp, because it caught Rae's attention.

"Is everything alright? Do you require assistance?" she asked, looking up from her tablet.

"Well, nothing's wrong, not exactly. But could you come here and, uh, take a look at this?"

Big Sis stepped over and I handed her the goggles, "I've got it on microscope setting, and I'm looking at the Bright-Eyes' skin, or fur, or whatever. Tell me what you see."

She studied my little friend for a few minutes and let out a low whistle. "Whew! I begin to get an idea of what you mean! These guys are even more incredible than we thought. The greenish portions of this skin seem to have photosynthetic properties, while the reds and oranges exhibit anthrocyanitic characteristics." Which was just her way of saying that the BrightEyes' hide not only looked like jungle plants, but seemed to be actually MADE of jungle plants, at least to some small degree.

"Yup, that's what it looks like to me, too!"

Rae coaxed the other BrightEyes onto her hand and gave it a microscopic once-over as well. "And this one. The yellow and tan sections of its skin actually have a silicon crystal structure, and the blue-hued parts—if I'm looking at them correctly—are composed of electro-bonded liquid. That is to say, it *looks* like sand and water because it *is* sand and water!"

"I would almost say that this is a case of 'you are what you eat,' but these guys don't actually seem to eat anything."

"Affirmative. Instead, they simply appear to incorporate attributes of their immediate environment into their own physical structure at a molecular level! In other words—"

"Yup. In other words, the BrightEyes are actually made up of the same stuff that is all around them. But there's obviously more to it than that, otherwise they would both have the same structure, color, and so on, instead of each having a unique makeup!"

Wow. Just wow.

After that kind of a discovery, it was hard to concentrate on our primary mission of getting out of our prison paradise and back to our lab, but by the time the sun went down and the moons came up, we had progressed about as far as we could without more resources. I had managed to salvage quite a bit of material from the burnt-out sections of our original equipment and Rae had pulled together enough schematics that I was pretty confident that I could figure out how to rig something up for a quick and dirty one-time transport back to Earth or to our own dimension or wherever our home was.

All the while, however, something very disconcerting was on our minds. Every couple of hours or so, the ground would shake. Nothing like that first trembler that had knocked me on my *tuchus*, but big enough so that we couldn't ignore them. But there was nothing we could do about those sporadic tremors so we had to file them under the category of 'Something to Worry About Later.'

Neither of us had gotten much sleep the night before, because we had been watching the BrightEyes watching us. But Rae put on her 'over-bearing-and-over-protective big sister' hat and wanted me to turn in, to go to bed, while she stood sentry.

"Look here," I snapped at her. "I think at this point some real sleep is more important for both of us than wasting time keeping watch through the night." I was exhausted and I could see that she was pretty much wiped out too. Then, as usual, I felt bad about barking at her, so I smiled. "Besides, we've got our very own special guardians to keep an eye out for us," I said, addressing the swooping and floating BrightEyes. "Right, guys? Since it doesn't appear that you need to sleep. Or eat. Or drink..."

The two floating fuzzies liked the idea. *"chirp-rrr!"* You'd almost swear they perked up at attention like a couple of soldiers on patrol! They really seemed to understand what I meant because they started slowly circling the perimeter of our camp, emitting a low buzzing sound and looking into the darkness beyond the ring of firelight.

"Okay, I guess you're right," sighed Rae, and from the look on her face, I could tell she really was tired. We curled up into little nests of leaves in our cozy campsite.

The fire was dying down to embers and Rae said, "I think this is just about the most peaceful setting I've ever experienced, in spite of the predicament in which we find ourselves."

Between the soft pink and blue light of the moons on the water, the faint roar of the surf and the glowing eyes of our little friends to watch over us, I thought she was right and I was just about to tell her so when I heard another sound. At first, I thought it was the seismic rumbling again, but there was no vibration to accompany it. My brow furrowed as I concentrated to try and identify the source of the low-pitched grumble.

That's when I realized that it was the sound of my big sister snoring! For about five seconds I considered getting up and using our gear to record the sounds, thinking how funny it would be to play it back for her in the morning. But before I could bring myself to climb to my feet, I dozed off myself into a deep sleep.

Chapter 5

DANAE'S LOG 4:
Food for Thought

"**W**ell, that's the end of that!"

I threw down my tool kit in frustration. I felt just about ready to cry. We'd gotten up at dawn and I really thought that with all the material we had been able to scavenge up, I'd be able to figure some sort of work-around to get things operational despite the fact that my Widmanstätten circuits and my battery were out of commission. But the more we worked on it in the morning, the clearer it was just how close—and how far away—the solution was.

Pretty much most all of the components were there. They might only hold up for one engagement before going all kablooey, but that was all we would need in order to get back home. But I was missing some vital elements that I just couldn't do without and no matter how hard I tried, I couldn't come up with any replacements that would work for us.

"Hmmm." She didn't show it, but I knew Rae was pretty upset too. When she stops talking, you know something's wrong. "What if—no. Maybe—nah. Perhaps?—huhnt-nuh."

"My thoughts exactly," I said. "Without a Widmanstätten meteorite, or an awfully good replica, we're stuck. I could hook this platform up to all the electricity in Hoover Dam and it wouldn't move us an inch. On the other hand, even if a meteor fell right here and landed in my hand," I pounded my palm with my fist, "it would still be just a stupid chunk of useless rock, since we don't have anywhere near the level of electrical power current that we need to run through it." I flopped down on my back in the sand and closed my eyes in defeat. Yes, a bit melodramatic, I know, but I was awfully depressed and didn't much care. "That's it. I'm done. Wake me up when Colin has successfully stolen our life's work and decides to bring us home to rub our faces in it."

Rae sighed. "I guess we can use the time to learn more about our perplexing little acquaintances here." She's one of those kinds of people who always makes the best of things. Yeah, she's a perky pain in the neck, but I love her. "I wonder if we can use your empathy loop research and your helmet to communicate a little bit better with them?" she continued, and I heard her fiddling with the helmet as she asked "What should I say to them?"

"See if you can get them to bring me some shade," I called, without opening my eyes, "I'm getting awfully hot here in the sun, but I'm too bummed-out to move under the lean-to." In all actuality, I probably was setting myself up for a wicked sunburn, but oh well. If I was going to be miserable, I might as well be really miserable.

"Hmmm, let's see," I heard Sis muttering. And then, through my closed eyelids, the glare of the sunlight dimmed.

I thought maybe she was standing over me and blocking the sunshine, but when I opened my eyes to look, it was the two BrightEyes—hovering in the air about half a meter above me—who were shading a bit of the sun from my face. "Um, Rae? Did you do that?"

"Wow, I guess so! I was thinking of trying to ask them to bring some palm fronds over to give you shade, but then I realized they have no way to carry them. Then I thought about how big their shadows would be and wondered if it would be enough for you to notice any difference in the amount of sunlight on your face, and... they must have received the image from the helmet broadcast!"

"Huh! I guess it works!" I closed my eyes again. "Pretty neat, but you're right, there's not much shade to be had from the little guys. I guess I'm doomed to just lie here and overheat for now." I started to doze and had just about drifted off when I heard Rae laugh and then a bunch of big fat drops of water splashed my face.

My eyes popped open and I was sure that *this* time I would see my sister standing there and splattering me with sea water, but she hadn't moved an inch. "What the what-what?" I sputtered, grabbed my walking stick and used it to help me climb to my feet.

"Can you believe it?" she said, still giggling, "I still had the helmet on and I thought about what other ways there might be to provide you with relief from the oppressive temperature, and the BrightEyes took it from there. Both of them flew over to the edge of the beach and plopped down into the water, soaking up the liquid. Then they flew back to you and shook themselves all over like a pair of wet dogs, spraying you with water drops!"

"Wait. So you told them to splash water on me?" That actually was kind of funny, and impressive that she could convey that kind of an idea to these little animals.

"No! I wasn't even thinking of the water, I was trying to figure out how they might be able to provide more shade for you, or maybe how to fan the air for a breeze in order to cool you off!"

Whoa. Whoa! "You mean they came up with the idea all on their own?"

"Right! Think about what this means! It shows that the BrightEyes would score pretty high on the Rodman Intellect Rating Scale. This is a clear-cut case of independent problem solving!"

I walked over to join Rae. "Yeah, that's some higher-level thinking. Say, let me see the helmet for a minute, will you? There's something I want to try out." I put it on and thought real hard. I realized my nose and forehead were all scrunched up, that happens when I'm really into an idea. Then both of the BrightEyes floated off toward the jungle at the edge of the beach.

Rae watched them disappear into the forest. "Well, they're doing something. Is there a particular task that you've asked them to accomplish?"

"I don't want to say quite yet. Wait and let's see what happens." After about 15 minutes, they returned. My little green and red friend flew around behind us and started nudging us toward the foliage, while Rae's yellow and blue buddy led the way, flying back and forth, looking for all the world as if beckoning us to follow.

"It seems as if they desire that we change our location. I mean, they want us to go someplace." Rae looked at me with her eyebrows raised. "Do you know what they have in mind?"

"I think so." I grinned. We started walking in the direction indicated. We worked our way through the underbrush and then, about 40 meters from the edge of the beach, the BrightEyes stopped at a large tree. It was tall and bushy. We couldn't see up into the branches, but I did notice several more just like it growing farther inland. The BrightEyes started circling it, spiraling up and around and into the leaves above. Then back down. Then up again.

"Give me a boost, Sis?"

Rae looked dubious. "I don't know, Danae. Maybe I should be the one to try and see what's up there..." Always the mother hen.

"Oh, come on! It's climbing a tree, not running a marathon! Besides, this was *my* idea."

She finally gave in. I told you I was stubborn. "Okay," she said, making a stirrup with her hands to help hoist me up to the lowest branches, "but you be awfully careful. There's not a single emergency room within shouting distance."

I only had to climb a little ways up into the branches. (And it's a good thing, too. I wouldn't admit it to Rae, but this stiff leg of mine can be a pain in the neck when it comes to activities like this.) The BrightEyes were hovering around a clump of large purple berries, and I could see several other similar clumps all within grabbing distance. I plucked them from the tree, called down, "Catch!" and dropped them to Rae's waiting hands. Once I had harvested all that I could reach, I made my own way back down to the ground.

"Bon appetite!" I announced with a grin.

Rae looked thoughtful. "I think that's pronounced *bon appétit*. The 'i' has a long 'ee' sound." I rolled my eyes. "And let me guess," she continued, ignoring my facial expression, "you concentrated your mental faculties upon the fact of how we were growing weary of a diet composed solely of bananas and these creatures decided to find some different and varied food for our consumption?"

"You got it! And so did they! And now, so do we! Got it, that is. Got food, that is."

On the way back to camp, we discussed what this all meant as far as the BrightEyes were concerned. "They are most def in the top quarter of the Rodman scale," I said, "able to recognize a concept such as food for us, even though they don't seem to 'eat' in the same way that we do. They were able to understand what I wanted and then they developed a solution to the problem. And all of this was based solely on me expressing a desire to eat something other than our bananas."

Back at the beach, my chem kit showed that the berries checked out A-OK. Although they looked a lot like grapes, the taste was more of a meaty mushroom flavor. "Odd, but good," I announced.

"Particularly after our decidedly singular menu over the past several meals," Rae agreed. Then she got a thoughtful look on her face yet again. "Say, Danae, you said the helmet provides a loop, right? It's a transmitter and a receiver, that is, we can project feelings toward the BrightEyes, and they could also project toward us. That is, in addition to their own natural empathic abilities. Is that correct?"

"Um, yeah...?" I wasn't sure where she was going with this.

"So, I'm just wondering if we could get the BrightEyes to communicate some more concrete data to us about this island. If they could, in essence, project information onto the holo-map?"

See, I told you before and I'll tell you again, my sister has a big, big brain.

It was worth pondering. "Hmmmm. If we could get the idea across to them, then yeah. I mean, if they can understand what it is that we want to know, I think it is def possible." I picked up the helmet. "And I think I know how to frame it so that they can grasp the concept." Adjusting the gear on my head, I addressed the two creatures, who both seemed to know that something was up. They were buzzing curiously around our heads. "Okay little buddies, you did great! Thanks for showing us these berries, they are very yummy. But I wonder... are there any more trees in the jungle that have those types of berries growing on them?

They both bobbed up and down in the air, very definitely communicating a *"Yes!"* to me. Then they started floating back toward the jungle, expecting us to follow them and find some new treats.

I called out to them, "Wait! Wait a minute, okay?" I gestured for them to come back.

"Blerp?" "Brbbt?" They sounded confused but returned to hover around me.

"Can you SHOW me where they are, instead of taking me there?" I reached up to the helmet on my head and flipped a switch on to engage the cartography projection app and *poof*, the topographical holo-map appeared in the air in front of me. The blinking dots marked the locations of the four of us. "Whoops, just a minute." I grabbed a connecting cord and linked the helmet up with my tablet and adjusted some of the software settings. The colors of the markers changed. I assigned yellow to me and blue to Rae (our favorite colors, natch!), then red to my friendly BrightEyes and green to Rae's.

The fuzzballs started buzzing in excitement.

"See? That's Rae, and that's me," I explained, pointing as I spoke. "And that's *you*, and that's *you*. And that's all the area around here." I concentrated and willed a new marking onto the map, a purple X. "And that's the place you took us to the yummy food."

Rae whistled in appreciation. "You used the empathy feedback receptor and *'felt'* some new information into the cartograph?"

I couldn't help but grin. It *was* a pretty nice bit of thinking outside of the box, if I do say so myself! "Thank you, thank you," I said, and curtsied. "But please hold your applause until the end of the presentation." Then I turned back to the BrightEyes. "I'm going to widen up the band of the reception so you can add markings on the map, too. Can you think of where some more food is for us? Can you look at the map and think of a marking for it there?"

Their response was very interesting! They looked at each other and swooped around and then put their heads close to each other as if conferring over the puzzle. Then they both turned toward the map projection and presto-change-o, just like magic, another purple X appeared, not far from the first. And then another. And another. When they were done, I could see a few dozen of the markers on the map.

"Great!" Rae laughed, "At least we know that we won't starve!"

I grabbed one of the bananas from our stockpile and held it up toward the BrightEyes. "That was perfect! How about these? Can you add them to the map too?"

"Brrrpbrbr!" It only took about 30 seconds this time for several little cream-colored X's to show up on the map. From where we stood, I could see that all of the markers

that showed up near our beach camp were accurate and seemed to correspond perfectly with the banana trees we already knew about.

Rae laughed again. "Wow, when these BrightEyes grasp an intellectual concept, they persevere and pursue it to its logical conclusion. I mean, once they get the hang of something, there's no stopping them!"

She was more correct than she realized, because all of a sudden, some two or three dozen *orange* markers appeared on the digital model. "What the what-what?" I wondered.

"Hmmm. They located the 'grapes' and the 'bananas' for us. I would almost be willing to establish a small wager that those new X's are yet another potentially edible fruit for us." Rae addressed the BrightEyes. "Is that it? Did you also put some 'oranges' on the map for us?" Both of them nodded and buzzed in agreement to confirm her guess and she grinned at me. "Great job, Little Sis! Looks as if we'll have plenty of food for the duration, as long as we can stomach that much fruit. That was brilliant of you to figure out how to get the little fellers to communicate with us via the empathy feedback loop." She glanced up at said little fellers (who were happily fluttering above our heads) and sighed. "But I guess it's time to return to addressing the overarching problem for now."

My sigh echoed hers. "Yeah. I guess I kinda hoped that my subconscious would come up with an answer while we were messing around with the map, but..." I looked at the platform and our small collection of components, "...it all comes down to two very particular things," I stuck up my index finger. "Power." And then another finger. "And Widmanstätten circuits. With nary a sign of a lightning storm nor a chunk of meteorite in sight." I reached up to take the helmet off my head and get back to work.

"Blrrp? Bpprt! Pttpt! Zzbbt!" All of a sudden the BrightEyes went frantic with activity, chirping like nobody's business.

"Huh? What is it, you two?" I couldn't tell what was giving them such a conniption fit, I just knew they were excited about something.

"D? Um, hey, Danae?" Rae tapped my shoulder. "Could I inquire as to whether you made a mental addition to the topographical representation? That is, did you happen to 'feel' and add something new to the map just right now?"

I was a little annoyed by her question. I wanted to figure out what was up with the BrightEyes and here my big sister was zoning off about the map. "No, what are you talking about?" But when I looked down at the projection, she didn't have to explain. There were two new X markings on the image! A light-blue one had shown up on the map just a bit inland from our campsite, up toward the mountain. And another was a metallic-silver color, near a small lake that was located close to the center of the island.

"Right immediately after you said 'lightning' and 'meteorite', the BrightEyes exhibited a frenetic behavior—I mean that they got all excited—and those marks showed up on the map," Rae said in a hushed tone, "and if *you* didn't think them onto the projection..." her voice trailed off.

I completed the thought. "If I didn't think them...then the BrightEyes must have put them on! We had just asked them to find food for us. So when I said we really needed that other stuff, they must have thought I was asking for their help again." I looked at the new X's. "But what do you think they're marking? You don't think they could really understand what we need to make the transporter platform function again... do you?"

Rae focused her big brain on the matter. "It is a possibility that they understood you. Or maybe not. In fact, *probably* not. And even if they *did* understand, I can't imagine that there is anything on this remote tropical island that would fit the bill of what we're lacking. Don't get me wrong, I would love to think so, but I just don't see how it could possibly be."

"I think you're right. I don't see how either, Sis. But I think we should check it out, because there's no other chance of getting back home before Colin lays claim," I swung my arms around to indicate the beach, the jungle, the BrightEyes, "to all of this."

Chapter 6

NOAH AND LEVI'S JOURNAL 2: "Into the Tunnel!"

The tunnel was wide enough for me and Levi to travel down it side-by-side for about 50 meters. One of the best features of our work uniforms is a communicator system that is built into the fabric of our masks. The slightest whisper by either one of us can be transmitted to the earpiece in the hood of the other. There is even a safety protocol included into the system so that if we're speaking at a normal volume, or if we have to raise our voices, it automatically regulates the decibel level so it won't blast out our eardrums. It was all designed by Danae... it's great to have a tech wiz in the family!

Yeah! Thanks, Danae!

The result was that we were able to carry on a dialogue all the while cautiously navigating the tunnel in a relatively silent stealth mode. And to make things even more secure, when we are on the job, we add into our communication a bunch of Yiddish that we learned from our Nana, and sometimes a bit of Salish, some Native speech that we learned from our Grandpa Mitchell. So even if anyone could hack into our conversations, the likelihood that they could understand us is practically nil.

We got the idea from the way some people would communicate in secret in the ghettos and camps during World War II, using special code words in Yiddish to share information, and from the Navajo Code Talkers in WWII, too! Like my little cousin likes to say, 'It's a fact, look it up...I dare you!'

Nothing seemed to be amiss in the tunnel, but I don't know what I would have expected to seem to be out of place, short of alarms and flashing lights. So I spoke in Yiddish to Levi through the communicator.

> "Vos maint es, Bruder? Tsoreh or bupkis?
> Tsoreh or alts iz gut?"

Or to put it into English, so people out there in Readerland who don't know the lingo can understand...

> ["What does it mean, Brother? Is there trouble or is it nothing? Is there trouble or everything is all right?"]

He replied the same way through the throat-microphone.

> "Ich vais nit. Es gefelt mir nit."
> ["I don't know. I don't like it."]

We reached the end of the tunnel and faced the door. It had a manually operated mechanism, so that in case there were a power outage, an EMP blast or some other catastrophe equally debilitating to technology, it could still be used for exit or entry. We crouched in readiness, text-book examples from our martial arts training, and Levi pulled the lever. The door swung open, smoothly and silently, to reveal another dim corridor beyond. I vocalized to my brother,

> "Azoy vayt, azoy gut."
> ["So far, so good."]

We followed the hallway, another 50 meters or so of concrete and steel, to an industrial-looking staircase leading up into the main facility. Thanks to our special footwear, there was no telltale clumping or footsteps as we ascended the stairwell for some 15 meters to encounter yet another heavy metal door.

Levi turned to face me and placed his hands on my shoulders and I heard his voice coming through the tiny speakers in my hood.

> "Shtelt zich op doh, vart a minut ... Fartig?"
> ["Stop here, wait a minute." *deep, calming breath* "Ready?"]

I gave quick nod and answered.

> "Fartig! Vos gicher alts besser."
> ["Ready! The faster, the better."]

We played the game known as *Rochambeau* for who got to be the first one to go through into the potentially dangerous situation. Levi won, with scissors over paper, so I'm the one who operated the handle and pulled the door open as he took a battle-ready crouch and stepped forward to scope out the situation.

> "Gornit. Kumnt arein,"
> ["Nothing. Come in,"]

he told me, and I don't mind saying that I let out a sigh of relief when this new hallway proved to be just as dim and deserted as the ones we had just come from.

We passed on through and I eased the door shut behind us. As we started down the corridor, I whispered to my brother through the communicator,

> "Hiten zich, un kuk arum."
> ["Look out and look around."]

Levi nodded in agreement.

> "Shpatziren pamelech un dervartn sakoneh."
> ["Walk slowly and expect danger."]

I replied,

> ["Gerrecht!"]
> ["Correct!"]

Levi gave me a thumbs-up. That's my twin bro. He might be a meat-eating barbarian, but he's pretty handy when it comes to a spy mission!

Thanks again, pal! You're gonna give me an ego that's more swelled up than a polecat in a water barrel if you're not careful!

Yeah, well don't get too comfortable with the accolades. I haven't gotten to the part of the story yet where things went bad. Real bad. And it was all our fault.

Oh, yeah. Hmmm, I keep forgetting about that.

So anyway, we gave each other a fist bump, and kept working our way toward the Operations Center.

Chapter 7

DANAE'S LOG 5: Challenges and Opportunities

"Portable electricity." Rae made a wish, crossed her fingers and spit ("Ptooey") over her shoulder.

"A Widmanstätten circuit." I did the same. ("Ptooey.")

We had no better options, so we had decided to check out the two new X's that the BrightEyes had put on our map. The blue one was closest, so that's where we decided to head to first. According to the map, it was just a few kilometers away, up in the foothills at the base of the volcano.

Oh, yeah. The volcano. All the while that all this was taking place, the ground tremors became more frequent and more severe. A couple of 'em about rattled my teeth right out of my head. "So what do you think, Rae, do we need to worry about Death Mountain up there?" Since she knew the treasure-chest melody from one of my favorite games, I figured she'd also know this reference.

"Mount Doom, you mean?" Touché. She scored one on me and called it by the name of the volcano in another one of her classic films, that trilogy with the hobbits and orcs and stuff. Although come to think of it, she might have actually been reaching way back in her brain from the original source material, the Tolkien books. (And how did I know all of this, you ask? What, you don't think they made a video game out of the Peter Jackson movies? I'm telling you, I absolutely rocked Middle Earth when I played as Gandalf!)

I frowned. "Death Mountain, Mount Doom, Magic Mountain, or whatever you want to call it, I don't like all this shaking and baking." I'm not a big fan of trying to reconstruct delicate technological equipment in the middle of an earthquake.

"Well, I didn't want to make a big deal of it and worry you, but I've been running a little algorithm on my tab ever since we got here." That's the thing about my sister; she's all artsy and stuff, but she also knows her way around a computer. "It's been collecting details on the volcanic activity and cross-referencing that info with a database of scientific research of historic seismic activity. If Mount Doom up there follows the normal pattern of volcanic activity as recorded by vulcanologists back on Earth, it's a better than even chance that we're going to experience a significant event before we even get a chance to return home."

Argh. Sometimes she really is a little more protective of me than I can stand. I glared at her. "Point number one. You 'didn't want to worry' me? I oughta kick your rear end for saying something like that. Either I'm your partner or I'm not, am I right?"

Rae stared at the ground, shuffled her feet, kicked a pebble and mumbled, "You're right."

"Point number two. You're saying that Death Mountain is likely to blow its top before we get the comeback equipment from Colin?"

"Affirmative."

"How likely is likely?"

"It's 73.4 percent likely." She smiled. "On the bright side, that means that in about a quarter of the possible scenarios, this place will still look like a tropical island instead of like a lava lamp when we get the replacement tech from Colin, and we'll still be able to beam out of here." Then she grinned even wider at me. "Partner."

I grinned back. I just can't stay mad at her. "Oh, let's be wild and crazy and ignore the 'nearly' part. We'll call it a solid one-in-four chance. What's 1.6 percent between friends, am I right?"

Rae whispered softly to herself, "Yup. 'We are two wiiiiiild and craaaazy guys.' Steve Martin and Chevy Chase, classic Saturday Night Live."

Even in a situation like this, she just can't keep from pulling up obscure entertainment quotes! I ignored it and continued, "But I would much prefer to beat the odds and transport out of here early. Partner." I was glad we weren't ticked off at each other anymore.

So on we trudged, following the map. (I wore the helmet and kept the projector on. As a result, the map seemed to be floating in the air, keeping pace with us as we made our way.) The BrightEyes were flitting around us the whole while, kind of leading us toward higher ground. We kept the pace slow, both to conserve energy and so that I could maneuver through the underbrush with my leg and walking stick. The first kilometer or two were the worst, but once we got through the jungle and started to gain some elevation up the slope of the volcano, the vegetation thinned out a little bit. There didn't seem to be any more tremors, but I did notice a rumbling sound that got louder the higher up the mountain we went.

It took us about an hour to get up into the thick black air that wreathed the mountain. It turns out they were neither exactly storm clouds nor volcanic smoke, but instead, a weird combination of both. Once we were in the volcano smog, visibility dropped to about 20 meters, the haze was just that thick.

"Hey. What's that?" I rubbed my eyes and looked again. "Hey, Rae. Do you see that flickering, or am I just really tired?"

"No, I see it too!"

The closer we got to where the light-blue X on the map was leading us to, the more visible the flashing light was. It lit up the clouds, and I realized what the rumbling sound was.

"Thunder! Rae, that's thunder. And that flickering is lightning."

Sure enough, as we came into a clearing, a pretty little mountain meadow on the side of the volcano where the steamy smog wasn't quite so thick, we could see the actual streaks and flashes light up the sky.

"It's... beautiful." Rae leaned against a boulder and gazed at the light show.

"Yeah," I agreed. "In a dramatic and intense sort of way."

"Now if we just had a bottle that we could catch it in, either metaphorically OR literally, we'd be that much closer to achieving passage on our way back home."

I held my hand up and my little BrightEyes settled onto it and nuzzled me. It gave a questioning little *'bllrp?'* like it was trying to figure out what in the heck my sis was trying to say. "She means that even though there's electricity right in front of us, we don't have any way to use it. Well, it was a good try, Phoebe. Thanks anyway."

Rae looked puzzled. "Phoebe?"

I felt my cheeks get hot. It was a little embarrassing to get caught being so sentimental. "Yeah, I decided this little critter needed a real name. And I thought, well it's red and green. Like flames and leaves. Or to get poetic about it, like a fire and briars. Fire-Briar. But that's a mouthful. So Fi-Bi. Or more conventionally, Phoebe."

"Wow! That's a convoluted train of thought! By which I mean, what a complicated way to come up with a name. But it works!"

"What about yours?" I guess I didn't want to be the only one being all mushy.

"Hmmm, let's see. Part of the makeup for this one is a sandy sort of silicate. So I'll call it Sandy!"

I laughed. "Simple, yet effective!"

Both of the BrightEyes seemed delighted to have acquired names; they swooped and bounced in the air around our heads.

I turned back to the map. "Well, I guess we can keep this lightning storm in mind in case we can ever figure out some way to capture and store the power. Should we go ahead and check out the other X, the silver one?"

But this seemed to distress Phoebe and Sandy. They were very agitated and tried to herd me closer to the storm, as they had when leading us to the grapes. "Yes, Phoebe, I see the lightning. But there's nothing I can do with it right now."

"Blerp! Blerp! Blublerp!"

"What are we missing?" Rae scratched her head. Then, "Hey, Little Sis. Look at the map. We aren't quite yet to where the X marker actually is..."

She was right. We were at the lightning storm, but our actual destination seemed to be over near the far edge of the meadow. "Okay, let's check it out." We walked over toward where the BrightEyes wanted us to go, to where we would be right on top of the map's blue X. And as we approached a pile of large rocks at the base of a cliff, three electric streaks flashed right by my head, coming within a breath of hitting us.

I dropped to the ground and dragged Rae with me, covering my head and expecting a crash of thunder to follow at any second. But... nothing happened. No crash. No shaking. Not the slightest rumble beyond the constant background thrumming of the storm.

"Open your eyes, Danae, you've got to see this."

I looked up and squinted. The three "lightning bolts" were, believe it or not, circling overhead. I looked more closely and could finally make out three little balls of electricity, bouncing around in the air above us and... playing with Phoebe and Sandy?

I'm sure that you out there in Readerland have probably already figured it out. And I should have tumbled to the fact of what was going on a lot sooner than I did. But to put it very simply, Rae and I had just met some more of the island's BrightEyes. Lightning-based BrightEyes. BrightEyes that had internalized the same sort of energy that makes up lightning. In other words... PORTABLE ELECTRICITY BrightEyes.

Chapter 8

DANAE'S LOG 6: Something Shocking

R ae: "Portable electricity."
   Me: "Yup. Portable electricity."
Rae: "Hmmm."
Me: "Yup. Hmmm."
With the help of Phoebe and Sandy, it only took about ten or 15 minutes for us to become friends with the new trio of lightning BrightEyes and I adjusted the theta-wave sensor on the helmet so that they each showed up individually on the map, three light-blue markers instead of just one. We studied them as best as we could, and it was still hard to believe it. We looked at them, touched them and felt the power pulsing within them, and checked 'em out under the Ruggoggle microscope. Or as my sis put it— examination via visual, tactile and enhanced optics.

"Well," I finally said, "we've seen a BrightEyes that has an affinity for the beach—that's Sandy—and its body has utilized both sand and water into its cells. We've seen a Bright-Eyes—Phoebe—whose environment is the jungle flora and it has plant fibers in its cellular makeup. So I guess that we shouldn't be surprised to find some BrightEyes who live in an electrical storm," I cocked my head and raised my eyebrows, "and have incorporated lightning into their DNA."

Rae laughed. "So these BrightEyes here are living, breathing electrical power cells." Then she paused. "Hmmm, except maybe for the breathing part; I still haven't figured out whether or not they respirate." She cupped Sandy in her hand and addressed the little critter. "I've got to hand it to you, you guys really came through!" And believe it or not, that little blue and yellow fuzzball actually looked pretty smug about it all! (Not an easy thing to do when the only feature that you have with which to express emotion is a pair of eyeballs...!)

And so it was that we set out for the final X marker on the map (the silvery one), me and my sis accompanied by nearly half a dozen BrightEyes; Phoebe and Sandy and the three new ones, who Rae tagged with the names of Snappy, Crackly and Poppy. (Don't look at *me, I* didn't pick 'em! Rae said she'd explain it to me once we got back home. For some reason though, it made me hungry for breakfast.) Our path took us around the base of the volcano and toward a small lake that sat at the interior of the island. As we walked, we discussed the potential of the lightning-type BrightEyes. "I really ought to run some tests and do some experiments to learn more about the parameters and limitations of these little fellows, but given what we've seen, I don't think there is any reason they wouldn't be able to provide enough juice for us to transport back home. Fingers crossed and knock on wood."

"It certainly does look promising," Rae agreed, "Fingers crossed and knock on wood." (Yeah, we're scientists, but at the moment, we figured we would take all the good luck we could find!) "They do seem to have complete control over their electrical output." We had discovered that the trio of glowing BrightEyes could lower their voltage so that we could handle them and never feel even the slightest shock. And that they could also increase the power so that it tickled, and then they could even pump it all the way up to being just too shocking to be able to touch them. "And as fascinating as it seems, this ability is actually one of the least confounding aspects of the BrightEyes. Creatures with control over electricity are not unheard of even back home."

"What are you talking about? There's a yellow mouse who shoots lightning and lives in a red and white ball and has battles with other crazy creatures, but I've got news for you, Sis, those Japanese cartoons are fictional."

She snorted (yeah, actually snorted!) and grinned back at me. "No, really, listen. Similar electrical characteristics can be found in members of the animal world back on our own Earth. Think of the electric eel, and that's only the best known of several species that can create and discharge electricity. But of course, nothing back home comes close to having the amount of control and sheer power that our new, local friends have demonstrated."

I figured I'd take her word for it. I didn't much care if every animal on Earth shot lightning out of their nose every time they sneezed, just so long as *these* guys were willing to help us get the electricity that might help us to get back home.

Of course, for that to happen, we still needed one last missing piece of the puzzle, a piece that our BrightEyes friends seemed to think we might be able to find. Although how in the world they thought they might be able to provide me with Widmanstätten circuits, I couldn't imagine. Unless... Hmmmm. Unless...

"Rae?"

"Yah?"

"You don't think maybe, just maybe, Phoebe and Sandy might be leading us to a meteorite that crashed here, do you?"

"Shhhh! I don't want to jinx it! But that's what I'm hoping, especially since they really came through on the 'portable electricity' bit..."

See? Even more proof that scientists can be awfully superstitious! Well, I figured that if my keeping quiet would bring us luck (or at the very least, not jinx us), I was all for it. So I didn't pursue that line of thought any further. Instead, I focused on watching my step as we forged ahead. My stiff leg made things tough enough without adding a twisted ankle into the mix.

We made our way down and around the foothills of the volcano and finally reached the small lake, just like the map showed. It was pretty as a postcard, with dark, mysterious water and a tiny little island about 150 meters out in the middle...the little chunk of land sticking above the surface was about the same size as a basketball court and with a couple of palm trees growing right up on it. Phoebe and Sandy guided us to the edge of the water and then hovered around as if waiting for us to do something.

I wasn't going to make the same mistake as before, when I hadn't paid close enough attention to exactly where the BrightEyes were trying to take us, so I double-checked just where at the lake this silver X was located. Although I had a sinking suspicion about where it was going to lead us, and I'll bet you have a pretty good idea, too. Yup, you're right, the silver little X was blinking right on top of the island.

I grabbed my Ruggoggles and pulled them down over my eyes and gave the controls a little twist. Sure enough, the silver striations against the deep black body of the island showed up plain as day. "Rae, that's no island. That's our Widmanstätten meteorite."

She took a turn with the goggles and confirmed it. "Incredible. Now that we know what we're looking at, it's so obvious. Look at the shore and the hillsides around the lake —this isn't a natural depression collecting rainwater and springwater. It's a crater that was formed when this meteor slammed into the island, maybe millions of years ago, and it later filled up with fresh water!"

"Pretty crazy odds against it making landfall right here on this speck of land, especially when there's all of this ocean for hundreds of miles around," I noted. And glumly added, "Probably about the same odds against us finding a piece of the meteor small enough to take back to the platform and fit into the Tesla coil. And I just don't have any tools that I can use to chip a little right-sized chunk off that monster, it's even bigger than the meteorite that Grandma and Grandpa Rugg discovered. The BrightEyes again found what we needed, but I'm afraid this time it's just not going to work for us."

"I'm ninety-nine percent confident that you are exactly correct. But—" Rae cranked the goggles up to full power,

"—maybe, just maybe there is a small piece of it that has broken off somewhere in those cracks and crevices along the island meteorite's surface?"

"Yeah, but it's like a football field and a half away from us, and those are some unknown waters." A swim would actually feel great, my leg was aching from the hike, but on the other hand, I didn't feel like serving myself up as lunch to some behemoth-sized fish from the depths. In a world that contained such incredible creatures as the BrightEyes, who knew what else could be lurking about in water too deep to see to the bottom? There could be something down there, something not too friendly, something that would just love to make a snack out of a teenage girl, and I told Rae so.

She agreed. "I'm with you on that! I thought we might inquire as to whether our newfound acquaintances could peruse the premises for any appropriately sized mineral specimens."

I gave her a look. *The* look. The look that says she needs to dial it back on the big words just a tiny bit.

"Meaning maybe the BrightEyes could float on over and give the island a look and see if they can find any small pieces of meteorite," she translated.

Oh. Okay. And it was not a bad idea, actually. If they found anything, then we could figure out a way to get over there, maybe build a raft or something, but we wouldn't have to waste the effort if there was no point in it. The fuzzballs must have thought it made sense too, because, as soon as she said it, Phoebe and Sandy bobbed in agreement and flitted over the water toward the large black lump of island.

It was too far for me to really see them very well, and Rae was watching with the goggles, so I played with the lightning trio for a little bit until I heard my sister gasp.

"Danae? As far as we know, the BrightEyes can't really carry items, and definitely can't levitate them, right? Like when they tried to cool you off, they couldn't bring leaves or palm fronds with them, right?"

Argh, get to the point, Sis! "Right, right, right! What do you see?" I shaded my eyes but still couldn't make out what was going on over there.

Rae was enjoying my frustration. "Wait for it. Waaaaait for it..." I was tempted to grab the Ruggoggles off her face and take a look, but restrained myself. That's a gold star for me, I figure.

And it was just as well, because it was only a second or two later that I could see blue-and-yellow Sandy and red-and-green Phoebe merrily floating their way over the water back toward us, and each was trailed by a similarly-sized black lump floating along in their wake. I *squeeeeee*-ed with delight. I'm not proud of it, but I did it. "They found TWO meteorite chunks, and it looks like they are both just the right size! But how in the heck are they managing to bring the rocks back with them? Can they levitate stuff after all and we just didn't know about it?"

Rae didn't answer, she just shook her head and grinned at my bewilderment.

You've probably already figured out what the whole deal was. Again. I mean, it's really kind of obvious. But just like with a television gameshow, it's a lot easier to get the right answers when you're just playing along at home. Being there on the spot and in person, I couldn't wrap my head around it until they were actually right back next to us. The black lumps weren't rocks. (Duh.) They weren't small pieces of the meteorite. (Double duh.) They were (of course!) a pair of BrightEyes that had adapted the composition of the meteorite into their own physiology; iron-ore, with nickel-iron crystal striations and all.

Rae: "Widmanstätten circuits."

Me: "Yup. Widmanstätten circuits."

Rae: "For all intents and purposes."

Me: "Yup. For all intents and purposes."

Rae: "Hmmm."

Me: "Yup. Hmmm."

Rae, again: "Widmanstätten circuits."

Me, again: "Yup. Widmanstätten circuits. For all intents and purposes."

Rae: "To go along with the portable electricity."

Me: "Yup. To go along with the portable electricity."

We all made friends with the new BrightEyes in no time at all and they happily joined our merry little band of adventurers. (Hmmmm. We're going to need to figure out just what the right word is for a group of BrightEyes? A flock? A herd? Maybe a pack?) Anyway, it was great because it allowed us to do some on-the-spot experimentation. I adjusted the sensor to track each one of these two new fellers individually. By using the empathy helmet, we seemed to be able to lay the groundwork for all the new critters to understand what we wanted, and then Sandy and Phoebe seemed to be able to help out as well, to fill in the gaps when we tried to see if the lightning BrightEyes could send power through the 'circuits' that were apparently embedded into the bodies of the meteorite BrightEyes. (Who we started calling Rocky 'n' Roll, because, you know, we first had thought that they were rocks. Yeah, corny, I know!)

We started with a super low trickle of electricity. I asked Rocky to get right up next to Snappy, who gave off a few tiny sparks. They thought it was great fun, but nothing seemed to happen. So we asked Snappy to provide more juice. When he did, Rocky seemed a little confused, and then the silver streaks in its skin pattern began to glow. The little critter was delighted! We didn't even have time to say anything else, but Snappy-the-Lightning-BrightEyes cranked the power level up into the double digits, and Rock loved that even more.

The next thing we knew, Crackly and Poppy were playing with Roll, all on their own, the two lightning BrightEyes shooting pulses of electricity into the meteorite BrightEyes. The naturally occurring circuits that ran throughout its coloration pattern glowed and pulsed with a beautiful luminescence.

"Eureka! That is, I'm ready to declare this a success!" Rae crowed.

"Maybe it's because both of the components—the circuits and the power—are basically woven into the DNA of the little fellers," I marveled, "but it's as if the meteorite BrightEyes patterns were practically MADE to channel this electricity!"

"Great! If your leg feels up to it, let's make all due haste to return to the worksite."

"Yeah, Rae. My leg feels up to it." At least that's what I *said*. In real life, it was aching up a storm, but I wasn't going to admit that to ANYONE. "But hold up a sec. Sit down, will you, I need to talk to you."

Sis folded her legs and settled down on the grass, while I found a rock outcropping and rested my rear end on it. "Shoot, partner," she said, with a concerned look on her face, as the whole colorful, burbling, friendly flock— *Oy, this problem again. Are they a pack? A herd? No, let's go with flock, after all. If Rae can name them something crazy like Snappy, Crackly and Poppy, I can pick a totally normal name to describe a group of them all bunched together, right?* Anyway, the flock of BrightEyes flitted over and around us like a bunch of big, round butterflies. "Something bothering you?"

"Rae, I think we have a decent chance of cobbling something together that will get us home. And this chance is given to us entirely by these amazing, wonderful little creatures here in the OtherWorld. These creatures that Colin didn't know about and didn't know how they might help us. Without the BrightEyes, Colin's plot would be absolutely airtight and we'd be defeated. *With* the BrightEyes, we have a fighting chance."

"Just like how the Ewoks on the forest moon of Endor were a complete game-changer for the Rebellion," Rae murmured.

"What?"

"Nothing, nothing, sorry. I mean, I agree with you one-hundred percent."

"Well, the thing is, we have to have the help of Snappy, Crackly and Poppy, and the Rocky 'n' Roll twins—or at the very least, one of each type of those BrightEyes—for this to work. They need to replace the parts of the transporter that went kablooey."

"Affirmative, I am still able to follow your train of logic."

"Those parts of the transporter aren't part of the external framework. They are integral to the platform and they actually make the trip—they *physically travel* from one world to the other—along with the platform. If we put this together, the Widmanstätten circuit and the batteries— or in this case, the BrightEyes that are helping us—will be transported back to our Earth with us." I sighed. "I want to get back and keep all of our work away from Colin more than anything in the world, but I just don't know if it's right to yank these cute little fellows away from the OtherWorld. If everything works out okay back home, then maybe later we could return them here. But what if it turns out that we couldn't? And is it even fair to use them like this?"

Rae didn't say anything. She just kind of fidgeted and traced doodles into the sand.

After a few minutes of silence, I verbally nudged her. "Well? I was thinking maybe you had not quite realized that our success would mean that some of them would have to make the trip with us..."

She finally sighed. "I realized it."

"And?"

"Um. This is something I wanted to bring up with you when we got back to the beach. I, uh, actually think that maybe we should bring them ALL back through with us."

My jaw dropped. "Wow. And here I thought I was being thoughtless by considering going through with the project when it meant a couple of them would get displaced. But now you think it'd just be cool to round them all up and take them who-knows-how-many miles or dimensions away from their home?" That didn't sound like the sister I know. She's usually super-sensitive to animal welfare and all that.

Rae paused, put her palms together, looked up at me and then spoke slowly. "That's one reason I didn't bring it up yet. I do realize that it does perhaps stretch the envelope of ethical scientific protocols."

"Gee, do ya think?" I said. Yes, I know that sarcasm is an ugly character flaw. But I'm just so GOOD at it.

"Knock it off and listen up!" Rae snapped back at me... I was finally getting under her skin. Good. But I did shut up and let her continue. "I was also waiting because I didn't want to worry you with the REASON that I think maybe we should take them all."

Good ol' Big Sis. (That's more of my famous sarcasm.) "Oh, by all means then, please deign to let me in on the oh-so important reason we should act like poachers on the African savanna and treat the native life as our own personal property to bring home as a trophy!"

Rae took a deep breath. I could see her mentally counting to ten. I do have to give her credit, she can do a good job of controlling her temper when it's really important to her. Finally she replied, "Let me ask you this... Have you noticed any ground tremors since the time we first encountered the new BrightEyes near the base of Mount Doom?"

"What in the wide world of sports does that have to do with anything?"

"Just answer the question!"

"Ummmm..." Let's see. Come to think of it, the answer was no. I had had some tough hiking, but none of it had been because of the ground shaking, not since... hmmmmm, not since we left the meadow. "Okay, so you're right. No tremors since then. So that's great, right? One less thing to worry about?"

She shook her head. "It would *seem* so. One would *think* it was a good sign, but in this case, looks can indeed be deceiving." She put the palm of one hand over the closed fist of her other. "When the pressure in the volcano gets released, the surrounding area rumbles. Just like a tiny burp."

She spread the fingers on her upper hand to indicate cracks to let out the volcanic buildup. "But when something happens to block that release valve," she started pushing down with her palm while pushing up with her fist, "the pressure builds and builds and builds, until finally something has to give." Her fist slipped past her palm and it was like she was punching the air. "And you have not a tiny burp, but an extraordinarily large belch, and perhaps even some chunky stuff comes up."

"Be a little grosser, why don't you?" But I was starting to see what she was talking about. "You're saying because the tremors have stopped, that means we're getting closer to the big belch? This place is going to blow up? Like as in magma and smoke and ash and destruction?"

She bobbed her head in agreement. "I've run the simulation three different ways. According to all of the data, both historical from other similar oceanic volcanos, and from what I've managed to collect here in the field, this island is likely to experience an eruption that very well may cover the whole land mass in three to five feet of lava. Or the chances are just as great that the force of the event will completely disintegrate the entire place."

I didn't need her to translate that. She was saying this whole island was probably going to be a very, very bad place to be. "When?"

"Best case scenario, in a week or so. Worst case situation... well, put it this way, we *should* have just enough time to make a brisk march back to the platform, to accept the help of our new friends, and to engage the transport back home. Barely. Say with a couple of hours to spare."

My shoulders slumped and my leg started to REALLY ache. "And you think we should take the BrightEyes home with us, all of them, because—" My voice trailed off as I finally understood what she was getting at.

Rae finished the sentence for me. "Because even these incredible creatures may very well find this place to be unbearable and unlivable in the near future. It's very possible that this island will cease to exist within two weeks. I propose that we transport them with us, not out of selfish intent, but in order to keep them safe, and then do what we can to return them to this world when possible. The fact that the integral makeup and physical characteristics of the lightning BrightEyes and the meteorite BrightEyes are components that will help to make this escape possible actually means that these creatures will be taking an active role in their own self-preservation."

Big-brain Sis has an explanation for everything. Big-brain Sis is usually right.

"But it's up to them, right?" I wanted to make this absolutely clear. "We explain it all the very best we can, and if they don't want to be a part of it, or if they don't want to go, we don't make them, right?"

She climbed to her feet and nodded again. "Most definitely affirmative. We've already established their very high scores on the Rodman Intellect scale. We won't force them into anything. Or deceive them about anything. Okay, partner?"

"Okay. Partner. But when we get back home, we're gonna have a long talk about this 'not wanting to worry me' problem you've got." Then I noticed Phoebe, who had been buzzing around my head since about half-way through our discussion. Both of our 'special' BrightEyes had gotten very agitated. "And speaking of getting worried, check this out. What's up with them, do you think?"

Rae frowned. "Yeah, I saw that. It started when I got to talking about the possible destruction of the island. I can imagine that would be a bit distressing to them."

Maybe. But I also thought maybe it was a little bit more than that. "I'm going to try the helmet." It was still fastened to my head and I turned my attention to the feedback loop. Yup, they were definitely worried. But with the help of the technology, I could sense that it wasn't a self-directed worry. Instead, it was worry that was aimed outward; concern for something or someone other than themselves. The map program toggle was still flipped to 'on' and the projection caught my eye. In addition to the X's for Rae and myself, and the markers for our little friends—seven BrightEyes in total by now—there were also a new trio of blinking markers. They were located at the far western edge of the island past the lake where we currently stood.

Rae looked down and also saw them. The new X's even had specific colors; one was yellow and two were a bright red. Rae said to me, "Okay. Three more objects or entities that are somehow a source of worry or stress for our new friends," then she addressed Phoebe and Sandy. She asked them some questions, trying to get some more detail, while I used the helmet to monitor the emotional flavor of their distress.

"More components for the platform?" *No, no, no*, the BrightEyes 'felt' toward us.

"Another type of food for us?" *No, no.*

"More people, similar to Danae and myself?" *No, no, HA HA, no!* Even though they were worried, this question seemed to be hilarious to them.

"More BrightEyes, beings similar to the two of you?" *YES! Yesyesyesyesyes!*

"Bingo!" I called out, "There must be three more of them over there!"

Rae studied the map some more. "Little Sis, this is a bit of a... quandary."

"What?! Spit it out!"

"Bear with me as I lay out a logical progression. Point number one: We agree that the BrightEyes can help us get home and that we have a duty to take them with us (pending their approval, of course) because of point number two: The island faces imminent destruction by volcano. Yes?"

"Yeah, yeah." I made a 'speed-it-up' twirling gesture with my hand.

"Point number two is the sticking point. Said destruction of the island may take place as soon as, let's see, honestly, it could be in as soon as six hours, according to my assessment. Which, *previously*, would have put us well within the safety zone, figuring the hike back to camp, some tests and experiments, and then implementation of the process. We could do it all with a couple of hours left over for good measure."

Aha. Once again, I was beginning to get the picture. "The key word here being, 'previously,' right?"

"Correct. But now, if we were to travel to the far coast, to find and collect what I assume are three additional Bright-Eyes, my best estimate of the time required means that we would get back to camp EXACTLY at the time that the volcano may very well erupt. That's a worst-case scenario of course, but one that has to be taken into consideration. Hence the quandary. We have a duty to help save all of these creatures. But by attempting to do so, we may create a situation in which they—and we—face destruction along with the island. By trying to save them *all*, we may, in fact, lose the chance to save *any* of them."

"Right. But..."

"'But' what? No 'but.' Yes 'quandary.' "

Sigh. Sometimes Big-brain Sis isn't so big-brain after all.

"Right. BUT. You said if *we* were to travel to the far coast. I know it's risky to split up into smaller groups when we're in unknown territory, but if *you* were to head out there to retrieve the other BrightEyes, and *I* were to head back to camp and run the tests and prepare the transporter, then everything would be ready to go and we would all be set *before* the earliest time that the volcano is predicted to blow up. Right?"

The look on her face was priceless, but sweet. She just couldn't imagine her little sis with a bum leg making her way through the wilderness alone. (And to be honest, I was just a tad bit nervous about it myself, but you don't have to be Einstein to see that the math on this situation just didn't add up any other way.) Rae argued and fought me on the idea for a little bit, but when I pointed out that her waffling was cutting into our already *very* slim cushion of time, she finally gave in.

All of the BrightEyes had been following our conversation as if they could really understand it. Since a lot of the course of action for the next few hours depended upon whether they could comprehend what might happen to the island and whether they would agree to go home with us, I hoped that they really did have an idea of what we were saying. I used the helmet and began to 'think' it all at them, but I didn't even need to bother. They sent back a vibration of complete understanding and agreement at me and Rae, and they even added a side vibe of warmth and appreciation for our concern about their well-being. They were all so nice and kind and friendly about it all that it almost brought tears to my eyes.

I looked at my sister and said, "Shut up. I'm not crying. You're crying."

She took the helmet/map, her rucksack and Sandy, while I took the Ruggoggles, my bag, Phoebe and the rest of the BrightEyes that currently made up our little flock. (Yes. *Flock.* I think it works nicely!) We hugged each other, and Rae took off at a trot, canvas bag slung over her shoulder, making her way toward where it seemed the island's last few BrightEyes should be. I adjusted my own rucksack, took a firm grip on my walking stick and started retracing our trail back toward our beachside camp. I'll tell you this, and no one else, I didn't feel nearly as confident as I let on. In fact, I was downright scared. But off I went.

Chapter 9

NOAH AND LEVI'S JOURNAL 3: "Into the Bowels of the Research Facility!"

*U*gh! Just ugh!

"Bowels"? You know how gross that is, right bro? Aside from being bad, clichéd writing?

As if you know anything about good writing. Back off, bro, or I'll slap you upside YOUR bowels.

That makes absolutely no sense.

Anyway, on our way to the Ops Center, we passed by one of the cousins' larger laboratories. It had a big side-by-side platform in the middle of the room with half of the floor missing and the air smelled of electricity, like someone had been welding nearby, but no sign of any people. But then Mister 'That-makes-absolutely-no-sense' Levi had a pretty good idea. (It does happen now and then.) We located one of the security cameras in the lab and Levi did a little creative hacking to see if he could backtrack the signal and get into the security recordings for the facility. If we could get those files, it would be a huge help toward figuring out what had happened here. Plus, he could check to see if maybe anybody else was tied into the security system with their eyes on *us*. So he grabbed some computer tools from his possibles bag and went to work on the camera.

About 15 minutes later, he grunted, "Well, gol-durn it all to heck!" In an old-timey prospector voice. Out loud.

I couldn't understand why he was breaking out of our super-spy silent mode. I whispered back through the communicator in Salish,

> "Hayo tam es nx̣con! T stem u kʷ sck̓ʷɫpáx̣t since?"
> ["Uh oh, that doesn't sound good!
> What's the idea, brother?"]

He tugged the hood back from his face and head and let it hang down the back of his neck, speaking out loud and in English. "No need for stealth, at least not for the time being. Nobody's using *this* security system to monitor us." Packing his tools away, but keeping his small tablet out, he continued. "The whole system is about as worthless as a dry well in a drought. All of the security footage for the past month is degraded and unreadable. It almost looks like someone tried to wipe the records."

I followed his lead and took my hood off. "Wow. You sure about that?"

Levi pondered. "I guess maybe it could just be a corrupted file. *Maybe.* Probably not. I did, however, manage to get just a few minutes of footage, let's take a look." He pulled it up on the tablet screen and touched the right-facing triangle 'play' icon. The image was fuzzy and streaked with static, like an old broadcast t.v. show, but we were able to make out a couple of figures running down one of the halls.

"Ok, that's the cousins!" I yelped. "Can you tell when this was recorded?"

My partner in crime shook his head. "Nope. No time stamp, no meta data, none of that stuff survived. All I know is that it was within the past 30 days."

As we continued to watch, we saw Kane scrambling to keep up with Rae and Danae. Then the scene flickered and we were looking at the inside of a large workspace, almost like a small warehouse, easily recognizable as the same lab room we were currently sitting in right at this very minute. "Check it out, pardner! Danae set the monitoring equipment up to automatically track movement, and then bring that feed to the forefront during playback! Man, that kid doesn't miss a trick!" Levi doesn't hand out compliments lightly, but me and my bro know that both of our cousins are the real deal when it comes to the science-adventure game.

Through the white haze on the screen, we watched the three of them enter the workshop. Kane situated himself at a control panel at one side of the room, while our cousins climbed up on that odd-shaped platform I had noticed. It was almost as if someone had pushed two trampolines together, one large and one small. In the center of the larger one was something that looked for all the world like a four-foot cyborg fungus. More specifically, it looked as if a robotic chanterelle mushroom and a robotic bolete mushroom got married and had a baby.

*Dude, it was just a Tesla coil and toploader on a short platform. Not *everything* in the world is connected to herbs and roots and mushrooms and stuff!*

Well, sure, you know that NOW. But at the time, I swear on a stack of pine nuts, it looked like some sort of mechanical fungus. (Nothing wrong with that, by the way. I mean a bolete is high in fiber, low in saturated fat and a good source of a whole bunch of healthy minerals.) So anyway, I could see it in the video, but looking over at the platform that was in the same room with us now, the cyborg mushroom—

—Tesla coil and toploader—

—wasn't there. Just a hollow spot in the floor of the platform. In the security video recording, Kane worked the controls while the cousins climbed onto the larger of the two platforms, one on either side of the mechanical toadstool—

—Tesla coil and toploader—

—each with a gear bag draped over their shoulders, and then—a big flash of light. Everything on the platform disappeared...girls, gear and the whatchamacallit, the Tesla coil and toploader.

—Tesla coil and- oh! Good boy!

As soon as Rae and Danae vanished from the scene, leaving only that hollow spot on the platform, their operations manager left the lab. The cameras followed his progress down the hall and back to his Ops Center, where we saw him sit down at his desk and just...kind of collapse. He looked miserable.

Yeah...he looked like I would feel if someone told me I could never eat another hamburger again in my life!

Yup, that's literally what it looked like. He even started crying. As the recording ended, he laid his head down on his desk and teardrops were blotting all of the paperwork there.

We sat there in silence until Levi muttered a single word. "Interesting." That's my bro, master of the understatement.

I finally shook my head to clear my thoughts. "Well, we don't know when this was, but given the current situation, I'm willing to bet this was the last time the cousins were here at the complex."

"Seems like a good working assumption," Levi agreed. "And Kane was still here after they left, all on his lonesome. That fits, too, since he's the one who contacted the family."

"So we're still on our way to visit the Operations Center, but at least we've got a little bit more information to help parse out the state of affairs," I said. "Knowing all of this will help us to, 'be prepared,' as suggested by the Scottish poet William Letford." (Levi groaned, but he wouldn't know good poetry if it punched him in the face.) Ten minutes later, we found ourselves at the Ops Center door. After getting back in covert-operations mode and pulling our hoods on, we played another round of Rochambeau. I lost again and worked the mechanism for entry while my brother took point.

He whispered, using Yiddish again,

> "Gornit dorten."
> ["Nothing there."]

I agreed in Salish.

> "čn wičm i X̌il."
> ["I see that it's still and quiet."]

So we both slipped in like ghosts, a pretty sweet trick, if I do say so myself. In fact, I was congratulating myself on how undetectable we were when a voice came from the dark side of the room and scared me about half to death.

"Hello, boys."

Whoops. We were not as undetectable as I had thought. Obviously.

Levi recovered more quickly than I did and I've got to hand it to him, his voice hardly quavered at all when he called back aloud, "Um. Howdy? Who's there?"

A desk light came on and revealed Kane sitting in exactly the same spot where we had just seen him on the recording, although he had different clothes on now. In the security footage, he had been wearing a tweed suit. Now, it was a rumpled sweatshirt with the word 'Oxford' across the chest. "It's just me. Michael. Erm, that is to say, Dr. Mike Kane. We've met. I have to say, whenever Rae and Danae talk about you, it often seems as if they are, uh, exaggerating the extent of your skills. But you really are as good as they claim. How on earth were you able to gain access to the facility?"

"Oh, you know," Levi shot back, sounding as cool as a cucumber, "Lots of sleep and a good diet. Red meat, fresh air and plenty of water."

Although I'm not a fan of the 'red meat' bit, I followed my brother's lead as far as the witty banter went. "The whole healthy lifestyle thing," I agreed. "Like the Bard says in *Henry IV, Part I.* 'Live cleanly, as a nobleman should do,' right?" Highly trusted longtime Operations Manager or not, the secret tunnel was strictly a need-to-know-family-business kind of thing, and I wasn't going to tell ol' Mike about it, so I figured that quote from Shakespeare might distract him from asking any more questions, what with him being British and all. "But, ah, we were kind of hoping we might find our cousins hanging around. You haven't, um, seen them lately, have you?"

Kane slumped even further down into his chair.

Yeah, he did. He already looked so sad that I would have bet that wasn't even possible. That fella looked lower than the belly of a rattlesnake.

"Hmmmm. Yes. Well, it's a short story and, um, not a very happy one, I'm afraid." Kane described the break-in by the Null Rats, how they sent monitoring equipment some-place and how Team Rugged Stuff had decided to turn the tables on Null and protect their discovery, something they called 'the OtherWorld.'

When we heard this last part, Levi and I both looked at one another and we both whispered,

> **"YenehVelt!"**

... the Yiddish translation for the English phrase of

> ["OtherWorld!"]

Then we turned our attention back to the sorrowful old guy slouched behind his desk was saying.

We realized that last part of the whole process he was talking about was what we had seen on the surveillance film, apparently.

Yup, when the cousins set off to perform the ol' switcheroo.

And then Kane told us what had followed. "I don't know that they completely understood the severity of the situation. The girls, uh, seemed convinced that what we had seen on the security tapes was Colin Null's employees installing some sort of remote monitoring equipment at the far side of the portal, and that they would be able to reverse the situation within minutes. But they did not return within minutes, or even within hours. They...they did not return at all."

Levi and I planted ourselves in a pair of office chairs facing Kane's desk, while he sat in his straight-backed wooden-slatted chair and continued to describe what had happened. (Rae once told me that chair had come from his family's estate in England...I couldn't help but think that he might cheer up just a tad if he wasn't sitting in such an uncomfortable-looking piece of furniture.) "I had just returned here to my office, despairing of what to do next. I didn't know if the girls had met with some technical mishap or perhaps had encountered some sort of, hmmm, hitherto unknown natural threat in the OtherWorld. Or something else entirely. But then I received a message from Colin Null himself!"

Levi and I glanced at each other yet again. We knew that couldn't be good.

"The message was coded Priority Red, so of course I answered it. Null bragged to me that he was the driving force behind the disappearance and the subsequent failure of the girls to return home. He told me that what we had, ah, seen in the lab was not his henchmen installing monitoring technology, but was instead a devious trap for Rae and Danae... It was designed to lure them to the OtherWorld, where the equipment required for their return would be destroyed. The result is that they have been captured and trapped on that side of the portal."

"Hold up there, old hoss." (Levi's 'rustic-frontier-cowboy' twang was thicker than ever. That's a sign that he's either getting very angry or having a very good time. And I'll tell you what, between those two options, I knew he wasn't having a very good time right now.) "Our cousins—Team Rugged Stuff—developed the technology to get there in the first place, why don't you just use that to open another portal and go retrieve them?"

"I'm, ah, afraid, ah, that it's not that simple. It could be done, it could be done, yes, but it would take weeks, months even, of fine-tuning the special circuits that Danae has developed."

I was puzzled. "Then why aren't you doing it? You should have people working on it right now, instead of having the whole place shut down. I mean, like Maya Angelou said, maybe we can't control events, but we don't have to be reduced by them, either."

"The, ah, girls will be back long before we could get, um, even the first stage of the new portal completed. Let me explain," Kane fidgeted, rubbing his hands together, almost nervously. "Null told me why he had rigged this trap, it's a deviously disturbing situation. He is going to take credit for the entire discovery, the entire project, at a conference at his, ah, headquarters in New York. Once he has presented the work as his own, on the world stage, it will, *de facto*, become HIS. In the eyes of the public, in the eyes of the media, in the, in the eyes of the world's scientific community, this research and everything that derives from it, will be a Null Corp project. Massively unfair, yet, unfortunately, a fact of life."

"Science by press release," I grumbled.

Levi nodded. Then scowled. "But how does that stop you from working to get the cousins back here to the Rugg homestead?"

"Oh, don't you see?" Kane was almost moaning now. "Once Null has made his announcement and secured the fame and acclaim and the credit for the OtherWorld project, at that point, he wins. And once he has won, he doesn't need to keep the girls, um, out of the picture any longer. He'll send them the equipment that they need in order to return. Because they'll never be able to convince anyone that THEY are the researchers responsible for the science of the OtherWorld." He sighed.

It would have been heart-wrenching to watch, if I wasn't already madder than a wet hen...

"It is all very cut and dried," he continued, "but Colin still belabored the point, *ad nauseum*, when we spoke. He made it very, ah, very clear that he will facilitate the return of the girls if and when—and ONLY if and when—he is not hindered in any way in completing his press conference."

I swear, right here and now, he started sniffling and tears started dripping out of his eyes, just like we had seen in the security video. This ex-military guy with a reputation for being as stern as they come and he was crying. Nothing wrong with that, it just didn't fit the image that he's always projected.

"So I (sniff), I sent a message to the girls' parents that Rae and Danae would be out of communication for a bit due to some new research demands. And then I shut (sniff) everything down. I didn't want Colin to think that we were trying to, uh, to circumvent his wishes. I didn't want to put the girls at further risk! So I made it very clear to him that the Team Rugged Stuff organization was NOT working against him on this. (Sniff.)"

Levi was mad. Angry enough to practically yell at the old guy, and still using his movie-cowboy voice. "Step down, pilgrim! What were y'all thinkin'? Colin is one of the black hats here, one of the bad guys. You can't trust him! What makes y'all reckon he'll actually help get them back once he's made his announcement and absconded with all of their work?"

This actually seemed to put some pep back in the old fellow. "Oh no, my young friends." (We weren't actually feeling very 'friendly' at the moment, but we let it slide.) "No, Colin Null is indeed a scoundrel. But he is a villain of the, ah, the old school, which means that he operates by a very strict, if twisted, code of honor. He stated the conditions by which he will facilitate the return of the girls, and he will stand by those conditions, I would bet my very last dollar on that." Then he started getting weepy and sniffly again. "The other side of that coin is that, should we violate those conditions, we may very well never see your cousins—my employers—those dear girls—again."

Chuck scowled, but relented. "Well... okay. I guess that does make some sort of sense."

"Yeah. I guess," I chimed in. "But knowing what the situation is, I don't know how we're going to be able to just sit around and wait for that little hooligan to keep his promise. I think it might drive me crazy. I think—"

WA-HOOOOOOGA! WA-HOOOOOOGA!

I was interrupted by a very loud and raucous alarm—

Nice sound effects, bro! It was shore enough a ruckus, all right!

—complete with a flashing red light that strobed the room from its location on the ceiling. The din surprised both me and Levi, but that was nothing compared to Kane's reaction. That geezer was absolutely flabbergasted. He jumped to his feet with his jaw hanging open.

"Mike, old hoss, what is it?" Levi yelled over the claxon of the alarm.

The Ops Director didn't answer him directly, but only shouted, "It...it...it can't...it just can't be! It's just not possible!" Then he sprinted from the room. We followed close on his heels. The route seemed familiar and I was sure that Levi also recognized it as the hallway leading to the Portal lab, the same one featured in the hacked security footage, where we had been less than an hour ago. Kane slammed open the door to the lab and ran to the computer station. Everything in this room looked the same...at first.

Then a pinpoint of light blazed in the air right where the missing section of the platform had been. The bright glow grew to the size of a basketball, then the size of a pup tent, then the size of a compact car. Then the whole room—the whole world—went bright-light white and we couldn't see anything through the glaring flash of energy.

Chapter 10

DANAE'S LOG 7:
Back to the Beach

So remember how I said I was a smidgen scared about making my own way back to the beach?

Well, the short story is that I had nothing to worry about.

I just started hiking—one foot in front of the other, as they say—and several hours later, I came out of the jungle and onto the beach where our platform sat. Don't get me wrong, my leg was just about howling at me by the time I got there. And I'll admit that once I got back, I did give in to temptation and take a quick soak in the ocean water, right at the sandy beach where it was really shallow. It did my leg a world of good and helped me feel a bit cooler and calmer. Then I felt guilty that I had a chance to refresh while Rae was working her tail off to go retrieve the other BrightEyes, so I buckled down and got started on my end of the job.

If Rae was making as good of progress as I was, I figured she should be getting back here to the beach within a few hours, with her Sandy BrightEyes in tow, and along with three new BrightEyes, if we had been right about what our little friends had been trying to tell us. And that was just about the same time that Death Mountain might decide to blow its top. (Of course, it might turn out that it would just never, ever explode, too. That's just one of the problems of working with scientific models—they are, in the end, still just really good guesses about what is going to happen.) I needed to make sure that the lightning BrightEyes and the meteorite BrightEyes really could serve as living components to my OtherWorld equipment. And that they understood what it meant if it did work...that is, that they would be making a trip over to our Earth with me and Rae.

The thing is, they really did seem to understand what I was asking of them. They really seemed willing to come on over to our side of the Portal, back over to our home. They even seemed pretty excited about the whole thing. But since Rae had the helmet in order to use the map to locate the remaining BrightEyes, it did take a little time for me to be confident that I was really communicating the right ideas to Phoebe and all the others, the whole crew of Snappy, Crackly, Poppy, Rocky and Roll. And before I knew it, that was yet another hour gone, another hour closer to the potential volcanic big bang.

Over the next few hours, I did more practical electrical work than ever before in my life. Everything worked perfectly...in theory. In reality, however, the electricity produced by the sparkling trio was just a *little* bit different than what my now-destroyed batteries had provided. And the Widmanstätten circuits in the skin of Rocky 'n' Roll were just a *little* bit different than the Widmanstätten circuits that had been embedded in my now-melted meteorite.

This state of affairs was awfully frustrating. It was even worse than if everything had been not a *little* different, but *entirely* different than what I was used to, because then the failure points would have been more obvious. As it was, everything was just so very close to my normal material that it was extremely difficult to track down where the differences were. A lot of trial and error. A lot of tweaking or changing one tiny factor and running through the whole test again. Don't get me wrong, I love science. But sometimes the process can be boooooooring.

But I was getting close. I just knew it. I checked the time, and *if* Rae hadn't encountered any problems, she should be showing up sometime within the next 15 minutes to a half an hour. (I know, I know, to assume the absence of problems is always a big and potentially fatal thing to 'if' about!)

RUMBLE!

All of my tools shook and bounced on the floor of the platform near the Tesla stand. The sand on the beach vibrated and swirled, and the jungle trees rustled. It was another seismic tremor.

I wasn't sure if this was a good thing or a bad thing. Maybe this meant that the pressure in the volcano had been released, and it would just give a little burp instead of a big, chunky belch. (And I reminded myself to 'thank' my sister very much for that absolutely disgusting and terrible visual image.)

On the other hand, maybe this meant that we were getting close to the big event, the explosion that would bring dread and destruction. I was afraid this was the more likely situation, given that the timing matched Rae's worst-case prediction almost exactly.

I didn't have the wiring completely adjusted to compensate for the differences presented by the living circuitry and the living electricity provided by my new little friends, but I didn't return back to my work just quite yet. Instead, I addressed the BrightEyes.

"Alright Rocky 'n' Roll... which one of you is going to actually play the role of meteorite in today's production?" They looked at each other and honest to gosh, actually nodded. When we get back home, I have GOT to give some serious study to how these critters communicate with each other! Then Rocky floated over to the Tesla toploader. I had the lid resting in the 'open' position and Rock settled down into the little nest-like area in the center of it all, right where my poor lost space rock had previously been positioned before Colin made it go all kablooey and melted it.

"Now you sparkly little lightning bugs!" I called up to the electric BrightEyes who were hovering in the air above me. "Can you climb into the stand there and just kind of pile three high?" I could swear they were laughing as they flitted over to the cylinder and popped in, one-two-three. They looked just like that candy, Pez, all stacked up in a funny little dispenser. That is, if Pez was, you know, alive and full of lightning instead of being little tablets made from flavored sugar.

"Phoebe and Roll. I need to ask you to climb into my rucksack now." I know, I know, it seems wrong to put these creatures into a bag. But Rae and I had talked about it, and we wanted to be super-duper-double-dog-dare certain that none of the BrightEyes could accidentally fly up into the plasma field when the platform was activated. So the BrightEyes who were acting as a part of the equipment would be contained within the framework of the platform itself and the others would wait inside my ruck. We had also agreed that the BrightEyes with Rae—that is, Sandy and whatever additional puff balls she managed to find—would be safely tucked away in her own bag. There was plenty of room in there, even when you considered that Rae would probably also have the helmet stowed in there by the time she got back here to the beach with me.

Once this was taken care of, once the BrightEyes with me were all in place as snug as a bug in a rug (or as snugg as a bugg in a rugg, as the old family joke goes... it doesn't make any sense and it's not a very funny joke at all, but we like it!), I turned back to my electrical work.

RUMBLE-BA-GRUMBLE!

Another tremor! This one was much bigger, much stronger and it very nearly knocked me down.

Smoke started pouring out of the top of the mountain that loomed up over the island. I stared toward the jungle treeline. No sign of my sis. "Come on, come on," I muttered.

Then I remembered; even if she plopped down on the platform beside me right now, I still didn't have the equipment up and running! I grabbed my tools, scrunched up my face and focused on the job at hand. Purple wire to purple wire. No good. Darn. Red to yellow and green to black. Nothing. Purple to red to black to green to yellow to phooey. I was *this* close, I knew it, but I just couldn't get the right pathway connected to accommodate the new flavor of bio-electricity that the BrightEyes were generating.

BOOM!

I looked toward the huge explosion up near the peak of the volcano. Red-hot lava was pouring over the lip of the crater. It was flowing down the face of the mountainside with the speed of a proverbial freight train. And not just any proverbial freight train but a proverbial freight train made of deadly magma and consuming anything unlucky enough to get caught in its path!

"Oh, dagnabbit," I muttered under my breath. Okay, maybe that's not exactly what I said, but hey, I'm trying to keep my memoirs G-rated here. Let's just agree that what I said wasn't very nice. Then I turned my attention back to the set of wires I was working on. I fiddled with them and then glanced at the computer monitor. Nothing. Well, nothing good, anyway. There *was* a slight crackle and the stink of burnt ozone, but the monitor just continued to flash its red low-battery symbol. Huh. The small power source in the computer was still putting out a trickle of juice, but nothing was coming through from the other platform.

Double dagnabbit.

I frowned, kneeled down as best I could on my left leg, with my stiff right leg stretched out beside me, and got back to work on the connections.

"DUH-NAAAAAAAAY!"

Hearing my name being shouted, I jerked my head up and looked toward the treeline.

Rae busted out of the jungle and onto the beach, directly between me and the volcano. She was running full-tilt across the hundred or so meters of sand, right toward me and the platforms. She yelled, "I got them! I GOT THEM! The time has come for us to vacate the premises! That means go go go GO GOOOOOOO!" And that girl's got a set of lungs on her, so when I say she yelled, I mean she YELLED!

"Argh! It's not ready yet!" I hollered back.

"Well, it needs to GET ready at this point in time, or the window of opportunity is likely to be closed forever.

In other words, it's now or never, Sis!" Rae finally reached our OtherWorld Portal equipment and jumped up on the platform to stand next to me. Her bulging canvas rucksack hung from one shoulder.

I looked past her and saw the glowing wall of lava burbling its way toward us, swallowing up the trees right where she had emerged from the jungle just less than a minute ago. It went something like this: Tree. Then lava. Then *pffft* into ash and smoke. Tree. Then lava. Then *pffft!* Then—well, you get the idea. A massive flow of painful molten death. Heading straight for us. I gulped, trying to push my heart down from my throat and back into my chest where it belonged, and said (as casually as I could), "Hmmm. I see what you mean."

Fingers shaking, I tried another combination of the wire strands. And felt a glimmer of hope because there was a slight tingle of electricity between my fingers! From the corner of my eye, I saw the computer screen brighten and begin to flash with the green "Battery A-OK" icon. From where I knelt, I looked down at the small panel door that was open at the base of the stand. Three fist-sized glowing spheres of energy stared out at me. I spoke to them in a trembling voice. "Okay guys! Now's the time. Fire it up and give it all you've got!" In response, they began to glow brighter. And brighter and brighter. I gave them a quick thumbs-up and closed the panel.

Then I pulled myself to a standing position and turned my attention to the black little lump at the center of the metal tube around the top of the stand. (It's called a toroid, by the way, just in case you were wondering. The metal tube, that is, and not the lump. You already know that the lump was called Rocky.) Speaking of Rocky—who was the same size and shape as its three counterparts who were *in-side* the toroid stand—well, Rocky gazed at me with such a look of confidence that I started to feel as if this might really work, after all. Right on time and according to plan, the silver patterns that criss-crossed over the surface of Rocky's black body started to glow and spark. Electricity began to flow into the little guy, electricity provided by its companions who were wired into the stand below. I quickly closed the lid over the top of the snug metal nest and fastened it tight.

Fingers of lightning snaked out from the Tesla-coil equipment and began to encircle the whole platform, including me and Rae and our gear. As it made a complete plasma globe of sparks centered around us and the coil, I looked at Rae and squeezed her hand. "See you on the other side, Sis!" My voice was confident and brave. I mean, the voice coming out of my mouth, *that* one was brave. But my inner voice, the one bouncing around inside my head, *that* voice quavered as I mentally added, "...I hope!"

A brilliant white light engulfed the center of the toroid and almost instantly swelled large enough to fill up the entire plasma globe. It washed over us with a barely audible little snap, like when your bubblegum pops. At the same time, I could see the first ropy tendrils of lava approach the edge of our platform. They began to melt everything they touched, but before they could reach us, the world disappeared in a blinding flash.

Chapter 11

DANAE'S LOG 8:
Home Again and
Home Again

"**B**right light. Bright light." That's what Rachel was mumbling under her breath as the nearly silent explosion of white engulfed us, just before a wall of red-hot molten lava washed over the spot where we had been standing. I thought at first she was saying, "BrightEyes, BrightEyes," but then I recognized it as a line from one of those old movies she likes. *Goblins*, or *Gnomes* or something like that. But anyway, I'll bet it was the only movie quote recital that was ever started on one world and finished on another! Because what she actually said on the platform on the OtherWorld beach was, "Bright light. Br—" And then it finished up as, "—ight light!" on the platform in our lab. At home. On Earth.

It wasn't a smooth transition. The equipment was still having a hard time coming to grips with the different circuits and power that I was asking it to work with. But any landing that you can walk away from is a good one, right? Because when that 'bright light' faded away and we could see our surroundings, it was obvious that the trip had been a good one...we were back home again!

And while I wasn't surprised to see Mike at the control station, I couldn't believe my eyes when I saw our cousins, Levi and Noah, in the room, all suited up in their work clothes like super spies. And the feeling must have been mutual, because their jaws were hanging wide open like they were looking at a couple of ghosts. (Which, come to think of it, I guess we would have been, if we hadn't been able to beam out of the OtherWorld just before the lava caught up with us!)

The whole room was pretty quiet. It was like everyone was kind of in shock. Then my sis was the first one to speak up. (Not surprising. She's got some pretty good reflexes!) "Hi guys. How do the two of you find yourselves to be in the current circumstances? I mean, what in the heck are you doing here?" We both gently set our rucksacks down on the platform floor near the base of the Tesla stand, mindful of the gear—and the BrightEyes!—that were still safely stowed away in each of them.

Noah laughed. "We could ask the same of you! You've both been reported as M.I.A., Missing in Action!"

The other brother grinned and piped up in his trademark Western drawl, "Yeah, the whole setup looked worrisome, so we dropped in to see if we could lend a hand. But we should've known that you'd be riding herd on everything and have things under better control than a sheepdog in a pen full of lambs!" Even though they both spoke in a joking tone, you could tell they were incredibly relieved to see me and my sis all safe and sound and in one piece.

"Well, I wouldn't go so far as to call it under control, but things are now immeasurably better than they were some fifteen minutes ago," Rae commented dryly. As we clambered off the platform and stepped over toward our cousins, she called out to our Ops Manager, "What's the situation, Mike?"

"Oh. Ah. Oh. Ah, yes. I can only surmise what transpired on, uh, that side of the portal, but it appears that the Null Corp monitoring equipment was a ploy, a ruse to lure the two of you over to the OtherWorld?"

"Yup." I couldn't help but growl. "He didn't even try to disguise it, over there on the island. It was straight-up designed to catch us and hold us."

Under her breath, Rachel muttered, "We should have listened to Admiral Ackbar. He warned us. 'It's a trap!' he said." I swear, she just can't help herself. Popular-culture quotes are an addiction to that girl. But then again, the boys heard her and they both grinned and nodded, so maybe it's not just my sister who is the weirdo.

"Mmmm, ah yes. And as your cousins can attest, Colin soon afterward spoke to the press and stated that he had an important declaration, an announcement of a scientific discovery that would be the sensation of the century, that it would, ah, it would 'rock your world' is the term I believe he used."

I grimaced. "Yeah, he left us that little gem of info over in the OtherWorld, too." Remembering that hologram message made me mad enough to spit, all over again.

Mike continued. "He, ah, that is, he also messaged me here at the Team Rugged Stuff complex in a secret communique. He stated that the two of you would be retrieved unharmed, if and only if, our organization took no steps to circumvent his plans. Nor were we to attempt to recover you ourselves. As I told the boys here, he may be a cad, but he does keep his word. So, ah, I, um, put all Team Rugged Stuff projects on hiatus, sent all employees home and made announcements to all concerned parties that you two were on a special research mission that would keep you out of communication until late next week."

"Hmmmmm." It sounded as if Colin had told Mike all the same information that his hologram had delivered to us over on the other side of the OtherWorld portal. "Well maybe he didn't plan it to be a permanent trap, but he almost got rid of us for good without even realizing it." I still couldn't get the image of that lava washing over the edge of the platform out of my mind. Even from here, I could see that part of the platform floor was burnt and melted at the edge. If we had been one second slower, we would have been toast. Literally.

Rae spoke up again. "Well, it sounds as if you handled things to the absolute and utmost impeccable level of your ability, that is, you did everything that you could, Mike. Thanks for taking care of things." She patted his arm, then looked worried. "Mike, are—are you *crying?*"

"Oh, ah, just (sniff) tears of joy. I admit that I half thought that I might never see the two of you again. (Sniff.)"

There was a long, awkward silence, and finally, Rae turned to the twins and said, "But that doesn't explain you guys. What circumstances prompted your presence, and all dressed up in your finest clothing, none-the-less. In other words, why are you here and why are you in your work outfits?"

"Oh, you know us. We keep our ears to the ground, listening along the ol' trail, and when we heard the far-off rumblings of trouble—"

"—we didn't want to miss out on any of the fun! And it's probably going to be a ton of fun—"

"—when we all catch up to our favorite little hornswoggler Colin and teach him a lesson!"

Rae and I both grinned at each other. The cousins really would be a big help in turning the tables on our obnoxious nemesis!

But then Mike yipped like a puppy that just got its tail stepped on. "What?! No! His press conference is set for New York in less than, um, three, ah, days! There's nothing that you'll be able to do to stop him now. I hate to say it, girls, but I think you are, uh, going to have to throw in the towel on this! Chalk it up to, ah, experience and try to defeat him on whatever science project that you come up with next time."

"No, Mike." Wow, Rachel sounded firm. And confident. Ready to kick some tail. "We've got some very good reasons why we can't possibly let Colin claim control over the OtherWorld project or the portal." We both knew that Null would exploit the little BrightEyes in a heartbeat. "Reasons that are a lot more important than who gets credit for the discovery and the research." And several of those reasons were sitting in our rucksacks and inside the framework of my OtherWorld portal transporter at this very moment.

"Ahem," I cleared my throat. "Although that getting credit thing, that's a pretty darned good motivation, too," I reminded her.

"So we can't just give up," Rae continued. "Besides, we have faced situations in the past that appeared just as, if not more, dire and we still managed to emerge triumphant. In other words, we've beaten the odds before and we can do it again. If my calculations are correct, we still have time to thwart Colin's plans."

Mike sighed. One of those big deep sighs that comes from the gut. "Right then. Ah, stiff upper lip and all that. If you are determined to do this, then I guess that's all there is to be said. I'll begin gathering resources and setting up the necessary logistics. I'll be in the Ops Center, should you need me." He shuffled off out the lab door toward his office. I glanced at Rae with a look that said, *He must've really been worried, R. He really seems down.*

She flashed me a look back that seemed to reply, *Yeah, D, this isn't the same 'can-do' Mike that I remember. He really seems defeated.*

I went over to my computer and fired things up. My work station here in the OtherWorld lab isn't quite as robust as my work lab, where I've got three monitors side by side and a wall-sized smart screen, but it's still a pretty sweet setup. "Thanks for coming down from Alaska to check on things, guys. It really means a lot to us that you would drop everything to help us out."

"Well, maybe we can do something to assist in stopping Colin's press conference, because we haven't been any big help yet," Noah said. "You two obviously were able to escape from his trap without us doing anything!"

Levi chimed in, "Yeah, from what Mike told us about the whole situation, it sounded as if you guys getting back here on your own would be tougher than drawing to an inside straight! I know that your Ops guy, Mike, certainly didn't expect it. How'd you manage such a stunt?"

The cousins are older than us, they're even older than Colin, but I've got to hand it to Rae, she never lets that stop her. She took charge of the situation like a boss. "We'll explain all of that later, and you guys are going to love it. But right now, can you catch us up on what's been happening here on this side of the portal since we've been gone?"

"Sure," agreed Noah. "So when was it that you transported over? Sunday, right? Well that's when Null made his announcement. 'Hear ye, hear ye, don't miss my big press conference next week!' I'll tell you what, we just about had to brew up a pot of service-berry tea in order to calm down after seeing his smug face on the news."

"But I don't understand," said Levi. "Why? I mean, why would he want to wait? I would think he'd want to jump on it just as soon as possible after dry-gulching the two of you. Why not just hold the press conference that same day, as soon as you two were out of the way, and claim all the research as his own right then?"

Rae answered, while I scanned the interwebs for more news. "He wanted to give all the business journals and science publications time to be prepared for the story. If he sprang it on them too quickly, the news would be scattered and not have as much impact. But this way, he could wait until he was one hundred and ten percent sure we were out of the picture and then set up a big media circus for his presentation. And by setting the press conference to take place on Thursday, it will give all of the news outlets time to get the story in their weekend editions—more viewers and readers—but not enough time to do any real background investigation that might turn up anything fishy about his claims."

Levi let out a low whistle. "Whew. That fella is one devious li'l polecat."

"Most assuredly. This way, he controls the entire narrative of what he is presenting as *his* discovery. It hits every news and media outlet in the world at the same time. No one will miss or be able to ignore his announcement. And according to his planned timeline, when Team Rugged Stuff," she gestured to herself and to me, "finally returns to Earth to challenge his assertions, we sound either delusional or as if *we* are attempting to steal *his* research."

Levi ran his hands through his short hair and looked thoughtful. "Okay, it all makes sense, when you put it that way. But what I still don't understand is how he could have duplicated your project closely enough to trick you into getting stuck over there, and how he could have all the equipment and knowledge already developed to the point where he could claim it as his own? I had a little palaver with Nessa about it, and even she didn't know what was going on. And you know how serious she is about knowing EVERYTHING."

Noah nudged Rae glumly and tilted his head toward his twin. "He's got a date with her. Burgers in NYC." I rolled my eyes. Okay, granted, Nessa is pretty. And smart. And rich. But as far as I'm concerned, none of that can make up for being a Null. Even given the fact that *she* can't stand her brother any more than *we* can, I'm not a big fan of that girl.

In fact, I was just about to announce to my cousins that when it comes to dating, I thought they could do better—*much* better—than Nessa Null. But just then, the room went dark! Everything shut down. My computer and screens, the overhead lights and all the LEDs and indicator bulbs for the entire lab went black!

Chapter 12

DANAE'S LOG 9: Another Day, Another Trap

We all stood in stunned silence for a moment or two until Rae spoke up. "Well. THAT is not supposed to be able to happen." Told you...she's got good reflexes. I peered into the darkness over toward where her voice was coming from as she continued. "We have backup generators. We have backup generators on the backup generators. We have triple-level redundancies to make sure that an unintended power outage and blackout just. Can. Not. Happen."

"Yeah," I called out, "but we also have triple-level redundancies on the security systems, and those Null rats not only got in to the lab, but they got in to the lab and they used our own equipment to set a trap for us."

Two small beams of light appeared, and when my eyes adjusted, I could see that it was Noah and Levi. *That's right!*

I thought to myself. When I helped design their super-spy suits, we wired small flashlights into the hoods. Pretty smart thinking, if I do say so myself! They adjusted the focus to provide a softer ambient glow, rather than a tight beam, and it lit the lab with a very low, dim, pale light. We all went quiet, and I knew that all four of us were thinking like crazy to process what had just happened and to figure out options for what we could do next. The silence was (if you'll forgive a cliché) deafening. And then that silence was broken by a loud, metallic 'CLICK!'

Uh oh.

"Um, Rae?" I managed to keep the quaver out of my voice. "Was that what I think it was?"

"Affirmative. Our 'Fortress of Solitude' deadbolts." She sounded confident, but I knew she had to be worried, too.

One of the guys finally piped up, I couldn't tell which one in the gloom. "Clue us in, cousins."

Then the other. "Yeah. 'Fortress of Solitude? Like the comic-book super hero?"

Rae answered. "Oh, sorry. It's our special security proto-col. It's a set of deadbolts that seals the lab up tighter than your favorite Kryptonian's secret hideout. Which means that once again, we find ourselves in a situation in which our freedom and liberty has been severely curtailed. That is, we're trapped again."

I couldn't believe it. "So the Null Corp agents must have had a contingency plan for if we got back before the press announcement? Is that what is happening?"

"But...we sure didn't see any of Colin's goons hanging around." Noah sounded confused.

"Yeah. We didn't run into anyone besides old man Kane," Levi agreed.

"Dang," I said. "Those Null Rats are trickier than I gave them credit for. And the 'Solitude' security subroutine can only be initiated from the Operations Center. That means Colin's spies have captured Mike!"

"Right. Okay. Here's the situation." Rae took control. Like I said, she's got a knack for it. It's reassuring to know that being a bossy older sister has given her a skill set that's useful in the outside world. "The good news is, with the power out, they can't use our own security monitors to keep tabs on us while we plan (a) how to get out of here, (b) storm the Operations Center and (c) rescue our head of security, namely Mike."

Noah: "And the bad news?"

Levi: "Yeah, there's always a passel of bad news that comes along with the good news."

Rae: "The bad news is that getting out of here is impossible."

Noah: "Impossible, you say?"

Levi: "Well, I'll be doggoned. That IS bad news."

Rae sighed. "Well, hypothetically impossible, at least. We designed this thing's protocol so that once the solitude locks are in place, there is absolutely no way to breach the lab doors. Add to that, we have no power. And the lab equipment is all pretty specialized, so we don't have many tools that are helpful."

I made my way from the computer to the transport platform. "Well, I might be able to re-purpose some of the lab gear into something useful. And we have the tools that we had in our bags, the ones we took to the OtherWorld with us." I grabbed our rucksacks from the platform floor and gently opened the flaps. Then to the twins, I put on my radio-announcer voice. "But wait, there's more!"

A flock of BrightEyes popped out, a few from each bag, and started flitting around my head, happily chirping and blerping up a storm. Phoebe swooped down and nuzzled my cheek, and Sandy made a bee-line for Rae.

Noah and Levi were obviously surprised, but maintained their composure and took it all in stride.

"Well, looks as if the cat—or something—is out of the bag." Then Noah raised his eyebrows, looked askance at us and said in a low, inquisitive tone, "OtherWorld, huh? *YenehVelt?*"

Rae and I just grinned in reply. We don't know one-tenth the amount of Yiddish that our cousins do, but that old phrase had def been on our mind when we came up with the name for this entire project.

Levi rolled his eyes at our response. Then he gestured to the little creatures floating in the dimness that surrounded us. "Whatever you want to call it, now I really can't wait to hear about what all happened on yonder side of the portal!"

I stepped over to the platform and opened the panels on the Tesla equipment to let the meteorite and lightning BrightEyes out and about as well. "Since the power is out and Null can't spy on us, I guess we don't have to hide our little friends any longer."

Rae made the introductions, pointing to each person or creature as she named them off. "Noah Rugg and Levi Rugg, please meet the BrightEyes. This is Sandy. And Phoebe. These three guys are Snappy, Crackly and Poppy. This pair is Rocky. And Roll. And these last three are a few that I met on the other side of the island—a plant type that I've decided to call Flora, and a pair of beach types, one of whom I've named Baloo and this other is a beach type called—" She stopped mid-sentence. And just stood there, pointing at a BrightEyes that didn't look at all like the other sand-and-surf creatures.

"Um, Sis?" I nudged her.

She didn't even answer me, she was so focused on what she was looking at. "Well, well, well, what do we have here?" She coaxed the final BrightEyes down from the air and into her hands, the creature that she had said was a beach type. But it wasn't blue and yellow. Instead it had colorations of deep brown and olive green, or at least that's what it looked like to me in the dim light.

I wasn't quite sure what Rae's problem was. She had misidentified a BrightEyes, so that was maybe a little embarrassing, but it didn't seem worth the speculative expression that had come over her face. "What's up, Sis? So you just made a mistake when you saved those guys from the island? Instead of a plant type and a couple of beach types, they were a plant type and a beach type and some other type? That's not a big deal, we've seen that they can come in all sorts of different configurations."

"N-no, Danae, that's n-not it." Her voice was shaky with excitement. I didn't know what was up, but I did know it must be something big! The BrightEyes in question, meanwhile, was loving all the attention it was getting. "This was most definitely a beach-type creature when I found the three of them. I secured them in my bag, quick-timed it back to meet you at our campsite and then we transported back here, with flames literally nipping at our heels. And now, this BrightEyes is most definitely NOT a beach type." Rae scrounged into my bag and grabbed the Ruggoggles. She used the microscope function to examine the little guy and then announced, "In fact, it has taken on characteristics of canvas and brass. Just. Like. My. Rucksack."

Sigh. Well, we had seen over half a dozen impossible things over the past few days. What's one more?

Rae summed it up pretty well. "So the BrightEyes' adaptation and internalization of their environment doesn't take place on a generational scale. It can take place within hours, perhaps even within minutes. Their DNA can literally rewrite itself, right before our eyes." If you are reading this, you probably understand how incredible something like this is. This one characteristic alone, in a living being, is as wild and fantastical as the entire concept of the OtherWorld portal. As the full implications of what Rae had discovered exploded into my own brain, my game leg felt weak and I had to sit down before I fell down.

Rae took off the goggles and set them on my table. "But why? Why did this one BrightEyes transform from sand and water to brass and canvas? What is the causality relationship? Why didn't the other beach type of creature also change its characteristics?"

The twins had been standing by, just taking it all in. There wasn't much they could contribute to the conversation, since they didn't have any of the background information that we did. But Noah finally spoke up. "Um, we'll bite. Why?"

Levi joined in. "Yeah. We have no idea what's going on, or what these little varmints are, or what in the world you're talking about, but if it will help things along, then, 'Why?'"

I felt as if another one of those cartoon lightbulbs went off over my head. "Actually," I announced to the group, "it's all very simple. I'll bet you a hundred bucks I can show you why this one changed!"

Of course, no one took that bet. They know me too well! Rae said, "No dice, Sis. If you think you know the reason,

I'm not going to disagree. But might you be inclined to share with us your thought processes?"

"Yup!" I grabbed my empathy helmet. A quick adjustment, and I had tweaked it so that it could read the theta waves present in the room and project them onto a small display of the OtherWorld lab. The mini-projection showed the layout of the room, tiny X's for each person and for each BrightEyes, and with a slight adjustment, the brightness of each X was linked to the individual's theta-wave activity level. (It sounds more complicated than it really was. It was almost the same data we had been monitoring about the BrightEyes back on the island, but I just gave it a visual representation to go with the map hologram.)

("Check it out, bro," one of the twins muttered to the other. "Yeah, this is another project the girls are going to have to get us up to speed on, bro.")

With my best P.T. Barnum flourish, I announced, "Once you wrap your head around the fact of these incredible creatures, these Bright Eyes Bushy Tails—"

("Cool name." The twins muttering to one another again. "Catchy AND descriptive.")

"Ahem. Attention please! Once you wrap your head around the fact of their very existence, a little detail such as changing their makeup is not very far behind." I held my hand up like a bird perch and Phoebe swooped down and landed on it. I held my BrightEyes friend near my rucksack and said, "Watch the theta waves." The projection showed me moving the BrightEyes to close proximity with the bag, but there was no change in the intensity of the Phoebe X that indicated Phoebe's emotions.

"Sandy, can I have your help for a minute?" I repeated the actions with the other BrightEyes and again, there was no change in the marker that was the avatar for Rae's special friend.

"Now watch this." I called out to the little BrightEyes that used to be a beach type but was now brown and green. "Hi buddy." It floated over and settled into my palm. "What do you think of this?" I held it near my computer monitor, and no change in the theta waves. I held it near the Tesla coil on the platform and no change. I held it near my rucksack, and the theta-wave marker on the projection just about doubled in intensity!

"Ta-dah! *This* BrightEyes has a real affinity for the materials that make up my bag. It LIKES the canvas and the brass rivets that make up the rucksack. So it decided to CHANGE itself, to adapt its makeup, to match the external environment that it was attracted to! My empathy helmet gives us a representation of how that external environment impacts its feelings and emotions!"

Rae nodded in wonder. "Self-directed transmogrification at a cellular level. Every time I think these creatures just can't be any more amazing..."

Then I had another idea. All of the other BrightEyes were floating around, watching my experiment. I called Phoebe over and nuzzled the little fuzzball against my cheek. "Hey buddy. Want to try something for me?"

"Brrupt!" Yes!

"Okay, see how Olive here," (I had decided that would be the rucksack BrightEyes' name!), "see how Olive changed to be like this material?" I held Phoebe next to the canvasback BrightEyes. They greeted each other with cheerful chirps. "I wonder if *you* can change, too? I know you like jungle plants the best, right?"

"Brrupt!" Yes!

"But I just want to see if YOU can change your skin to be like the rucksack, too, just like Olive did. Not a permanent change, but just if you can change for a couple of minutes. Do you understand?"

My BrightEyes friend looked at the bag, looked at the other BrightEyes that had happily nestled itself into the canvas and then looked back at me. *"Brr-e-e-ept."* Another affirmative response, but this time more thoughtful, as if pondering.

"Okay, can you give it a try? Pretty please, with sugar on top?"

"Brrupt!"

I set Phoebe down on the bag next to its counterpart. All four of us humans watched as it wriggled around as if to get a feel for the material. Then its eyes narrowed as it focused on its goal. And... nothing. A minute passed, and then two. I used the helmet to check Phoebe's emotions, and it was still giving off a happy glow.

"You're doing great, Phoebe. But I don't want you to hurt yourself. Maybe we should just try this later?"

"Pppptt!" No! *"Hmmmmmph. Chrrrrpt."* It sounded as if it were muttering in concentration. Then *"Da, dadahhhh!"* in excitement. Little patches of brown appeared among the reds and greens of its skin. The brown was joined by blotchy olive-green spots, and the new colors spread until the entire exterior of Phoebe resembled my rucksack. My special BrightEyes friend floated up and circled my head in a victory lap. *"Broot, da-drrrt!"*

I laughed while Rae and the boys just stared. "You guys are all lucky you didn't take me up on the bet that I could explain the change in Olive's skin from beach to bag!" I crowed. Then to Phoebe, "That is great, just great, thank you! Do you want to change back to your normal self now?"

"BRRUPT!" Phoebe's natural colors and patterns returned within seconds.

I looked at Rae to see if this new development had her thinking the same thing I was thinking. She caught my eye and smiled. Yup, she had caught onto the possibilities of this new-found ability just as fast as I thought she would.

The twins, on the other hand, were still in the dark, figuratively speaking. And other than for their hood lights, literally speaking as well. Noah said to me, "Well, that scene probably ranks on the top ten list of most mystifying things I'm ever going to see in my life, right up there with the way a raw bitterroot plant can cure poison ivy. But my bro and I don't understand how, even though this is really and honestly astounding, it will help us out of our particular current dire situation."

"Although," Levi added, "my bro and I have absolutely no doubt that y'all do have something in mind that will get us all OUT of this lab and back INTO the game."

"Right and right!" I replied. "Let's get to it, Big Sis."

Chapter 13

DANAE'S LOG 10: Busting Out

I grabbed the Ruggoggles while Rae addressed a small, select group of the BrightEyes. She called five of them over to her—Rocky 'n' Roll and the three electric ones— "All of you li'l fellas, and your friends, have been an enormous help to Danae and me and we are very grateful! We could never have made it home without the power and the circuits and support that you all provided!" Rae has a real knack for making people feel good about themselves. And I guess it applies to non-people, too!

Out of the corner of my eye I saw the twins put their heads together and begin to puzzle out some of what had happened on the other side of the OtherWorld and how we had escaped from Colin's trap.

The little flock of BrightEyes buzzed and chirped around Rae. "Now we need to ask for more help from you, and it might even be a little harder than what you did for us to make our platform work back on the island."

Her audience burbled and plipped, as if to say *What, what is it? How can we help?*

"There are some circuits embedded in those doors over there. They are very special circuits that carry the signal to make the big tungsten deadbolts move in and out from the doors to fit into the door frames and the surrounding walls. They are powered and controlled from the Operations Center which is in another room. We can't get to the controls, and we have no electricity to power the signal."

While she was talking, I pulled out some tools and made a few adjustments to the goggles. I saw Noah mouth the word "electricity" to his brother, who nodded and gestured at the lightning trio.

"What we need to do is re-create those circuits here inside the lab, connect them to the door and power them up. Then we can re-activate the deadbolts, disengage them and get out of here. Can you understand what I'm describing?"

"Blmmmp." "Mmrrrrpp." "Bxxxxxzt!"

"So I'm hoping that you five BrightEyes can help with this. You three—Snappy, Crackly and Poppy—it will be just like before, when you provided electricity for the platform. This time, you will just be providing electricity for the deadbolt mechanism."

They loved that! They buzzed with excitement and Poppy even did a little loop-de-loop in the air.

"And now for you, Rocky, and you, Roll, it will be very similar to what Rocky did before, back on the island, with you taking the electricity from your buddies and running it through the circuits in your skin."

Now it was the pair of meteorite BrightEyes' turn to be excited! The two black-and-silver creatures did a jiggly little dance in the air that made us all LOL. (I mean we laughed out loud for real!)

"I'm glad you are all so eager and willing!" Rae complimented them. "But this time, it is going to be a little harder, because the circuits that we need don't already match the circuits on your skin. Over on the other side of the Other-World, your patterns already matched the electrical paths that were necessary; you have Widmanstätten patterns, and that was exactly what we needed. But this time, we need a different pattern."

I finally had the goggle settings right where I needed them. I focused the eyepieces toward the door and engaged the X-ray application. With a little fine-tuning, I adjusted the field to six inches, which allowed me to look into the interior of the door's structure and see the circuits that controlled the solitude deadbolts. Then I connected the goggles to the helmet so that I could run the image through the holography projector. Sure enough, there it was—a life-sized, one-to-one ratio hologram of the internal circuitry. In other words, we were looking at the guts of the door. And I was pleased that everyone seemed suitably impressed.

"Wow, cuz! Pretty cool!" Noah stated.

"Yup, we're gonna need to put in an order for a couple of those fancy sets of spectacles of yours!" Levi agreed.

I really do love my cousins. Not JUST because they appreciate my genius, but I have to admit, that appreciation is a big part of why they are among my favorite people in the world!

Rae directed the BrightEyes' attention to the projection. "Okay now, Rocky and Roll. Do you see those circuits there?"

"Brppt, bpt." Yup.

"They are different from the Widmanstätten circuits that you have running through you. But did you see how Olive changed skin to be different than before? And how Phoebe changed skin to match the rucksack, too?"

"Brrrppppt... bprptpt..." Yes...?

Rae took a deep breath. "So here's the hard part. Do you two fellas think that you could do something similar? Do you think you could change your skin, just a little bit? Could you maybe change your silver patterns from what they are now, to match what we're showing you *here*? You wouldn't have to keep it up for long, just enough time for your lightning pals to run some power through the new circuits for a few seconds?"

"Brmrmrm." The two BrightEyes put their heads together and we could hear a low buzzing. Finally, they turned back to us and gave an emphatic *"Brrppt!"* Yes! *"Brmrbt."* Or at least, we'll try!

Rae clapped her hands. "Thank you! That's wonderful! And if you can't do it exactly, that's okay. We're just proud of you for trying."

Rae turned to those of us in the room who had arms and legs and motioned for us to get ready. "I'm going to have one meteorite BrightEyes sit on each side of the door jam, and work on shifting their circuits to match the ones shown in the projection. Danae, you're more familiar with the wiring in the deadbolts—"

"I *should* be familiar with it. I designed the darn thing!"

"Exactly, so I'd like you to monitor their progress and let me know when—or if— they have changed enough that they are a match for the system. When you give me the high sign, I'll ask these three living battery packs," she nuzzled the lightning trio, "to pour some juice into Rocky and Roll, just like they did in order to power up the platform."

"And you guys," she turned to address the twins, "if— or hopefully, *when*— you hear the solitude deadbolts retract and disengage, please IMMEDIATELY open the door and keep it open! I am just about sick of being trapped in places."

"You bet your boots, Rae!"

"Doorstop Number One and Doorstop Number Two, that's us!"

"Okay! Let's do it!" She gathered Rocky and Roll up, one in each hand and set them on the top opposite corners of the ledge of the doorframe. Then she turned the helmet's holo projector so that it shone the image right onto the door...the effect was as if part of the structure were actually cut away and as if we could see, with our unaided eyes, the interior of the solid matter. "There you go, buddies. That's the pattern we need you to copy. Can you change your skin to match that?"

Almost exactly as before when Phoebe had concentrated on transmogrifying into a canvas-like material, the two furrowed their brows and narrowed their eyes. We could all see the effort they were putting into it. The silver markings on their hides didn't change... at first. Then I noticed a small shift, a little wiggle in one of the stripes on Roll, who was sitting over on the right-hand side of the door jam. Noah and Levi had their eyes on Rocky and I heard them both gasp at the same time. Afterward, Noah told me it was like watching ice melt, as it slowly transforms from crystalline solid into a fluid liquid; first one tiny bit, then another, then several in a quick cascade and before you know it, one thing has entirely changed into another.

Within five minutes, the circuitry patterns on the two black-and-silver BrightEyes matched the special proprietary design that I had developed for my Fortress-of-Solitude security measures. I pointed at my sister and called, "Now! Go, Rae, go!"

"Guys," she called to our cousins, "you're not going to want to stare directly at this! Listen close and when you hear the deadbolt, do your thing!" Rae shielded her eyes and spoke to Snappy, Crackly and Poppy, who were hovering in the air in front of the door. "Okay, now it's your turn. I know you and your friends on the door there like to play the game where you fill them up with electricity, so go ahead and do that now. Between the three of you, try to put an equal amount of lightning into both of your pals there!"

She didn't have to tell them twice! They were ready, willing, and boy-oh-boy, were they able. The place lit up like Dr. Frankenstein's dungeon during a lightning storm. I wanted to look, but I'm way too smart to do something like that without wearing welder's glasses (or the Ruggoggles with the right setting, but that particular resource was currently being used to give us the schematics of the solitude circuits). Even facing away from the lightning BrightEyes, I had to squint against the flashes of light that filled the room and I knew that the silver etchings on Rocky and Roll were sparking and glowing as bio-generated electricity sped through the metallic pathways of their skins.

You would have expected there to be a buzzing or a sizzling sound, but the whole process was strangely silent. It made it that much easier to hear the big, metallic "CLICK-KA-CHUNK" sound that suddenly came from the door.

It took me totally by surprise, but Noah and Levi were absolutely ready for it. They hit that door like a couple of linebackers (I don't even know sports, but it sounds like a phrase that Levi would use!), swung it open and braced themselves against it to hold it away from the frame. "We got it!" one of them yelled.

Rae called out to all of the BrightEyes at the doorframe, "Wow, that was wonderful! You did perfect, but you can stop now!" The flashes of light died out, with just a few last little flickers as the three of them dialed down their lightning.

That meant I could turn to face the door again, and I stepped up to see about Rocky and Roll. "You were great, too! You managed just the right patterns, and you held them for just the right amount of time! You can change back to your regular circuits now, if you want to." They both flew down to my cupped palms and wriggled in excitement as I petted them. They did seem to be returning to the Widmanstätten patterns, but slowly, a more gradual process than when Phoebe returned to being plant type after shifting to canvas.

The quintet of BrightEyes who had just been instrumental in our release all flitted off to play with the rest of the flock as Rae came over with a big grin to stand next to me. We gave each other our special sister high-five, slapping palms up high, then swinging on through to slap again at hip level and back up for a fist bump explosion. Cheesy, I know, but fun!

"Nice job, Rae!"

"Nice job, Danae!"

"Hey, what about us?" called one of the guys.

"Yeah, are we chopped liver over here, or what?"

"Nice job, Noah!" I called.

"Nice job, Levi!" Rae echoed.

Rae and I each grabbed opposite ends of one of the lab desks and push/pulled it across the floor to the door, where the guys helped us lodge it into the doorway so that there was no way short of an atomic blast that the door could swing shut again.

"Now what?" I asked Rae.

"Now we really need to be on our toes. Someone, probably someone working for Colin Null, arranged to have us locked in the lab, and they most likely will not be particularly happy to find out that we have reversed the situation. That is, we got free and they're gonna be upset."

Our cousins already had their hoods up on their heads, but now each one adjusted the headwear to the point where it covered their faces, leaving only their eyes visible. Noah spoke up. "Rae and Danae, do you mind if Levi and I handle this next part?"

His brother chimed in, "Yeah, we weren't really much help on getting out of the lab—I mean, anyone can hold a door open—and we're starting to feel more useless than a bell on a bobcat."

I did a little stage bow and gestured down the hall, "Be our guest!" We watched as they went into stealth mode, working their way toward the Operations Center. As they passed out of sight around the corner, Rae asked me, "Well, what are the chances, do you think, that the Null Rats are still around and those guys will be able to get Mike free from them?"

I didn't have to ponder it for long. "I don't think they would be stupid enough to hang around for long after they cut the power and locked us in the lab. The question is, did they just get the drop on Mike and then knock him out, or did they tie him up and stow him out of the way in order to engage the Solitude lock? Or did they maybe grab him as a hostage to take back to the Null Corp headquarters and to question him and learn even more about all of Team Rugged Stuff classified info?"

"If we're lucky, maybe they don't think he has any other knowledge for them, since they seem to know plenty about our operations already! They seem to have full access to our complex, know all our secret projects, have info on things like the Fortress of Solitude lock and who knows what else! Their level of proficiency at infiltrating our facility is infuriating! That is, I hate the way they just seem to be able to come and go at will..."

Tucking my walking stick under one arm, I held up both hands with middle fingers resting over index fingers in the time-honored 'good-luck fingers-crossed position' and said, "So here's hoping that they don't feel like there's a net profit to be had from grabbing Mike as a captive."

Rae grinned. "And as long as we're hoping, let's give some good thoughts toward the possibility that Colin's guys are dumb enough to still be hanging around the Ops Center. They might be attempting to partake of even more espionage and larceny. I mean, maybe they are trying to steal even more info and equipment. That would be great!"

"Huh? It would be 'great' in what sense of the word?"

"It would be great because then Noah and Levi could wipe the floor with them! Then maybe *we* could interrogate *them* and find out just how they managed to defeat our security so thoroughly!"

She was right. Those Null Rats wouldn't stand a chance against our cousins!

Chapter 14

NOAH AND LEVI'S JOURNAL 4: "Into the Ops Center!"

Leaving the laboratory behind, me and my bro worked our way down the hall, each of us hugging opposite sides of the corridor. Around a few turns, we finally got back to the door of the Operations Center, back where we had first met up with Mike Kane just a bit earlier in the day. Levi kept a lookout while I reached over and gave the handle a gentle nudge. I fully expected that the door would be locked and the handle wouldn't turn, because let's get real...who would capture an enemy post and then *not* lock the door behind them? Even the numbskulls that Colin Null hires to work for him wouldn't be *that* stupid. So you can imagine how surprised I was when the handle moved smoothly with no resistance.

I whispered in Salish into my mask communicator.

> "Tas x̣e!"
> ["Not good!"]

Levi replied in Yiddish,

> "Yo, dos iz shlekht."
> ["Yeah, that's bad."]

I put pressure on the handle again and inched the door open. As it slowly swung inward, it revealed the room inside to be dark and quiet. We advanced and positioned ourselves inside the doorway, all the while scanning the interior. Then I hissed to my brother, this time in English, "Pssst! Thirty-two!" (That's our code word for 'Freeze!', as in 32 degrees Fahrenheit, when water turns to ice.)

I came up with that one!

Yes, and you are inordinately proud of the fact.

Anyway, we both went motionless. I could sense Levi examining the room, trying to figure out what had caught my attention. And when he noticed it, his body tensed up a bit, just ever so slightly. At the far end of the room, behind Mike's desk and hidden in almost complete darkness, was the outline of a figure slumped over in that uncomfortable chair of his.

We both stayed so still that statues would have been jealous of us, and all the while we communicated back and forth. Although we still used our subvocalizers, given the situation, we didn't bother using Yiddish or Salish.

Levi: "Is...is that him? Is that Kane, I mean?"

Me: "It looks like it could be."

Levi: "I hope he's just unconscious, and not, you know..." He broke his frozen position just enough to mime pulling a finger across his throat in the international symbol of what Shakespeare referred to as shuffling off the mortal coil. Or as the mystery writer Raymond Chandler called it, the Big Sleep.

Me: "Yeah. I hope so."

Levi: "Let's wait for about three more minutes and if nothing happens, if he doesn't move, I'll give us some light so that we can take a better look at things?"

Me: "Three minutes sounds good."

One-hundred and eighty seconds later, Levi eased his hand into his possibles pouch and slowly withdrew a little item that was the size and shape of a golf ball. *We sure could use one of those glow-in-the-dark critters that Rae and Danae have with them,* I thought to myself. My brother tossed the 'golf ball' in an arc up toward the ceiling in the center of the room. As soon as it touched the panels over-head, it stuck tight and began to emit a light that totally illuminated everything in sight. Half the room was bright and stark and the other half—anything facing away from the light—was draped in knife-sharp shadows.

Now we could see the figure that was slumped in the chair.

We looked at it. We looked at each other. "We'd better go get the cousins," said Levi. Out loud. In English.

I just nodded and made my way back to the lab, and I didn't bother to keep quiet about it. There was no longer any need for stealth.

Chapter 15

DANAE'S LOG 11:
Colin Null Goes
Too Far

Rae and I were cleaning up the lab, bathed in light that was being provided by the trio of electrical BrightEyes when Noah showed up at the doorway. "Did you find Mike? Is he okay?" I asked.

My cousin didn't answer directly, but just said, "The Operations Center is secured, but you two need to come and see this."

I glanced over and caught my sister's eyes. *Well, that doesn't sound good, R.*

No. No, it doesn't, D.

We followed him back down the hall to the large room that serves as both the brain center of our operations and as Mike's office. Each of our particular BrightEyes friends—Sandy and Phoebe—accompanied us, while the rest of the critters seemed to be content to flutter around our lab and explore their new surroundings.

We entered through the main door and saw Levi standing on the far side of the room, near Kane's desk. Everything was illuminated by a bright light attached to the ceiling near the center of the room, a light that I recognized as a device I had designed for the cousins. It was very effective, but gave everything a harsh, cold appearance, not at all like the friendly and colorful light provided by the lightning BrightEyes. As we made our way across the room toward our cousin, our eyes were drawn to the chair behind the desk and the figure slumped there.

When we stopped in front of the desk, I glared at Levi with the most withering expression I could conjure up. "Excuse me, but just *what* in the world is *that*?" The *'that'* in question was a scarecrow of sorts, a manikin sitting in Mike's chair and made from crumpled up papers stuffed into a shirt that I also recognized as belonging to Mike, a crisp, white button-down with his initials stitched into the pocket. The figure was sitting there like a department-store dummy, all kind of slumped over, and an envelope was paper-clipped to the shirt. The envelope was addressed to "The girls of Team Rugged Stuff."

"This is... unexpected," said Rae. "I guess there's nothing to do but read what it has to say."

I let my sister take the note from the dummy; for some reason, the whole set-up made me uneasy and I really didn't feel like handling the message. She opened the flap of the envelope, removed and unfolded the sheet of office paper, holding it so that it caught the light from the ceiling. She cleared her voice, "Hmm-hmph," and began to read it out loud, while Sandy and Phoebe sat on her shoulders, looking at the letter for all the world as if they were following along and reading the words in time with her.

"My dear Rachel and Danae,

Kudos and congratulations on your return. Team Rugged Stuff has exceeded even my high expectations for your resourcefulness. I would have bet money against your being able to escape my trap. (In fact, I DID bet money against it, and as a result, lost a considerable sum.) And yet, here you are. I regret to inform you that you have forced my hand and caused me to do something distasteful. I have directed my henchmen to take your beloved and esteemed Dr. Kane as a hostage. I had hoped to just keep you out of the way and stranded at the OtherWorld Point until I had made my announcement to the press. But now, I am forced to use the threat of violence against your longtime and extremely loyal friend. Let me be blunt. If you move, plot or plan against me and/or my press conference, Dr. Mike Kane will suffer the consequences. Severe consequences. Dire consequences. You have been warned.

Most sincerely,

Colin Null.

P.S. Dr. Kane probably deserves a raise, too."

The room was quiet as we stood around in a kind of stunned silence. Noah finally exclaimed, "What a rotten little jerk that kid is."

"What a twerp," Levi agreed.

"Brrg! Prrpt!" growls and hisses from Phoebe and Sandy.

I, on the other hand, wasn't too sure about the whole setup. "I don't know, guys. This just doesn't seem right, somehow."

My sister agreed with me. "Yes. I don't know what it is. There's something about this letter. I don't know, just kind of a bit *off*, somehow."

I grabbed up the envelope and the letter. "I know. For one thing, when has Colin ever referred to us by the correct name? I mean when has he ever called us 'Team Rugged Stuff'? He always tries to get us riled up by calling us 'Team Slugged Rough' or something else just as silly. He must be more desperate than he's letting on if he passed up a chance to make fun of us."

"Desperate is the word for it," said my sis, "I mean, to take Mike as a hostage? That's just not like him at all. Taking a hostage is...well, it's vulgar. This behavior indicates an unprecedented level of anti-social behavior. That is to say, Null must be freaking out about us being back here, if he's sinking to this kind of low-brow tactic."

"Yup." I sighed. "Well, I guess we can marvel at his decline and fall later on, but right now, we've got a flight to catch." I motioned to Rae and the boys with a 'come-on' gesture.

Noah stared at me and his jaw dropped. And honest to gosh, his mouth just flopped open like in the comic books. "I'm sorry, I must have missed something. A flight? A flight to where?"

I gotta give credit to Rae, she didn't miss a beat. "To New York, of course. We've got a press conference to sabotage." That's my sis. SHE knew what I was talking about!

Levi joined his brother in looking as if someone had just popped him on the top of the head with an ax handle. "But, but what about all that 'consequences, dire consequences' palaver that Colin mentioned? Aren't you afraid he'll do something to your amigo Mike if you all of a sudden show up in New York?"

Rae pooh-poohed that. "The very last thing in the world that Mike would want is for Colin to be able to use him as a tool against us. Besides, all we have to do is keep a low profile, and Null won't even know that we're on our way."

Suddenly I laughed as a funny thought struck me. "Besides, oh-cousin-of-mine, you can just think of us as chaperones!"

"Huh?"

"We'll just be along to keep an eye on you. Or did you forget? You've got a date in NYC for burgers with Nessa!"

Chapter 16

DANAE'S LOG
INTERLUDE 1:
Nessa Null Profile

Hmmmmm. I just realized something. For the narrative to make any sense from here on out, anybody reading it needs to be more familiar with the Null family, so I've got to put in some background info on Nessa Null. There is a problem, though: Thinking about her makes me want to puke all over the room! So I made Rae put together a dossier on her. (Rae's a much nicer and more forgiving person than I am. (That's my polite way of saying that she's a sucker!)) But no matter how you look at it, the Null family has had a big impact on me and my sis ever since we brought the Ruggs back into the science-adventurer game, so it's pretty important to try to figure out whatever we can about them.

Profile: Nessa Null
Compiled by: Rachel Rugg
Profile Editor notes:
Verifiable Fact is presented straight type
Assumption/Supposition is presented in italic type
FACT:
Name: Nessa Null. Named for an ancient Irish queen who was known as Ness, the daughter of Eochaid Salbuide, the King of Ulster in Northern Ireland.

Nessa is the older sister to Colin Null by two years. When both were still in their early-to-mid-teens, Colin began his adventurer-scientist career, using the bulk of the family fortune to build labs, hire scientists and develop a world-class research organization, with himself at the head of it. Nessa turned her attention not so much to the field of pure scientific exploration and research but instead poured a small fortune into acquiring silent (but controlling) partnership in several newspapers, news media stations and websites.

At the time of the writing of this report, one out of every five journalists in Europe and North America works (either directly or, as is more commonly the case, indirectly) for Nessa Null.

ASSUMPTION:

We believe that she has leveraged her influence here so that the databases of all of these news media and journalism businesses feed into her own personal computer information system. This includes even UNPUBLISHED notes and conversations by the unwitting journalists—if they write something on a company-provided laptop or say something on a company-provided cell phone, that info is captured and duplicated into Nessa's files.

FACT:

The relationship between Nessa and her younger brother Colin goes beyond sibling rivalry and all the way into bitter hatred. The source of the enmity between the two stems from the actions that Colin took in order to fund his startup. When Nessa was 14 and Colin 12, their parents disappeared while on an African safari. After a year passed and no sign of the adult Nulls was forthcoming, the courts declared them legally dead and the massive Null family fortune passed to the children.

ASSUMPTION:

This, apparently, was what Colin had been waiting for. There are even rumors that he bribed people within the legal system in order to speed up the process. And with some world-class financial fraud, he was able to substitute a false will into the legal proceedings.

FACT:

The multi-million-dollar inheritance that would have normally been split equally between sister and brother and held in trust until they reached the age of majority was now suddenly divided 10 percent against 90 percent, with the vast bulk of the estate going to the younger brother, Colin. Nessa received only a (comparatively) small stipend, enough to live on comfortably.

ASSUMPTION:

She might have been content with this, but after the financial affairs were settled, some sources report that Colin actually bragged to her about how he had, in effect, stolen millions of dollars from her, money that their parents had intended for them to share equally.

From that day on, she began accumulating information, with the primary purpose of revenge against her brother.

FACT:

Early in the course of her networking, she happened upon some unpublished information regarding a new offering from one of the up-and-coming software companies. Armed with this knowledge, she invested her entire monetary allowance for the year into seed money for the business and when the new product development finally got to the stock market in an Initial Public Offering, she found that she had suddenly increased her net worth by hundreds of thousands of dollars. A few more purchases on the market grew her fortune exponentially.

ASSUMPTION:

She always invested in new products that her research indicated would provide the highest amount of return for the least amount of risk, and because her research was flawless (illegal, but flawless), she rarely suffered a financial loss.

FACT:

It didn't take too long for her to build her own fortune.

ASSUMPTION/CONCLUSION:

A fortune that nearly, but not quite, rivals the amount that her brother had cheated her out of. But she considers it just a side-effect of her main goal, which is to crush Colin Null and his entire organization. No matter what. She knows it might take time, but she is smart, young, rich... and very patient.

END of PROFILE

Chapter 17

NOAH AND LEVI'S JOURNAL 5: "Into NYC!"

T he doorman announced the arrival of "Misters Rugg and Rugg" and we heard Nessa's voice over the intercom telling him to send us on up. Me and Levi have been to New York a bunch of times, but I never get used to how big it is and all the activity of the place. The guy at the front door asked if we needed help with our luggage, but we thanked him and said no. We each had on a backpack and we were also each pulling a huge (and I mean *huge*) steamer trunk behind us, but these were on wheels, so they were pretty easy for us to handle.

Aren't you kind of starting in the middle? How'd we end up in New York all of a sudden?

Oh, okay, okay. Let me back up a little bit.

When we found that dummy manikin that the Null Rats left behind after the Kane kidnapping, our cousins Rae and

Danae were determined to take the fight straight to Colin. And after all, Danae was absolutely correct; we *did* have a ready-made excuse for going to NYC already, since my brother had an evening engagement lined up with Nessa there.

Remember what I said to you at the time? "Hurry up, let's not be late, 'cuz me and Nessa have got a date!" Pretty clever, right? Maybe you're not the only poet in the family, huh?

Hoo boy. Yeah, right. I think you'll be better off sticking with rude limericks, bro.

So anyway, we all went from the labs over to our cousins' house, cleaned up a bit and grabbed a bite to eat. They clued us in about what had taken place over on the other side of the OtherWorld portal, and we filled them in on everything that had happened back here in the real world. Then we had Levi place a call to Nessa Null.

When she picked up the call and her face showed up on the video screen, my brother did his best to get the rural twang out of his voice as he greeted her, "Hello, Nessa!" From over his shoulder in the background, I waved a greeting to her, but we made sure that the girls were far enough off to the side that the camera wouldn't see them.

"Hi fellows! An' what's happenin'? You're not callin' to break off our hamburger date now, are you, Levi?" (I can't even describe how incredible she sounds, with that slight Irish accent. She's got the most beautiful voice this side of Imelda May!)

Levi got all flustered. "Oh, no! Not at all! I mean, unless *you* want to cancel. But you don't want to, I hope?"

"No, silly. I'm buildin' up a big appetite, so you'd better not flake out on me."

Levi sighed in relief. "Oh, well, good! No, the date's still on, but there's been some activity that's taken place on that *other* subject that I had spoken to you about. You know, that, um, well, that other subject."

Nessa's eyes went big. "You mean with your cous—"

Levi cut her off, "Yeah, with that." Just in case Colin could somehow have the conversation bugged, we didn't want to give anything away over the phone.

Nessa seemed to pick up on what my brother was talking about and gave a low whistle. "Well, well, well, what do you know. As it just so happens, I, too, have some new information regardin'...that matter."

Now it was me and Levi's turn to whistle. My bro put an innocent expression on his face and replied, "Hmmm, you don't say," then he looked over at me and I nodded to him. He turned back to the pretty face on the phone screen. "Well, Noah and I would like to come into the city a little earlier than I had originally planned and chat with you some about the, um, the, um, about that other matter."

Nessa was a little puzzled. "I don't see why that would be a problem. When were you thinkin' of flying out here?"

"Right now. We'll be staying in town for a couple of days, we've got a buddy from space camp who lives in the city and he said it'd be okay with his folks if we bunk with him for a while. And we're going to have some big suitcases with us. I mean, *big* big. Like huge. Like ginormous. Like—" Levi held his arms as wide apart as they would stretch in an effort to give her a sense of the scope of scale that he was talking about.

"Okay. I get it. Big suitcases." But she still sounded puzzled. Like she couldn't figure out why in the world we would be telling her about the luggage we would be bringing with us.

Levi rubbed the back of his neck and looked sheepish. "So. Yeah. But no matter what, our burger date is still on, right?"

I called out from behind him. "Or not! I mean, you shouldn't feel obligated to keep the date! Besides, cattle farming for beef is really bad for the environment. And also, maybe you won't feel like going out to dinner after chatting about... other stuff." Then Levi elbowed me in the stomach. Hard.

Yeah, well, maybe next time you can just line up your own dinner date, instead of trying to sabotage mine!

After performing this heinous act of bodily harm to my mid-section, Levi continued the conversation. "Don't listen to my dimwitted brother here. Dinner will be great. But what do you say, maybe as soon as our flight gets in, could we stop by your place? I mean, even before we go over to our space-camp friend's house?

"Sure, an' I'll be expectin' you!" Did I mention that Nessa has a great voice? I could just sit and listen to her talk all day long, and it wouldn't even matter what she was saying.

Yeah! She could be reading the phone book out loud for all I care, and it would still sound sweeter than molasses!

So we got an overnight flight from the very convenient Reno/Tahoe International Airport into JFK Airport in New York. Me and Levi felt kind of guilty, riding in the first-class section with our backpacks in the overhead storage, while the pair of big steamer trunks that we brought with us got schlepped into the cargo hold. Six hours of airtime later, we had traveled from the Biggest Little City in the World to the City that Never Sleeps, but with the time change, it was already mid-morning by the time we collected both of the big ol' trunks from baggage claim and got into the city, to Nessa's apartment building.

And that finally brings us back to where you started this chapter. Now that you have filled in the blanks, you may continue y'all's story..

Gee, thanks for your permission, bro. Hashtag sarcasm.

The elevator took us, along with our luggage, up to Nessa's Midtown Manhattan penthouse loft. It had 360-degree views of the city, and the Empire State Building was visible at an angle through the skylight.

"Quite a place you've got here! Not bad, for a research nerd!" I teased her as Levi and I wheeled our trunks in through her front door and she gave each of us a little European kissy-cheek greeting.

Sigh.

"Thanks. It'll do until I can find somethin' that's a little more chic," she teased back. In reality, it was obvious that she totally loved this place. The executors of the Null estate in Ireland think that she spends her time in America studying as a pre-admissions student at Empire State University and that she lives in the dorms there, but I think she only shows up on campus when she needs to pick one of the professor's brains about something. "But what about you guys? If that luggage is any indication, you're plannin' on staying here in the city for more than just a few days. More like a few months, from the looks of it."

Levi and I each gently tipped our respective trunks down off their wheels so that they rested on the floor right-side up. My brother raised an eyebrow at our hostess. "Oh, I'm afraid that these trunks are not really a good indicator of how long our visit will be. But I bet you already know that!"

"Yeah," I grumbled under my breath, "I didn't get to bring ANY change of clothes, I'm gonna need to find a laundromat pretty soon..."

Nessa just grinned. "Well now, I *did* kind'a figure as much. So don't you think we ought to get these things open?"

Levi returned her grin. "I *told* Noah that you would have deduced what we were up to before we even got here!"

I snorted and grumbled some more as I undid the latches to the steamer trunks. Then I grabbed my phone from my pocket and placed a quick conference call. "Eagle One to Baby Chicks. Baby Chicks, do you copy?" Two different female voices answered over the tinny-sounding speaker.

"Ten-four, Eagle One."

"Roger that, Noah."

I grinned. It was time for the big reveal. "Baby Chicks, prepare to hatch. Repeat, prepare to hatch." I flipped the final hidden latch on my trunk, while Levi did the same on his luggage. Each of the big boxes opened with a burst of mist and a low pneumatic *'hisssssssssssssssssssssssssss'*.

Suddenly, from the trunk on the floor in front of me, came a loud yell that nearly scared me out of my skin! "Ahhhhhhrg!!!"

Chapter 18

DANAE'S LOG 12:
Tea with Nessa

"**A**hhhhhhrg!!!"

Sorry. I just couldn't help it. When my travel pod finally opened up, I let out a loud groan. Like really super loud. My leg was absolutely killing me from not being able to stretch it for the past eight or so hours. Walking stick in one hand, I levered myself out of the crate and tumbled onto the floor of Nessa's apartment. Off to the side, Rae was climbing out of her own pod, stretching. She was groaning, too, just not as loudly as me.

Nessa was standing between the twins, smiling warmly. "An' welcome to the big city, girls. The powder room is down the hall, first door to the left, an' I'll go into the kitchen and put some tea on for you."

Rae returned the smile, then glanced my way. *D'ya mind if I go first, D? I have REALLY got to use the facilities!* Her expression was easy to interpret.

I nodded. *Go ahead, R, I gotta work a few kinks out of my leg before anything else.*

My sister headed for the "powder room" and Nessa headed for the kitchen. When Rae got back, I was using the sofa as a brace to lean up against and stretch my calves. Nessa wasn't back yet. "Little Miss Suzy Hostess, isn't she?" I growled under my breath.

Rae started her own stretching regimen and replied softly, "Yeah, well, I'm not her biggest fan either, but she *is* helping us out here, so we should be a little gracious about it."

"Phooey. She's just doing it because she despises Colin as much as we do," I murmured back. As an afterthought, I added, "And because she likes to see the twins, knuckleheads that they are, compete with each other over her."

The object of our conversation returned from the kitchen holding a tray with five mugs of tea. "I wasn't sure which you would prefer, so I've got both Irish Breakfast and Gold Blend. You two take first pick, and the boys and I will have whatever's left. Won't we, guys?"

The cousins almost fell over themselves to agree with her. Chumps.

I have to admit though, after a trip to the bathroom, then a cup of tea (with plenty of sugar) and a little time for my body to unfold, I did feel in much better spirits.

We sat around the living room, sipping our drinks. (Of course the tea was Barry's, a traditional Irish brand!) Nessa and the twins very patiently waited for me and my sister to begin to feel human again. Nessa gestured to the trunks and asked, "Do you mind?"

Rae said, "Sure, go ahead," and I gave a little mock bow, twirling my hand in the direction of the disguised travel pods. I wasn't really crazy about letting her get her paws on my tech, but on the other hand, I was curious to see what she thought of my newly invented emergency rescue pods. (Great for ships or submarines, or heck, even for space stations (they are TOTALLY self-contained); anyplace where a person might need their own little shell to stay safe in the case of some sort of catastrophe... if we had these along with us on the other side of the OtherWorld, I bet we could have even ridden out the volcanic explosion!)

The Irish girl set her cup down and gave the big "suitcases" a thorough investigation, murmuring to herself the whole time. "Hmmmm. An' look here, now. A reinforced frame, of course. Sealed, with an insulated environment against temperature changes. A nice three-stage re-breather for fresh air, with an extra tank in the base. In sum, the perfect way to travel incognito." She examined the trunks from all angles, probably memorizing all the details she could so that she could enter them into some sort of data file later. Finally, she turned and looked at us. "But only if you absolutely have to, because as really clever as it is, I'm sure it was a cramped, uncomfortable and terribly borin' journey."

I snorted. "You've got *that* right! We had our tablets, but there's only so much Minecraft you can play and so much time you can take being strapped in—and cooped up— before it starts to feel like you're going to go crazy!"

" 'Phenomenal cosmic powers; itty-bitty living space...' " Rae muttered.

The cousins and I ignored her, figuring it was probably another movie quote, but Nessa's face broke out in a grin. "Robin Williams as the Genie!" This drew a corresponding smile from my sister.

Great, I thought, *just what I need, a touching scene of bonding between my sis and that pain-in-the-neck Nessa.*

But I kept my mouth shut. (I guess the caffeine was starting to kick in a little bit, thank goodness!)

Noah gulped down the last of his tea (he was drinking some herbal stuff, too, of course). "Well, I'm relieved that your travel pod steamer trunks worked out so well." (I had *told* him they would, but apparently he only believed it now that Nessa had given her seal of approval. (Yes, I know I sound like an old grouch!)) "You know, people have DIED trying to stow away in the cargo areas of airplanes. I'm still not sure it was really necessary to take that kind of a risk, especially when you both could have just had seats up in first class with me and Levi."

Nessa put her tea down on a tasteful coffee table, sat down on a beautiful chair (obviously designed to be the focal point of the room), crossed her legs and put her hands on her knees. It was all very earnest and sincere as she addressed us. "As little leg room as they may offer, and as dangerous as it could have been," (I bristled at this, but held my temper), "I think this was probably the smart thing to do." (Oh. She was actually backing me up and taking my side of the debate. Well. Okay, then. That made me glad I hadn't lost my cool at her.)

The twins, as usual, hung on her every word. (Chumps. Boys are just chumps.)

"I know that my dear brother Colin managed to get a Homeland Security facial recognition alert put out on both Rachel and Danae. It hasn't gotten any public fanfare, of course, but both of you girls are currently on the No-Fly list. The minute you tried to get through security in order to board the plane, you would have been, to put it bluntly, snagged an' bagged. Colin really wouldn't have taken it very well had you just gone an' bought a pair of airline tickets directly to the site of his big announcement, so he made sure that it wouldn't be possible for you to take a commercial flight here to New York from out West. Or at least he *thought* he had prevented you from crashin' his big announcement. It seems you've discovered a workaround, at least for the first phase of your mission to stop his press conference."

She glanced coyly at me and Rae, and I wondered what she had on her mind. The way she was looking at us, so intently from under her big lashes, she obviously was about to unload some sort of bombshell on us. "Hmmmmm, yes, his big announcement. You know, the announcement... about his development of a portal to some other world."

Bombshell, indeed! The fact of the OtherWorld world was supposed to be top secret, that's why we were trying to stop the press conference in the first place! We all stared at her. The room went silent. I frantically locked eyes with Rae.

—R, did she say 'portal to another world'!?

—D, yes, she did! But how? None of Colin's public relations stuff has mentioned the OtherWorld! He only said he had a big announcement, but hasn't given any hint as to what the announcement is about!

All of a sudden, I felt like my brain was a squirrel bouncing off the insides of my skull trying to find a way out. *How'd she know about the OtherWorld?! Is she working with Colin?! If she knows about the OtherWorld, does she know about the BrightEyes?! Did we just walk into a trap?!*

The next thing I knew, there was a big crash of china. I looked down to see that I had dropped my teacup and saucer right out of my hands.

"Oh, don't worry about that, I'll clean it up later." Nessa was very clearly very pleased with the reaction that she had gotten by so casually revealing that she knew about our big secret project.

"How. How. How," said my sister (and it's not easy to put Rae in a situation where she's at a loss for words!). Finally, she managed to sputter, "How? In the world? Do you know? About the portal?" I could see the same thoughts flashing through my big sis's mind that were skittering in mine.

Nessa sat there, smug. Smiling.

I heard Levi whisper to Noah, "I told you she'd probably figure that part out!"

And the reply. "You're crazy, bro, I'm the one who told *you* that she would probably dig up that info."

I was so mad I couldn't even trust myself to speak, so it was good ol' level-headed Rae who finally set her teacup on the table, took a deep breath, looked Nessa in the eye and said, "Okay. We really need to talk."

Nessa finally gave in and explained how she had deduced the general outline of the OtherWorld Project. That's the thing about some people (myself included, unfortunately), we just can't resist bragging about what we can do with our big brains. I pressed the record button on my smart watch, trying not to make it look obvious. She probably noticed the movement, but just didn't care that I was getting an audio record of her explanation, because she was awfully proud of her research. And I guess she had a right to be. Anyway, I'm including here in my log a verbatim transcription of that recording, along with some notes added in by me and by Rae.

Chapter 19

DANAE'S LOG INTERLUDE 2: Nessa Null Transcription

Once he reached out to the press and announced the date for his big event, it was plain that Colin had somethin' very big planned, that was for a certainty. And then I got the phone call from Levi, askin' if I knew what was behind it all. That made me fairly confident that whatever me dear brother was up to, it had something to do with Team Rugged Stuff. This gave me the startin' point that I needed in order to begin my investigation. I have, of course, met both of you Rugg girls a few times before, but we have neither come into conflict nor worked together in any capacity. The fact that you are a source of irritation to Colin does, however, make me inclined to think favorably of you, very favorably indeed.

[Annotation by Danae: I also tend to think this is why she goes out on so many dates with Noah and Levi, 'cuz it's gotta drive Colin crazy whenever she spends any time with a Rugg.]

[Annotation by Rachel: And make no mistake—from my analysis of Nessa, EVERYTHING in her life is secondary to her ultimate goal of revenge against Colin. If she ever found herself in a situation in which hindering us would also hinder her brother, she'd not hesitate for one microsecond to turn her allegiance against us. What I mean to say is, she'd throw us under the bus in a heartbeat, as long as it turned out to be bad for her brother!]

So I put all my other projects on hold and began a crash investigation into findin' out just what the current connection was between Null Corp and Team Rugged Stuff, what it was that had caused Colin to become so smug and what it was that had caused the Rugg girls—that's you, I mean—to go missin'. I started with all of the obvious leads, knowin' that none of them would be likely to enlighten me, but I am nothin' if not thorough. It's what has made me the top researcher in the world, after all.

[Annotation by Danae: Oh yeah, THAT's what made you a top researcher. That and money! Lots and lots of money, LOL!]

Once the basics were out of the way, I started on my own personal favorite track of inquiry. I began to gather data *not* on the activities of Null Corp and Team Rugged Stuff, but on the activities of the major scientific equipment suppliers from around the world.

[Annotation by Danae: Now, THIS part of her story made me scratch my head and raise my eyebrows!]

One of the revered fables in the history of the science of astronomy claims that researchers deduced the presence of Pluto long before they actually physically spotted the tiny little 'planet,' because they observed the influence exerted on other space bodies that had already been charted. This 'Planet X' made the other planets move in minute little ways that they could observe and thus deduce the existence and location of what came to be known as dwarf planet Pluto. This is the way that I went about the present problem.

Both Colin and the Rugg girls did too good of a job of maskin' their own activities, but they couldn't hide the impact that they had on third-party vendors, university professors and other individuals and organizations.

[Annotation by Danae: At this point in the story, Rae and I looked at each other with an expression of "Whoops!"]

[Annotation by Rachel: Affirmative. It had never crossed my mind that even though our own activities were kept secret, our progress might be tracked and charted by the activities of other entities. That is, by checking out other people, someone could figure out what we were working on!]

I discovered that over the past year and a half, there were major purchases of scientific supplies shipped to an undisclosed location that I could narrow down to a delivery destination in the United States of America, somewhere between Salt Lake City in the state of Utah and Sacramento, California. Within that target area, I could track them to the Reno/Tahoe area in the state of Nevada. Knowin' that's where your laboratory is, I could deduce that those supplies were bein' used by you two sisters.

And I could spot other, similar purchases being ordered and shipped to a very familiar—*too* familiar— location in Ireland. These secondary purchases occurred almost simultaneously, but were much smaller in scope. It was clear to me that Colin was duplicatin' your efforts on a small scale, investing only enough resources so that he could follow and understand the original research on which you were spendin' a much larger amount of time and money. But his actions were taking place within hours, sometimes even within minutes, of your own. Somehow, he had real-time access to a database of your supplies and inventory.

Before long, I had a fairly complete picture. Rae and Danae were developin' a new technology, and based on the supplies, it involved exploring some new and exotic locale, some new world or setting, something along those lines. And access to this new world was not by conventional methods, but via some new mode of transportation. It wouldn't normally concern me very much, except for the fact that my dear brother Colin had a mole, or some sort of information bug, in their organization, feeding all the data to him just one step behind the Rugg sisters. With a little informed extrapolation, it wasn't hard to figure out that Rae and Danae had been successful. As soon as they had completed all of the hard work, Colin had snapped the jaws shut on his trap; his mole, his spy within the Rugg organization had done somethin' to get the sisters out of the way and Colin was goin' to step in and claim the new technology—and probably the new world, as well—as his own.

Because, as you surely understand, if Colin presents this new technology, new discovery, new location, (whatever it is) to the world as being a development of Null Corp labs, it will hardly matter that he has stolen it. He will get away with it.

Just as he stole my inheritance. And got away with it.

As far as the scientific community, and the world, will be concerned, it will be his.

[Annotation by Danae: We know! WE KNOW! That's what we've been saying all along and it's why we're so frantic to stop him!!!]

And if Colin wants it, I want him *not* to have it. So please consider me to be an ally—or even, dare I say, a member—of Team Rugged Stuff for the duration of the conflict.

END of TRANSCRIPT

Chapter 20

DANAE'S LOG 13: Colin's Plan, Revealed

When Nessa finished her story about how she had deduced the truth about our latest project, we all just sat there for a few minutes. I don't know about the others, but I think Rae and I were just too stunned to speak. ('Consider her to be a member of Team Rugged Stuff,' Nessa had said. Ha, yeah, right. Hashtag Never Gonna Happen.)

Finally, my sister shook her head as if coming out of a dream. "Hmmm. Brilliant. Do you think that's how Colin has managed to dog our trail throughout the entire project, keeping just one step behind, or in some instances, one step ahead? Did he use that 'Planet X' approach?"

Nessa frowned. "No. For one thing, his actions durin' that time period each took place almost immediately after yours. Real research takes time to produce results. And also, real research just isn't his style. He's much more direct.

Sneaky, but direct. He's got some sort of solid pipeline of information directly from inside your organization. And the fact that he was able to react so swiftly to your return from his OtherWorld trap makes me even more convinced of this. You were back in the lab, what, fifteen minutes tops, before his team swooped in and made off with your Ops Commander, that Dr. Kane of yours?"

Her frown deepened (in a way I'm sure the twins (chumps) both considered to be very attractive). "An' you're right, though, taking Kane as a hostage doesn't really fit Colin's *modus operandi*." A vicious smile crossed her face. "I wonder if he's becomin' unstable?" The thought of her brother losing his super-smarts really seemed to make her happy, and I can't say that I would disagree with her on that. But somehow, I didn't think that was the case. Something about Mike's abduction still stuck sideways in my brain and just felt kind of...off.

Nessa had already cleaned up the mess I had made, and now she started collecting the empty teacups and saucers from the others to take back into the kitchen. As she worked, she continued to dominate the conversation. "An' speaking of something that does nae fit his method of operations, I'm very surprised that he was so sloppy as to allow you to return from wherever it was that he had you trapped, that 'OtherWorld' place. He had obviously planned on you two being completely out of the picture until after his announcement. So...just exactly how *did* you manage to return to Earth?"

We had given her a very brief thumbnail sketch of our adventures. We had intentionally left out any mention of the BrightEyes. (The BrightEyes who were, by the way, now luxuriating in our year-round arboretum back at the Galena property, between Reno and Tahoe. There was no way we were going to risk them on a cross-country escapade at this point, and they absolutely loved our 10-acre greenhouse, so they were safely tucked out of sight for the present. They were being babysat (or should that be called BrightEyes sat?) by our other cousin, Izzy. She's the oldest of all of us Rugg cousins and she agreed to come up to our lab from her home in the SF Bay Area and spend some time keeping an eye on our new friends.) We also warned Levi and Noah—on pain of looooong and paaaaainful death—not to mention the BrightEyes to ANYONE outside of the family, and I think we got the point across to them. Rachel and I knew very well that Nessa was helping us *only* because it served her own purposes, and that it could be as soon as next week that we might find ourselves up against her as an opponent. So any mention of our new floating friends was strictly a big no-no.

And Nessa's current oh-so-casual tone wasn't fooling me. She didn't know how we got back, and to her, that state of not knowing something was a special torture all its own. Still, I guess we had to give her some sort of explanation, one that would satisfy her for the time being and keep her from pecking away at us for more information. So I matched her own level of casual conversation. "Oh, I just cobbled some technology together from the parts I had taken along with me in my bag. I'm sure you understand how it is, Nessa. I just made do with what resources I had available," I replied, carefully buffing and examining my fingernails. The very picture of nonchalance, that was me!

"Yeah, I guess we're just smarter than Colin figured we were!" Rae said brightly, putting on the most innocent smile that she could muster.

Nessa was still skeptical, though. "Hmmmph. Right. Well, an' I guess maybe later on, you'll let me in on what really happened. The fact of the way in which you managed to return can be something that *you* know about this whole situation that *I* don't." She made a big show of now examining *her* fingernails, in a deliberate and exaggerated imitation of me. "Sure, an' it's okay. It makes us even. Because there's somethin' about the whole situation that *I* know, and that *you* don't."

All of us Ruggs exchanged glances. Nobody said anything. We were all wondering what in the world it was that she was planning to spring on us now. Finally I spoke up. "Okay, I'll bite. What do *you* know that *we* don't?"

"Nuh-uh-uh." Nessa smiled sweetly and wagged her finger at me in a 'nope-nope-nope' gesture. "You tell me, an' then I'll tell you."

Rae jumped in, and a good thing too, 'cuz I was stuck. No way I was gonna spill the beans about the BrightEyes to this girl, but also no way was I gonna not find out whatever it was that she was holding back from us. My sister put on her very best reasonable-sounding voice and said, "Look Nessa, we really, *really* can't tell you right now how we managed to make the jump back to home. But I pinkie-swear, just as soon as we can clue you in, I'll give you all the details."

Nessa looked dubious, but Rae has a reputation for being scrupulously honest. Eventually, Nessa gave in. "Fine. But just remember, you owe me, and I *always* collect on debts. When you can tell me, I *definitely* want to know how you escaped from OtherWorld Island." She sat back down in her showcase chair, crossed her legs all dainty and ladylike and steepled her fingers together. I couldn't help but think that she looked like a James Bond villain. "But for now, here is what *I* do know and *you* don't know. I know what Colin's plans are for your OtherWorld Point once he has taken all of the credit for its discovery and development." Then she sat back in smug silence.

Rae and I looked at each other again, but this time in puzzlement. We had been expecting some big momentous revelation, but neither of us was quite sure what she meant.

I mean...Colin's plans for the OtherWorld Point? Wasn't that just about the most obvious thing in the world? He would be planning on exploiting it, of course.

Me and my sis glanced questioning looks over at the twins; maybe they knew what she was talking about? But both Noah and Levi had the same puzzled looks on their faces, the kind that said, "Don't look at *me*, I have no idea what's going on!" In unison, they each emphasized their lack of insight with a little shrug. No help from them, thanks a lot, guys.

So Rae finally broke the silence. "Hmmmm. I'm afraid we have to admit that we're not sure what you're getting at, Nessa. A whole new world, with Colin controlling the doorway to it? I imagine he'll want to explore it, search for minerals, strip it of its natural resources, stuff like that."

"And tourism, of course," I noted. "I'm sure he'll want to start to build up some hotels and resorts and charge people tons of money to spend a week or two at a time over there on the other side."

Nessa clapped her hands together and looked so pleased with herself, I wanted to punch that expression right off her face. "See, an' that's more proof of the puddin' about what I know that you don't. Neither of you has the wee slightest clue as to what his true plans really are, and you're both very wrong in your guesses."

"Okay smarty-pants. I'll bite again." I crossed my arms and stuck out my chin. "Why don't you put your money where your mouth is and tell us what Colin's got up his sleeve for the OtherWorld?" Rae nudged me, frowning at my rude tone. "Okay, sorry," I relented. "Will you share what you know about his plans? Pretty please?"

Nessa grinned and gave that little 'nope-nope-nope' wag of her finger again. Argh. "First, a wee lesson in economics. Let's think about it. In order to explore or to develop natural resources, or to build resorts—as you two seem to think he's plannin' to do—what do you need?" It was a rhetorical question, and she continued speaking with no pause or chance for us to answer her. "You need a PLACE to explore, or a PLACE with resources to exploit, or a PLACE in which to build that hotel. And yes, you have discovered a new PLACE, so I can understand why you would assume that is his intent. But what *else* do you need?"

This time, the question wasn't rhetorical, but I still didn't know what she was after. I just looked at her and shrugged my shoulders. The boys made a big show of being innocent bystanders with no intention of hazarding even the slightest guess. And Rae said, "Ummmmmmm?"

Nessa was more than happy to continue her lecture. "It's a trick question, because it's a two-part answer! And those two parts are," she held up two fingers like a peace sign or a victory signal, "Time an' Money!" Nessa's vicious, triumphant grin was all teeth. Like a shark. "In addition to the PLACE you also need TIME and you need MONEY," she repeated. "All of your ideas—exploration, natural resources, tourism—they all take an investment of both time and money, a lot of each, to pour into that PLACE before they start paying off. You've got to fund your explorations. You've got to locate, transport and refine those natural resources before you can get a return on the investment. And as for hotels and resorts, oh my!" She rolled her eyes dramatically. "Don't even get me started on the travel an' leisure industry! Do you have any idea of how long it is before you begin to see a profit on a hotel? Do you have the slightest inklin' of how small the profit margin is on a resort? Without a long-term plan, you might as well just stand on the beach and throw your money away out into the waves!"

"Okay, maybe so, but...," objected Rae, holding up her index finger in counterpoint, "but Colin has plenty of money to invest."

"Oh, he's got money, an' that's for sure," agreed Nessa. "But even with all of his money AND all the money he cheated me out of, he doesn't have enough cash that he's goin' to just go and dump it down a hole with very little chance of seeing a quick profit. And what he *isn't* sure of is how much TIME he has. So he's not goin' to tie his fortune up into investments that take a long time to pay off."

That made me perk up. "What do you mean, he's not sure how much time he has?" I asked, "Is he sick or something?" I had my fingers crossed that maybe he had contracted some sort of disease, something that wasn't deadly, but that would make him very, very uncomfortable. I mean, really, was a week-long bout of non-stop vomiting too much to hope for?

"No, nothin' like that," Nessa waved her hands, brushing aside the suggestion. (Dagnabbit.) "But he's a realist, and although he would never admit it, he does think very highly of your capabilities. He hid his activities, of course, but according to my research, I can see that he has been callin' on a lot of legal scholars and consulting firms. I can tell that he is preparin' for the possibility that the two of you would be able to mount a legal challenge to his anticipated control of whatever it is that exists over there on the other side of the Portal." Nessa uncrossed her legs and leaned forward toward us, speaking in a hushed and secretive tone. "It would appear that he has determined that there is a solid chance that you might be able to prove your side of the story, at least to the world courts, within three to seven years. If he controls the OtherWorld at the outset, you might never get public opinion and the scientific community on your side, but you might be able to get the law on your side... eventually."

"Remind me to thank him for holding us in such high esteem," I grumbled sarcastically, but Nessa ignored me.

"So long as there's a chance that you could stage that kind of a comeback, that means there's a chance that any money he invested in resource development or in tourism could be lost well before he could see a profit on it. It would be a gamble, and Colin does nae gamble. *Ever.* He puts his money on a sure thing, or else he doesn't put his money on anything at all."

"That's right, I forgot about that!" Rae snapped her fingers. "I knew something else bothered me about the note he left in the Ops Center. It said he had bet that we wouldn't be able to escape the OtherWorld. It even said that he had lost money on the bet. But that doesn't sound right, because, as you say, he never bets. Never on anything."

Sis was right. "Maybe he was just using a figure of speech?" I asked, just for the sake of argument. But I didn't think so.

"Maybe. But the note didn't make it sound that way." Rae turned back to Nessa. "Okay, I get your point. The way

Colin sees it, he doesn't have the time, and doesn't want to risk the money, to use the Portal and OtherWorld tech for any of the things that Danae and I thought of. So the big question is, what *does* he want to use it for? Or, back to the manner in which you phrased the question, what do *you* know that *we* don't know?"

Nessa clapped her hands together. Again. This is the type of stuff she just loves, being able to show off how smart she is. "Well, the big payoff, of course, is to steal your technology, to steal your research and your reputations. Stealin' what belongs to others, that just makes his day." On that last sentence, her voice changed from gleeful to bitter and she seemed to lose her train of thought.

Rae and I glanced at each other.

This girl has got SOME set of emotional baggage, D.

Yeah, and we thought these steamer trunks that we came to NYC in were a lot to lug around, R!

The Irish girl finally snapped out of it and focused back on what she had been saying. "But there's another way to make this project turn into an instant money machine for him. Forget everythin' you know about the other side. I can tell by the way you talk that you are entranced by whatever you saw over there, but for now, pretend you've never been there, never even seen any video footage. Imagine that, as far as you're concerned, the OtherWorld Portal is just a big doorway that opens to—well, to nothing. Or to blank space. Or to a big hole. If you had a doorway to nothingness, what could you do with it?"

"Ummmm. Send a probe?" Rae ventured.

I agreed. "Right. I mean, we'd have to do *something* to explore what's over there."

"And I'll bet that's EXACTLY what you did do, am I correct?" Nessa was right, and we both bobbed our heads in the affirmative. She nodded back at us. "We have some differences between us, you Rugg girls and me, but in this case, I'm right there with you. A whole new world, who wouldn't want to find out more about it? Who wouldn't want to learn new information, to find new data that either helps us to confirm our understandin' of the nature of existence or else opens up brand new paths of inquiry? Who *wouldn't* be enthralled and delighted and just want to learn everything they could?"

I couldn't see where this was going... She was losing me again. "Well, yeah. Anyone, everyone would want that, right?"

Nessa scowled. "Who wouldn't want to explore it? Who would be so cold inside as to have no curiosity, that's the question. And the answer is, my brother, Colin Null, that's who. That's who doesn't care one iota about true knowledge and pure research." By this point, Nessa was agitated as all get-out. She stood up and paced the room like a tiger, face flushed and fists clenched. "So *here's* what I know that you don't know. Let me tell you what other industry, what business other than science equipment and legal consultin', has recently been impacted and influenced by our very own 'Planet X', also known as Colin Null."

Finally! All four of her audience members—me, my sis and the twins—we all leaned forward in our chairs. I'll give her this much, the girl knows how to build up a story.

"Let me put it this way," she said. "The three largest waste management companies in the world now have a new majority stockholder, and there are a full dozen smaller, private companies that now have a new owner, all by the name of Colin Null." She flopped back down in her chair, sat back and waited for her announcement to sink in.

Again, more silence. Finally, the boys chimed in.

Noah: "Wait. What? Waste...management?"

Levi: "Wait. What? Like trash? And...garbage?"

Me (screeching): "Wait. What? You don't mean—You can't mean—You'd better not mean—! Do you mean—Colin is going to use the OtherWorld Portal as a GARBAGE DUMP?!"

Of the four of us, only Rae seemed to take the information in stride, but I recognized the look on her face, and it wasn't good. She wasn't angry. She was beyond angry. She was long past angry. She was all the way through angry onto the other side and still picking up speed. In a deceptively quiet voice, she said, "It makes sense, in a twisted, depraved and selfish way. Just open the portal and dump in the trash. No environmental regulations. No storage fees. No property taxes. It would be a goldmine just in hazardous waste removal alone, because he wouldn't have to pay for or to provide for proper decontamination measures. Good job, Nessa. We should have realized, but we didn't. And you did. Thank you and kudos to you."

Rae turned to the rest of us. Me and the twins all recognized that calm face and voice that really hid (as the saying goes) the fury of a thousand white-hot suns. "But I think you all realize that. This. Will. Not. Stand." The three of us nodded. For being all cheery and bright for the most part, my big sis can get pretty scary intense at times!

Chapter 21

DANAE'S LOG 14:
War Council

"**S**o you guys are doing okay for now?" Izzy asked, while Rae and I watched the BrightEyes buzz and flit around in the Team Rugged Stuff arboretum. Our older cousin was sprawled out on a creek-side bench back in Nevada, while Big Sis and I were in our hotel room in New York, a few hours after leaving Nessa's place. I was using my tablet to sync up with the large interactive screen that was in our botanical space back home. (Yup, I have EVERY-THING teched up at our place, even the greenhouse!)

"Affirmative. For now, at least," Rae replied. "Thanks so much for coming up to Tahoe on such short notice. Right now, there's just nobody else around to whom I could even begin to imagine entrusting the care of those little fellas."

"Oh, yeah! For sure!" She dismissed it as if it were noth-ing, but Rae and I both knew it was no tiny favor we had asked of her. It's a long drive up to our place from the Bay, four hours, maybe five if there's bad tourist traffic. At least with it being summertime, she wasn't missing any of her college classes by helping us out. The way she always talks like some sort of surf-dudette, you'd never know she's a hard-core philosophy grad student just about to earn her doctorate.

Sandy and Phoebe hovered in front of the screen some 3,000 miles and three time zones away, expressing their happiness at seeing us again. "Which," my sis noted, "shows that they can identify, discern and interpret electronic digital imagery, perceiving us through visual and audible input entirely separate from empathy waves."

"Yup," I translated, "Theta waves don't transmit through the communications link, so we know that they recognize us just from sight and sound. Another interesting Bright-Eyes fact for the encyclopedia entry!"

Nessa had offered us the use of a guest room at her apartment, but we (politely) declined. Not just because we didn't trust her (I think both of us Rugg girls were about half-and-half on how much we thought we could really rely on her), but also because we really needed some privacy and personal space after that cross-country trip cooped up inside the emergency pods. And this also gave us a chance to check up on all our new friends that we had had to leave back home at Tahoe. (Because we sure couldn't do that while we were anyplace where Nessa could see us!)

Watching the rest of the critters in the background— some zooming around the tree branches, some perched on plants, others floating around the little pond—Rae sounded thoughtful. "Say, Sis? You know how Snappy, Crackly and Poppy are what we have been classifying as 'lightning' BrightEyes, right?"

"Yeah. That's old news, elder sister o' mine. Get to the point, I can't bear to sit through another epic story like Nessa's big production!"

Rae laughed, even though I was only half-kidding. "Okay! The point is that now I only see *two* of the electrical— or also known as lightning—BrightEyes. And instead of the third one, there's now a plant-type BrightEyes who bears an awfully close resemblance to the ferns and rocks and moss at the edge of the little frog pond there. I think good ol' Poppy decided that it likes the riparian environment better than the lightning environment."

I looked more closely and be doggoned if she wasn't right. I guess Poppy changed itself into a whole different type of BrightEyes! Transformed itself from lighting to plant!

"Well, that's a load off my mind!" Izzy exclaimed. "I thought I was, like, losing it, ya know? The last time I checked on them, I couldn't figure how my count was so out of whack!"

"Once we get this situation with Colin taken care of, we've got a *lot* of research to do in order to understand our little pals!" I muttered.

Rae punched her fist into her palm. "Colin. Right. The BrightEyes are really something and if we want to keep their world from becoming the biggest garbage landfill in existence, we've got to do something about it!"

Not long after we thanked Izzy again and turned off the live video/audio feed from our home base, Noah and Levi showed up at the door to our hotel suite. In no time flat, they were both sprawled out, one of them on each of the big overstuffed lounge chairs that were in the front room. "Hey Bro, we messed up, crashing with friends instead of staying at a hotel like Rae and Danae are doing," Levi commented.

"Yeah, but think of the money we're saving!" Noah rubbed his thumb and fingers together in the international gesture of money. "These two cousins of ours might have to invest into Colin's garbage-dump scheme just in order to be able to pay the bill for this place!"

I threw a pillow at his head. "Ha ha. Very funny. Don't even joke about something like that. The thought of us trashing the OtherWorld, it's...it's...well, I don't even have the words for how much that would never happen."

Rae was more matter-of-fact in her response, and explained how it came to be that we were staying over in an absolutely luxurious hotel room. "We're friends with the owners of the hotel, actually. We helped rescue their son from an attempted kidnapping once, so now they always let us stay here when we're in the city. Which is really nice of them and we make sure not to abuse the favor." Then she scowled at the three of us, me and the twins. "But that is *so much* beside the point! We really need to be getting back to the whole reason we're gathered here today—Namely, how are we going to stop Colin?"

Noah sat up straight and got serious about things. "His conference is scheduled for tomorrow...Can't you just issue a press release right now, maybe get in touch with some of your journalist friends and beat him to the punch? Hold your own press conference before he holds his?"

"Naw, it won't work that way," I collapsed onto the shaggy white carpet that covered the floor and stared at the ceiling. "That's why *he* didn't just have a press conference the same day immediately after he trapped us in the OtherWorld. These things take a lot of planning, a lot of coordination, and all of that takes a lot of time. With us out of the way, he then had just a big enough window on the calendar in order to set up tomorrow's event. It's *time* that we would need if we wanted to circumvent him, and it's *time* that we don't have."

Levi pondered. "And y'all can't just brace him after the conference, can't go to the media and challenge what he said, huh?"

Sis looked glum. "No, if he announces this research and technology to the world in this venue, the truth won't matter. Enough people who count will believe him, and there will be no going back. He knows it, Nessa knows it, and we know it."

"Well," I amended, "both Colin and Nessa seem to think that we would be able to reverse it, at least legally, but that would take a lot *more* time we don't have, because while we finally worked our version of things through the courts, the damage would be done. Colin would have turned the BrightEyes' world into a trash dump, and then he would probably sell off his waste-management companies just in time to make even *more* money."

Rae stood up from the sofa and squared her shoulders. I could tell that she had processed the data and was ready to propose a course of action. "Okay. Here's my assessment of the situation." She ticked her points off on her fingers. "One, Colin has scheduled a press conference. Two, we can't hold our own conference first. Three, we can't correct the situation once he has held his conference. Therefore, the only viable option that I can determine is that we must prevent him from completing his announcement."

That started the brainstorming session on just how to accomplish Operation Press Conference Shutdown. We even patched Nessa in on it via weblink.

("You know, Nessa might have some good ideas about how to do this," wheedled Noah.

"Yeah, she knows the ins and outs of this here big city, she knows how Colin operates and she wants to knock him down into the dust almost as much as we do!" cajoled Levi.

"I guess we shouldn't ignore any possible advantage that she might be able to provide," mused Rae.

"Fine, whatever!" I grumbled. But I want to go on record and say that lovestruck boys are just *the worst*.)

The first thing that Rae and I tossed out as an idea was to see if we could get the Prof (short for Professor, natch) involved. He's kind of a freelance science adventurer who we've worked with before...he was sort of a young apprentice to our Grandma and Grandpa before they went missing. Think of an old Indiana Jones with an eyepatch and you've got a pretty good idea of what he looks like. He also carries a really cool cane around with him. One of his legs got all banged up on one of his adventures years ago, and when my leg got messed up in a car accident when I was younger, he's the one who helped me wrap my head around it and helped me learn how to use my walking stick. So, yeah, I really like the old guy.

"I already spoke with him," said Nessa. "As soon as I heard about Colin's press conference, I called the Professor up to see if he knew anything about it. He just laughed and said 'That obnoxious brother of yours recently paid me a large sum to stay out of his business for the next month. So if, in four weeks from today, you're still interested in talking, call me back and have your checkbook ready.'" She frowned. She doesn't very much like the Prof, 'cuz he doesn't fall for her cutesy act, she can't charm him like she does to other guys (ahem, I'm talking about YOU here, Levi and Noah!). Which, of course, only makes me like him even more!

But with the Prof out of the picture, that meant we had to come up with some ideas on our own. And two hours later, we had the outline of a plan. Not a great plan. Not even a good plan. I heard Rae mumble to herself something to the effect that she thought she had seen our plan once on an episode of *Get Smart*, whatever that meant. But we all agreed that it was better than nothing. Slightly better. *Maybe* slightly better.

We started with the supposition that our immediate goal was to stop the Null Corp press conference, so we tried to work backward and come up with strategies to make that happen. Several ideas were proposed, I'm not going to embarrass my family members by saying just who exactly suggested which hare-brained plots, but they included, in no particular order:

- Creating a kaiju scare to cause an evacuation of the city;
- Starting a rumor of a contagious plague resulting in the authorities quarantining the Null Corp building;
- Smuggling several hundred pounds of cheese into Colin's facility, resulting in an infestation of mice and then ratting him out to the health department (ha ha, see what I did there?);
- And even framing Colin for some crime bad enough to get him arrested and held in police custody for the next several days.

Rae finally sighed glumly, "Well, I can certainly imagine *Colin* using any one of these tactics to achieve his goals, but none of them are really *our* style."

Nessa rolled her eyes. I knew that she was more than willing to engage in any one of these ideas if the end result would be to cause problems for her brother. But it wasn't her call, it was up to us. (I kind of agreed with Nessa, but what kept me from endorsing any of these plans was *not* that they weren't exactly kosher, but that they just really weren't *realistic*, given our lack of time and resources.)

"So hear me out," I said. "Not that I advocate releasing a terrible disease into Null Corp, or even pretending to do so, but I *do* think that the building should be the focus of our efforts. Colin is using the conference center that is inside the building for the event, so if something happens to the event venue, he'll have to postpone, and that will give us the opening that we need. We'll be on even footing with him and can make our own announcement in time to fend him off."

"I find no flaw with this line of reasoning. That is to say, it makes good sense," my sis backed me up. Looking at our cousins, she said, "This sounds like it might be more in your wheelhouse than in ours. So let me frame it this way. The problem is: Large building in Manhattan's business district needs to be caused to be shut down, with no real danger posed to people or property, and no threat, real or imagined of monsters or disease. What is the solution?!" She pointed at Levi. "Go!"

He snapped his fingers and grinned. "That's as easy as possum pie! Power! Cut the power. A building like that loses power and everything comes to a stop."

Rae pointed to Noah. "Okay! The power. Yes or no? Go!"

Noah also grinned. "Well, if I remember correctly, it was Lord Acton who noted that, "Power corrupts and absolute power corrupts absolutely."

This time, it was Rae who threw the pillow at our cousin.

He laughed. "Sorry, sorry! Hmmm. Power. Yeah, my bro might be on to something there. But we have to take into account the fact that a facility like Colin's will most likely have a backup source of electricity, something to keep everything buzzing along with business as usual in the case of a failure in the city's main power grid."

Nessa's voice came from the computer speaker. "Good thinkin', boys, but I'm afraid that my brother is one step ahead of you." We looked to the television flatscreen where I was mirroring my tablet screen. She was seated on that fancy-schmancy chair of hers and tapping away furiously at her keyboard. She digitally pushed a new virtual window to my tab and I set up a split-screen image so that we could see her on the left side of the television and the blueprints that she was sharing with us on the right-hand side.

I frowned. It was a schematic of the Null Corp building. "Where'd you get that? I just ran a search on the county and state websites for construction permits, improvement permits and so on, and the engineering paperwork that *I* came up with doesn't show anything at nearly that level of detail for the property!"

She grinned. Fiercely.

I groaned and was just thankful she hadn't clapped her hands together again.

Her grin got even bigger, even more fierce, in response to my irritation. "Ah now, an' you've just got to know where to look," she said, all smug and innocent at the same time. "Colin pays a lot of money to the engineerin' firms who work on his properties so that they will submit bland, generic and oh-so-false paperwork to the governmental agencies who oversee that sort of thing. But unfortunately for him, his elder sister—an' that'd be me—can usually find some low-level office worker at each of those same engineerin' firms who are only too happy to forward a copy of the authentic documents to *my* research firm, in exchange for just a wee bit of financial compensation."

"Harumph," I grumbled. "Colin gets people to fake the paperwork and you bribe those people to give you copies of the authentic plans. Got it."

The pointer arrow on the screen moved to a spot near the bottom-right of the blueprints as Nessa continued. "However, the bad news for us is that Colin has *already* taken the Null Corp building off of the public power grid. Unknown and unreported to the government and utility officials, Colin's hyper-paranoia has caused him to devote a large portion of the basement level to his own in-house power generation. He has piped through the bedrock of Manhattan to tap into geothermal resources, which in turn generate electricity for his building. (All of which is incredibly illegal and unregulated, by the way). He doesn't have a backup power source, because, in effect, he is already using a backup power source."

Noah: "Oh."

Levi: "Dagnabbit."

Me: "Hey, that's MY cuss word.'

Also me: "Double dagnabbit."

Rae: "Hmmmmm."

Me (looking at Rae): "'Hmmmmm.'? What do you mean, 'Hmmmmm.'?"

My sister looked back at me, with a slight smile curling the corners of her mouth. "I *said*, 'hmmmmm' and I *mean* 'hmmmmm'. As in, 'Hmmmmmm, that's bad for us' because we can't shut down the building by cutting it off from the city power, but 'hmmmmm, that's good for us' because now all we have to do in order to shut down the building is to put his own interior generator, also known as a transformer, out of commission." Her slight smile grew into a full-fledged grin. "That makes for just *one* target, his own generator, instead of *two* targets, which would normally be—" she ticked her points off on her fingers again, "—one; the power supply, and two; the backup supply. Even better, we can plan something that is far more focused, with less chance of impacting other people or businesses in the area! Hmmmm, hmmmm, and hmmmm!"

Wow! Finally, some good news! Good news that was definitely worth a 'hmmmmm' or three! All of us there in the hotel room were suddenly feeling pretty good about the situation, until we heard "A-*hem*" from the computer as Nessa cleared her throat to get our attention. She sounded for all the world like a stern librarian trying to remind a pack of rowdy kids to keep the noise level down. We all turned back to look at her on the screen.

"Well, yes, I imagine that all of that is *technically* true," Nessa said in a thoughtful voice, "but I think you need to take a closer look at the schematic diagram. Do you see that room that the generator or whatever, the transformer, is housed in?" The computer pointer directed our attention to a spot on the blueprints. "That's not really a room, but a vault. You know, like a bank safe. An' that's not just any vault, it's a vault provided by and installed by one of the best and most secure vault companies in the world. It's a *TransVault* product. In fact, their corporate headquarters are not too far away, just across the river in New Jersey."

Our grins all faded. Levi groaned. "Never heard of them. But from the way you verbally italicized their name right then, I'm guessing their work is pretty much hunky-dory top of the line, huh?"

Nessa smiled wryly. "Yes, you could say that. Hunky-dory and top of the line. Perhaps the best in the world."

Rae looked thoughtful and drummed her fingers on the top of the coffee table. "Okay. Nessa, you're the one with the inside information. What are the chances that we could find a way to get to that vault, and once there, crack into that vault in order to decommission the generator?"

A pause from the other side of the internet connection as Nessa pondered. "Finding a way to get *to* the vault is the easy part. See this?" The little white arrow moved to a small square at the edge of the screen. "*That's* your way in. It's a totally low-tech secret corridor that Colin had installed so that he would have a way to get out of the building in the case of an emergency. But you could also use it to gain access *into* the property. Now, as for finding a way to actually crack into the vault itself, there are two answers to that. Answer number one: No chance. Answer number two: A very small chance."

I heard a soft scraping sound and was surprised to discover it coming from Rae. She was gnashing her teeth. *I'm* the one with a short temper, so when it's my sister who starts losing her patience, you know that we are in a frustrating situation! Nobody said anything in response to Nessa's last statement and the silence was really starting to get uncomfortable. The twins just sort of looked down at the floor, and I didn't really understand what Nessa's point was, so I couldn't think of anything to say in reply.

Rachel finally spoke. "Okay, we're all waiting for you to explain that, so you can skip the dramatic pause. I swear, you sound like Gollum guessing at Bilbo's last riddle, 'String or nothing!'"

Nessa laughed merrily. "Ha-ha, that's good! Oh my, I've got to remember that one!" And I think she really meant it. (Nerd.) "What I mean is that it is possible to make it *to* the vault door without much, if any, trouble, despite what my brother might believe about the state of his security. But once you are there, the chances of 'cracking' or 'breaking in' are absolute zero. It's one of the best vaults in the world. That's why Colin chose it. And unlike the Hollywood movies, there's no laser that's goin' to cut that metal, no secret decoder ring that is goin' to sort through a zillion potential options to find the correct combination."

"Okay, understood," Rae nodded slightly. "Answer number one, you said, means that there is no chance to break in. Now explain answer number two, when you said there *is* a small chance of success."

"That's where things get really interestin'," Nessa continued, "While there is no chance to *break* in, there is still a chance, a small chance, to *get* in, if you see what I mean."

I interrupted. "I *don't* see what you mean! What in the world are you talking about!? What do you mean; no, we can't break in, but yes, we can get in?!"

That got under her skin, I could tell, because then she addressed me as if she were talking to a toddler, speaking very slowly and over-enunciating her words. "If some-one were able to get a mas-ter code from the vault's man-u-fac-tur-er, then they would be able to o-pen the vault. It is only a small chance that someone could get that master code, but it is *not impossible*. With the master code, someone could open the vault door. Then they could GET into the vault, without BREAKIN' IN to the vault."

"Oh. Gotcha." I glared back at Nessa glaring at me.

"Hmmm. String or nothing. I get it," Rae murmured.

Levi ran his hand through his hair, making it all stand up from his head like a scrub brush, and leaned forward toward the computer screen. "So clue us in, Nessa. That small chance you mentioned, how would a cowpoke go about getting that master code? Could you hack into the TransVault system and track it down?"

Addressing my cousin, the Null girl instantly replaced her scowl with a smile and laughed yet again. "I know it's probably going to make at least one of the Rugg sisters upset, but the answer to that is... yes and no!"

I groaned. She was talking about me. And she was right. Much more of this kind of wishy-washy, yes-no, some-none talk from her and I was going to pop a blood vessel.

Nessa wanted to giggle at my reaction, I could tell. But (thankfully) she stifled it down to just that grin of hers and continued her explanation. "What I'm sayin' is that I can't hack into the company's computer system remotely. An' believe you me, I've tried. And tried and tried. But if I could get onsite, if I could physically get to the company's computer server, and if I could get just *one chance* to log into the TransVault intranet, it would be as easy as—how'd you put it, Levi?—it would be as easy as possum pie to get the master code!"

Levi grinned and scratched his head. "Well there ya'll go, then! You said the company has its headquarters facility fairly nearby, just a hoot and a holler away? Could we all go out there, infiltrate the site, get the code, come back and use the code to open the vault, then proceed with the rest of the idea to shut down the Null Corp power supply?"

Now, *that* sounded like a plan to me!

But when I looked back to the image of Nessa on the television screen, she daintily shook her head. "No, I'm afraid there's not enough time for that. It's too late to get there today while the offices are open, and the hacking would *have* to take place when the company's operational databases are bein' used, when they are online, which means during business hours. And while they *are* fairly close by, they are too far away to go there in the morning and get back to Colin's Null Corp building in time to get into the vault and shut down the power before his press conference."

"Argh," I moaned. "So close! If we had just been able to get here one day earlier."

Nessa cleared her throat in that librarian way again and held her index finger up as if to say 'wait a minute.' "Hmphm. Unless..." Then she was mumbling to herself, I couldn't quite make out what she was saying.

"Hey, Nessa!" I snapped my fingers to get her attention. (Rae hates it when I do that to her, so I hoped it would be annoying to the Null girl, too...) "Spit it out, this is supposed to be a brainstorming session, so let's hear what you've got on your brain." I was grouchy and past the point of being polite.

Nessa looked at us earnestly through the computer screen. "Okay. An' what about this? What if *I* were to go out to TransVault first thing in the morning and get the code from the mainframe, while at the same time, *you Rugg girls* were in the Null Corp building, right outside the vault door, waitin' for me to send you the master code?"

Rae pondered. "Hmmm. Sort of like being in two places at one time, huh? Taking advantage of working as a team. That sounds as if it might work!"

"Wait a minute," I interrupted. "*How* are you going to get that code, that digital version of a skeleton key? Just because you show up there at the business doesn't mean that they're going to let you waltz in and plug a laptop into their system, right?"

Nessa grinned at me. "Of course not! That's another aspect of—how did Rachel put it?—oh, yes, working as a team! I figure that if we can just get to the TransVault headquarters, Noah and Levi ought to be able to get me into the building and into the computer server room. Covert operations, that's your specialty, an' am I right, boyos?"

You never saw a couple of guys perk up so much as those two did at the thought of showing off for Nessa. If they had tails, they would have been wagging up a storm, like a couple of little puppies. Sheesh. Chumps.

My big sis looked at the schematic again. "Okay, hmmmm. First, you three at TransVault get the code, with Danae and me waiting at the vault door in the Null Corp building. Then you transmit the master code to us, we use it to get inside the vault and kill the power." She smacked a fist into her open palm. "Okay. That's our Plan A. Hopefully it will work. But if it doesn't, what's our Plan B? Any ideas, gang?"

Our cousins put their heads together and whispered for a few minutes. They paused and took a look at the blueprints. Noah was pointing at the screen with one hand and absent-mindedly playing with his long hair with the other, twirling it around his fingers. (He tends to do that when he's really concentrating, I don't think he's even aware of it!) Then more whispering. Finally, they came up for air.

"Okay, you want a Plan B? Here's a Plan B. It's not much, but it's the best we've got. If you *can't* get into the vault that serves as the power room and kill the juice—you know, what you are calling Plan A—then the next best bet is to get into the security room." Noah pointed to a room on the schematic that was on the second floor of the building. "If you can get into *here* undetected, then you can probably initiate a security lockdown. That would be like pushing a big 'pause' button on the whole building, and since Colin most likely has his system programmed to alert the police in the case of an emergency, this should bring the local law enforcement officers running as well. Any journalists who aren't already onsite for the conference would be locked out, and any who are inside will be far too busy wondering what is going on, they won't be sitting still for any con-ference. The result will be just what we are aiming for; the press announcement will be postponed." But he didn't look very sure of himself, and I might've been the only one who heard it when he added under his breath, "We hope."

Then Levi took over. "And for good measure, here's a Plan C. According to the blueprints, there's one more site from within the building where you could maybe manage to initiate a shutdown. Right *here*," he pointed to an office on the seventh floor, "is the spot. See, there's this one office set in amongst a bunch of other rooms that are *not* offices. *This* is an airway access room, *this* is a climate-controlled laboratory, *this* is a communications center, and *THIS* is an office. From the looks of it, it is probably Colin's own personal office, because from the wiring schematics on this plan, he's got a master panic button wired into the system so that he could initiate an alert of the building utilities and services right here from his desk if he wanted to." Levi didn't look very confident about this option that he was proposing either, but he finished up his explanation like a trouper. "Security lockdown. Press announcement postponed." Like his brother, he added, so faint that the others probably couldn't hear it, "We hope."

Gosh guys, nothing like a nice dash of self-confidence to raise a girl's spirits. (See, that's some of that world-class sarcasm I told you I was so good at...)

Nessa spoke up from the computer screen. "Huh. That is very interestin'. Colin is so sneaky, I'll bet his own staff doesn't even realize that he has that kind of a control button there in his office. He likes to keep all of his plots and schemes on the down-low."

"Yup, makes sense," Noah replied. "So there you have it. Plan B and Plan C. From the security center or from Colin's desk, you could shut down the building and create a lock-out situation."

I waved my hands as if I were pushing down the air, a classic 'slow down' gesture. "Hold your horses, cowpoke." Levi grinned; he loves it when other people also use his type of Western lingo. "If there's a security control room right there— or even two of them, if you count Colin's office— why don't we just start with Plan B or Plan C instead? Why not just skip the whole long, drawn-out, risky, convoluted, *meshugenah* bit about the vault?"

"Nope, not a good idea, cuz." Both of the guys shook their heads, and Noah explained it to me. "Plan A is the first choice because you can get *to* the vault relatively easily. Then if you get the master code, you can get *in* and accomplish your task without much hassle. *If* and *only if* that doesn't work, do we then go to Plan B, the security room. That's because the security room is harder. It's more difficult to get *to* that actual room, because it's not hidden out of sight; it's harder to get access to it without being seen. And Colin's office is even *harder* than the security room, being clear up on the seventh floor by the communications center like it is, so that makes it our *last* choice, our Plan C."

Levi agreed with his brother. "In a covert operation, you always take the path of least resistance, the option that throws up the fewest obstacles. If that option doesn't work, then that's when you move on to the next-least-resistant course of action. This is how you maximize your chances for success. If you go at it the other way round, you're putting all of your eggs into the hardest basket that you can find."

Huh, what do you know? Sounds like my cousins know what they are talking about!

"Okay, gotcha," I held my hands up in surrender. "I don't know if that analogy about eggs and baskets really works, but I get what you mean." Turning to include Rae and Nessa, I made a grand pronouncement. "I hereby declare that we have our Plans A, B and C established! Let's go stop a press conference!"

Chapter 22

DANAE'S LOG 15: Under the Null Corp Building

"It looks as if Nessa gave us the straight scoop about that secret entrance," I mused, as I peered down the dark hallway in which Rae and I found ourselves. "If anyone had asked me, I would've given odds that she was trying to make us look like chumps, or even worse, sending us right into a trap."

"Oh, I don't think she's quite as bad as you make her out to be," said my sis, closing the hidden entry door behind us. Then she frowned. "That being said, I have to admit I wouldn't have been overly surprised to find a whole platoon of security guards just waiting here to greet us, courtesy of one or another of the Null siblings."

I'll give credit where credit is due, Nessa really is without equal when it comes to research. Those blueprints that she dug up showed all the structures in the area of the Null

Corp building, from the original construction drafts all the way through every single improvement that had been performed over the past century. She had implied to us that she just bribed the contractors to give her updated plans, but from what I could tell, she must have cross-referenced every new renovation against purchase orders, time cards, pay stubs and more in order to have such a complete and accurate picture of the current layout of the building.

That's how she was able to direct us exactly to the subterranean tunnel that led into the sub-basement of Null Corp. Apparently, it had originally been an access passage from a side track on the subway system. But during one of Colin's improvements to the site's foundation, he had had all mention or reference of it deleted from all of the official records, and so no one knew of its existence. As a result, it was virtually invisible to the authorities, or to anyone else who might check any paperwork on the building.

Except for Nessa.

Her records showed not only that it was still there, but that Colin had worked to have it modified and reinforced, so that if any sort of emergency or disaster ever took place, it would be a secret way for him to get in or out of his corporate headquarters.

On a video call early the next morning from our brainstorming session when she was prepping us on how to get into the building, Nessa said that she had seen the tunnel on the blueprints but had never really given it much thought before now. "But I was sure that he must have an emergency entrance and exit to his building. I got the idea when Levi told me how he and Noah accessed your labs through a secret passage." Levi at least had the good grace to look embarrassed when Rae and I glared at him for blabbing about secret Team Rugged Stuff information. Nessa just smirked. "It's obvious, really, so don't beat him up about spillin' the beans. But I realized that if you two girls had planned for a crisis that might require a low-tech passageway in or out of your facility, then it was only logical that my dear brother had done the same."

I made a mental note to give Levi a hard time about his lapse in judgement once this whole mess was cleaned up, but for now, I held my temper. (That ought to be good for at least one more gold star!)

Nessa kept yammering, showing off how smart she was. "And just as in all research, once you understand that something *must* exist, it's not much of a challenge to find the evidence that it *does* exist. You simply have to work backwards from the known solution. So there you have it. The unmarked corridor off the subway tunnel. At the end of the corridor, a service door that can be opened by way of a turn-wheel. On the other side is the Null Corp sub-basement. Then down the hall to the vault that contains the power generator for the entire Null Corp building. Any questions?"

In my head, I replied, *Well, yeah, about a zillion of 'em. Like why are you so annoying?* Rae just smiled. "Thanks, Nessa. I think it's all very clear. We'll head over there, and you can pick the boys up and head over to the TransVault headquarters. We'll wait for you to signal us with the master code."

After we logged off the video call, Rae got serious with our cousins. "Noah and Levi, I urge you to exercise the utmost caution while in the company of Colin's sister. That is to say—Be careful! I know you guys think Nessa is great and all that, but you keep an eye on her. She wants to throw a monkey wrench in Colin's plans, sure. But it's more a case that she's *against him* than it is that she's *with us*, if you know what I mean. She's going to be picking your brains the whole time you're with her, trying to find out more about the OtherWorld and about Team Rugged Stuff confidential info. She just can't help herself; information is what she is all about."

I punched Noah on the shoulder. "Yeah, I think you guys have already given her plenty of insider details. Telling her about our secret passage! Sheesh!"

He protested. "Hey, that was all Levi! He was so giddy at the thought of his hamburger date with Nessa that he just sang like a canary, and it was a long, long song."

"Aw, come on guys!" Levi looked sheepish. "I'm sorry I blabbed, but look at it this way, it all turned out okay. It helped Nessa figure out a way you can get into the Null Corp building, right?" He looked back and forth at me and Rae. "I mean, right?"

"Yeah, well no more of that!" I growled at him. "And don't you even let one tiny little speck of a thought come into your head about opening your mouths about the Bright-Eyes! I am so serious!"

Both cousins crossed their hearts, then mimed locking their lips and tossing away their imaginary keys.

"Okay," I said, "I am holding you to that. Both of you."

We all filed out of the hotel room and went out to the street, where Nessa came by in her chauffeured limo and picked the boys up. Rae and I found the nearest subway station and caught a ride to a dank station near the location of Colin's corridor, both of us looking pale and sickly in the fluorescent lighting. When no one was looking, we ducked down the unmarked little passageway. To be honest, if we hadn't been looking for it, we never would have seen it. It was totally unnoticeable, just like Colin had planned it to be. Then it was a straight shot, underground, until my GPS indicated that we were directly under the Null Corp Building.

And just like Nessa had said, we came upon a door that looked for all the world like a submarine hatch. I leaned my walking stick against the concrete wall, grabbed the wheel set in the center of the door and started to turn it. It *looked* as if it were rusted solid, but I guess that was just some camouflage that Colin had in place, because it spun so smoothly, it was obviously well maintained. "Wow," I said, as the door swung open on recently oiled hinges, "I didn't expect *this* to be so easy!"

Rae handed me my walking stick and followed me through the doorway. "Yeah, how about that? I guess Colin likes to make sure that he has an escape route all set and ready at all times!"

I closed the door behind us and spun the wheel to fasten it. "Nessa also predicted that it wouldn't be locked. She said Colin wouldn't risk being in a situation where he needed his bolt-hole but couldn't use it for lack of a key or a code. That he would depend entirely on how well hidden it is to keep busybodies out. It's kind of scary how well she understands her brother, don't you think?"

My sister nodded vigorously. "Yes, yes I do. She may not be as evil as he is, but she is certainly as manipulative and conniving. All of which makes me loathe to divulge any more information to her than we have to. I mean, I see no reason to tell her about the BrightEyes!"

So here we were; no muss and no fuss, in the basement of Colin Null's headquarters. Down the hall, a quick turn to the left, and we found ourselves standing outside the very reason for our visit...the power room vault. The vault door took up one entire side of the wall and it had a digital key-pad set flush into it alongside the door handle. Yet again, Nessa's information seemed to be on the up and up. Rae gave an appreciative whistle and said, "Wow. This is what I imagine Fort Knox looks like."

"Well, at least we know that Colin takes the security of his power supply very, very seriously." Yup, the vault door looked as if someone might be storing England's Crown Jewels in there. Now it was just a matter of hanging out here until Nessa and the boys could send us the master code to open the vault door. Then we could turn off the power and *presto-change-o*, mission accomplished. We hunkered down with our teched-up smart phones (They were modified so that they could pull in a great signal anyplace, even way underground like now. One of my more useful innovations, if I do say so myself.) And we waited. And waited. And then we waited some more.

I played with the idea of punching in some random codes in the hopes of happening onto the right one, but my sister reminded me that it might be programmed to sound an alert after a certain number of failed attempts. Finally, Rae's phone gave a nearly inaudible little buzz and vibrated in her hand. "It's from Levi!" She smiled and gave the air a victory punch.

But when she read the message, the smile left her face like someone had slapped it clean off. "Confound it. Or to employ one of your preferred exclamations...Dagnabbit."

I looked over her shoulder and read the message from our cousin. "Double dagnabbit," I agreed.

Chapter 23

NOAH AND LEVI'S JOURNAL 6: "Into New Jersey!"

Once Nessa picked us up in her limo, it was a relatively quick drive from Midtown Manhattan over the bridge to an industrial park in New Jersey. The trip would have taken a lot longer, but her driver, a big bruiser named Henry, used to work for the Secret Service. He used to drive in the motorcades for the president and members of congress and stuff, so he knew all the tricks to find the quickest lanes and the smoothest routes. Of course, it didn't hurt that he was using a brand-new app on his GPS, one that Nessa had developed. It wasn't even on the market yet, she had it in beta-testing. It didn't just show where the traffic was heavy and where accidents were, it PREDICTED where slow-downs were going to take place. It didn't report in real-time, it reported in PRE-real time!

Pre-real time. PREAL time! We need to trademark that, bro!

In other words, our driver knew what route to take to avoid slow traffic before it even happened. We got to New Jersey in, as my brother might say, two shakes of a lamb's tail.

But for the short while that we were in the car, we discussed our plan of action. Nessa said we wouldn't be able to work our way to the computer databanks by entering the business through the front doors, so I told her that I would use my super-spy skills to find some sort of backdoor access and get us inside.

My brother was understandably flustered. "What do you mean, *you'll* use *your* skills? What about me? Maybe you meant to say, *we'll* use *our* skills?"

"You didn't let me finish," I told him. To Nessa, I said, "I'll use my skills to infiltrate the TransVault property, while my faithful sidekick here—he goes by the name of Mediocre-Intelligence Boy—will do his best to assist me."

Levi rolled his eyes. Nessa giggled. Score one for me.

If you hear a strange sound over here in the background, don't be concerned. It's just me gagging. Vomiting. Up-chucking. Losing my lunch. My brother's so-called wit often has that effect.

Ahem. Back to the narrative. So then I continued describing the plan of action, noting that once we got safely into the building, we would escort Nessa to the company's mainframe, where she would employ her considerable skill and intelligence to hack in and find the skeleton key (as it were), the master code to Colin's power vault. Nessa blushed at my description of her capabilities, and my brother rolled his eyes again. Score *two* for me!

Then I got to the wrap up. "At which point, I will transmit the code to the girls, who by that time will be waiting just outside the Null Corp vault door. They will use it to open the vault and shut down the power generator, resulting in the cancellation of the press conference. Nessa and I are heroes and I allow my minion—that's you, Levi—to buy us a celebratory dinner at a fancy high-end New York City restaurant. Preferably one with a great vegan menu."

Nessa beamed. "Yes. That's the plan. More or less," she giggled.

Then my brother piped up. "Oh, I'll be glad to make the dinner reservations, Bro. But if I do, don't be surprised if it somehow turns out that there's only room for Nessa and me at the table...and it darn tootin' won't have a vegan menu!"

Just then, Henry made a signal to Nessa and caught her eye in the rearview mirror. She leaned forward and gazed out through the windshield at the cluster of large industrial buildings about a half a mile in the distance. "We're just about there. Now you two duck down. Lie down on the floor an' I'll cover you with this blanket."

We both just kind of stared at her. "Huh?" I scratched my head, but couldn't remember this being part of the plan I had just laid out with such eloquence.

"I'm always goin' around everywhere collecting information, so no one will think twice about seeing me drive into this commercial park. I'm a known an' familiar quantity. But if I were to pull in with you guys visible in the car, it might raise suspicion, especially since you look like a pair of Hollywood ninjas in your covert operations outfits!"

"Hmmm. Alright, Nessa, I guess you're the boss on this mission." Me and my bro both pulled our uniform masks over our faces and did as Nessa had instructed. But as we lay there on the floor of the vehicle's back seat, with an Irish tartan wool blanket draped over us (very chic!), we whisper-chatted with each other via our subvocalization transmitters as the limo moved forward.

I wasn't sure that we really needed to duck down like this; I knew both of the Null siblings were super paranoid of everyone, but I couldn't help but think to myself, *Dude, really?* I even asked my brother in Salish through the communicator, too softly for Nessa to hear,

> "Ha es mił łu šey? t stem u kʷes ntelsi?"
> ["Is this too much? What do you think?"]

He murmured back in Yiddish.

> "Freg mich becherim? Match zich bakvem."
> ["How should I know? Make yourself comfortable."]

Huh. Sometimes, I've got to give my bro credit for his pragmatism. When there's nothing to be done about a situation, there's really no use fretting about it, I guess.

Before long, we felt the car begin to slow down. "An' can you boys hear me?" Nessa asked.

We both grunted out an affirmative reply to her question.

"Okay, good, here's how we'll play this," she said. "We are just about to drive around the back of the TransVault building. As we slow down, I'll open the right-side door, and you two can slip out of the car—do a tuck and roll or whatever it is that you man-of-action type people always do—into the area where the delivery docks are. My driver will continue around to the front and park there. I'll go in the front lobby and ask for Monsieur Thierault— he's the president of the company. I've met him a time or two, but I happen to know that he is NOT currently in the country. So the receptionist will regretfully notify me that he is not available. I will exit the lobby, return to the car and appear to leave the property. But in reality, as the car passes around the rear of the building again, I will slip out and join you in the delivery area, while Henry finds a parking spot nearby at one of the other industrial lots where he will wait for us. In the meantime, you two will have found a way to unobtrusively enter the building and will also have located an access point where someone who *isn't* a super spy—that would be me—can enter and join you inside. Then we will find an intranet terminal or connection. I will hack it. I will capture the master code. You will send it to the girls. Got it?"

I poked my hand out from under the blanket that covered us and gave Nessa a thumbs-up.

"Great! An' good luck! I'm openin' the right-side door in three... two... one... now!"

I pulled the blanket back and pushed it behind me. Levi dove out of the car, hit the pavement hand-first and used his momentum to roll across the lot, absorbing the impact across his shoulder and hip. I followed and heard a muffled 'clunk' as the limo door closed and the car drove on, turned around a corner and rolled out of sight.

We really *were* in our element here, even if it sounds like I'm bragging. We both crouched down in the shadows behind a concrete riser and gave the back side of the building a once over. I gestured to an emergency fire door at the top of a set of four cement stairs.

Levi eased his way over and tested it. "Nope." Neither of us had really expected it to be unlocked, but one of the first things a professional in our line of work learns is never to overlook the easiest and most obvious options, just like we had explained to the girls. All it would take is one faulty lock or one careless janitor, and ta-dah!...our job would suddenly be infinitely easier.

Of course, the opposite can also be true, and sometimes it just takes one guard to randomly cast a glance off to the side and spot us doing something we aren't supposed to be doing. Then, all of a sudden, our job just gets a lot harder! That's why the Rugg boys' motto is Hope for the Best, but Prepare for the Worst!

Since the door was locked—as we figured it would be—we both scanned the area for another access point. From my position, I could see a second story window and I pointed it out to my brother. He saw my gesture and nodded. He was standing right next to the building, and with no hesitation, he turned his back to the wall, leaned toward me and braced the base of his spine against the brickwork. He cupped his hands together with fingers interlaced, right at about the level of his bent knees. When I saw that he was ready, I ran full-speed toward him and when I got there, I stepped into the stirrup formed by his hands. As soon as he felt my weight, we both said "Alley-OOOOP!" simultaneously. He straightened up, using the power in his legs, back and arms to boost me skyward. I straightened my stepping-off leg, adding my own leg muscles and momentum to launch myself up over his head and against the side of the building, to a spot just below the second-story window. I grabbed ahold of the window frame. With my right arm and hand,

I clutched the sill, while my left hand tested the window itself. Bingo! It slid open, just as smooth as silk!

It's always about a fifty-fifty bet that windows on the second story of a building will be unlocked, because people just automatically think there's no chance of anyone trying to gain access to the site anyplace above the ground floor. Out on the range and in the forests, most animals will scan the area around them, side to side AND up and down, but for some crazy reason, humans just kind of ignore anything that is either above or below their eye-level range of vision. That's another thing that makes our job a lot easier!

With just a little upper-body wriggling and a kick of my legs, I was able to crawl through the window opening to the room inside.

Once I had made it to the interior, it was nice to see that our luck was still holding out; the room was empty. It looked as if it were some sort of records storage area, with shelves of files, boxes of documents, and a few odd chairs and desks piled in the corner. If someone had been inside, I would have had to figure out how to deal with them, maybe even to the point of subduing them and tying them up. But as it turned out, I could use the length of high-tensile rope in my possibles bag for a much better use.

Taking one wrap around my waist for bracing, I dropped the other end of the rope out the window and voiced a Yiddish message to my brother.

"Kuk aroyf!"
["Look up!"]

Just a few seconds later, he scampered up the rope like the squirrelly kind of guy he is and popped inside. He quietly slid the window shut while I coiled and stowed my rope away. "Okay," I said, still using the communicator, but slipping back into English, "now let's get down to that fire-door exit that was locked. We'll make sure it's not hooked up to any alarms, and then we can bring Nessa in through that access point."

We scoped out the hallway beyond our storage room and it was easy as possum pie (to use another Levi-ism!) to find our way to the stairwell and then down to the fire door. It took my bro less than a minute to clip and reroute the wires that were designed to sound an alarm when and if anyone opened the door.

But then he paused and gave me a strange sort of look. "Kind of odd, don't you think?" he asked me.

"What's that?" In all honesty, I hadn't noticed anything out of the ordinary.

"Well, this fire door. This alarm is totally old-school. And I mean waaaaaay old-school. It's kind of odd that a high-tech vault and security company has this kind of obsolete equipment in their own building. And not to mention, that window wasn't even wired for an alarm at all."

"Yeah. Maybe. I guess." I thought about it. "Or maybe it's just like that old saying about how the barber's kids are al-ways the ones that need a haircut the most. You know, 'cuz their folks are so busy cutting everyone else's hair? Maybe these guys are so busy providing security for other compa-nies that they just never got around to putting in updated security on their own building..."

My brother shrugged. "Could be. But there's another thing bothering me. High-tech companies usually want to show off. They take office space in newer buildings made out of glass and steel and marble. On the other hand, the brick construction of this site almost screams 'low-tech'."

I frowned. He definitely had a point. "Well, I'm not saying that I disagree with you, Bro. Let's keep our eyes wide open on this job. Let's get it done and then get the heck out of here."

I eased the fire door open and peered outside, just in time to see Nessa coming around the corner. She casually walked up the cement steps and slipped inside. I pulled the door shut behind her.

"Great timin'!" she exclaimed, "Did you have any trouble?"

"No, it was fairly quick and easy." Levi didn't mention his misgivings to her, and I followed his lead. I wanted her to be calm and focused on the task at hand, not worried about some silly little jitters on our part that probably didn't even mean anything.

"How about you?" I asked.

"It all went according to plan! Now, if you can guide me to the mainframe computer bank, I've got some research to do!"

I took lead, back up the stairwell and into the hallway. My two companions followed a short distance behind me, with Nessa about five meters back and Levi another five meters behind her, in the position that he always refers to as 'riding drag.'

It's an old horse wrangler term, Bro. It's the cowboy who rides at the back of the line to make sure everything is going okay with the riders and the pack string and the...

Sorry I mentioned it! Anyway, that was our lineup as we explored the building in search of the computer room. There were a few times when I peeked around corners when

I spotted employees in the halls and I gave the signal for the others to hold tight until the route was clear. It really didn't take long at all to locate a locked door that looked like a good prospect. After that, it only took about half a minute with my lock pick and *voila*, the doorknob rotated smoothly when I grabbed it and twisted.

Right now, I bet Rae and Danae are reading this and saying, "If you could pick the lock, why didn't you just do that to the fire door?"

Yeah, probably.

So I'll just note that it's all part of the covert ops protocol. An outer door that is locked is also likely to be wired for an alarm. And in fact, that was exactly the case in this situation. An interior door, however, that is locked is almost never also alarmed, so it's usually safe for us to jimmy it open.

Exactly. And cousins, if you already knew that, my apologies for the lesson. But what's the use of being the world's greatest covert-operations agents if we can't brag about it now and then?!

So anyway, I turned the knob and opened the door, slowly scootching it open about an inch. Cold air wafted out, a good sign, since the temperature is usually kept down low around mainframe servers. I peeked in and bingo, there was a big bank of computers humming away. I gave Nessa and Levi a 'follow me' signal and we all slipped inside, just as quick and quiet as a trio of shadows.

I closed the door behind us and Nessa started toward the monitor and terminal that were set into a space between two looming metal computer towers that were dotted with blinking lights of all kinds of different colors. Levi reached out and put his hand on her shoulder to stop her.

"Nessa, hold up a sec."

"Yes?" She was impatient and breathless; she just couldn't wait to get to that terminal. Her eyes were shining, she was totally in her element...she was in Acquisition-of-Information mode.

Levi hesitated. "Do you think this was maybe a bit too... easy? This place is supposed to provide the best and most secure vaults in the world to rich and powerful people, that's why Colin used one of their products to house his power generator, right? But we just waltzed in here like it was an insurance office or a shipping company or something."

Ouch. So much for keeping her focused on the task at hand. And yet, I had to agree. "He's not wrong, Nessa. In fact, I think an insurance office would actually have tougher security than what we've encountered here. Doesn't that seem a little bit... disconcerting?"

She just waved her hand in a 'shoo, fly, don't bother me' gesture. She was only half paying attention to us, and the rest of her mind was on the computers in front of her. "No, no, it's all good. Trust me." Nessa gently shrugged out from under Levi's hand and sat down at the rickety old chair in front of the keyboard and monitor. "It's really nothin' to worry about. TransVantage is always guarding the property of other businesses. They are never themselves a target, so they have never worried about putting stricter security measures in place for themselves."

Wait a minute. What did she say? Trans...*Vantage*? "Um. You mean Trans*Vault*, right?" I asked.

"Oh, yeah, right. Trans*Vault*. TransVault. Right." By this point, she was completely distracted from the conversation, pouring all of her concentration toward the computer screen and pounding away on the keyboard. Tap, tap, tappity-tap. "There! I'm in!" She finally turned to look over her shoulder at us. "An' now, boys, I don't mean to be rude, but I'm really goin' to need to concentrate on this in order to find what I'm lookin' for."

We got the hint and stepped back away from the desk and terminal.

Not to pick nits with your word choice, Bro, but I would say she did a lot more than 'hint' to us. She was pretty dog-gone blunt that she wanted us to get out of her way and leave her alone!

Yeah, true. Levi and I settled into a guard position at the door and chatted with one another, still in English, via our mask communicators so that we wouldn't distract her from her task.

"Okay, okay," Levi muttered, "I guess it'll all be okay. If she can just find that master code, now that she's into the system, then we can transmit it to Rae and Danae, and then we can skeedaddle out of here." He paused. "And I don't mind telling you, bro, the end of this part of the operation can't come fast enough for me."

"Yeah. I'm jumpy, too. Not sure why. I guess that when things go well, we should just accept it and stop looking for problems where they don't exist."

Since it really only took one of us to keep watch on the door, especially since we had re-locked it behind us when we came in, Levi went off to do a recon of the room while I stayed put. With one eye, I watched Nessa tear her way through virtual files and subdirectories, and the rest of my attention was alert for any sign or sound of unexpected and unwanted attention from the building's occupants.

From the far side of the room, behind more stacks of computer equipment, Levi subvocalized to me through the communicator. I heard a low and worried "Um, Noah?" in my ear.

"Yeah?"

"What's the name of this vault company again?"

"What do you mean? It's TransVault. Look around you, there's a big 'T-V' logo stenciled on just about every flat surface." It was true, it almost looked as if someone had been paid a penny for every time they could paint the stylized corporate initials onto a filing cabinet, packing crate or door. "Why do you ask?"

"Well, that's what I thought. TransVault. But some of this office equipment also has some additional info inscribed on it, just below the big 'T-V' graphic logo."

"Okay. So what's the problem?"

"Buddy, the problem is that the additional inscription says '*TrashVantage*'. Not 'TransVault'."

"Come again?"

"Trash-Vantage. Trash as in 'Trash.' Vantage as in 'Vantage.' TrashVantage as in NOT 'TransVault.'"

I just couldn't wrap my head around it. Trash...Vantage? "What are you saying, Bro? We broke into the wrong place?"

"I don't know about that. Thinking back to Nessa's little slip of the tongue when she sat down to the terminal, I wonder if it might actually be something worse than just being in the wrong building. But what I do know is that I think we need to get out of here, and I mean like yesterday."

Just then, Nessa gave a squeal of triumph. "Did it! I did it! It's done!"

I stepped over to her. "Great! Give me the master code and I'll transmit it to Rae and Danae! They're running out of time over there!"

"Ummm... Not yet! Let's get out of here first!" Nessa headed for the door.

"My thoughts exactly, Bro," I heard my brother's voice murmur in my mask earpiece. "It's time to get while the getting's good."

We all stepped back out into the hallway, but when Levi and I turned right, intending to head back to the stairwell and the fire escape, Nessa made a sharp left turn and went the other way down the hall.

"Psssst! Nessa! It's this way!" Levi hissed and waved frantically at her.

"You boys can exit that way if you want to," she called to us over her shoulder, "but I've grown sick and tired of sneakin' around this place."

Levi and I stared at each other. "I don't like the sound of that! What's up with her?" he muttered.

"I don't know," I replied, "but I'm not letting her out of my sight until she's given us that master code for the vault in the Null Corp building!"

We trailed behind her, bewildered and confused. At the end of the hall was a set of double doors; Nessa approached them and then marched right on through. Following her, we found ourselves on the second-floor foyer of what was obviously the front lobby of the building. A set of stairs led down to the receptionist desk and the front doors. Nessa strode down as if she owned the place. Levi and I trailed three steps behind, not quite sure how to play this whole scene.

We reached the front desk and the receptionist was an earnest young man, not all that much older than our cousin Izzy, wearing a suit and tie. He stood up and glared at us. "Now just see here! What is the meaning of this?"

During all of our missions, both in real life and in training, Levi and I had never run across a situation like this. I realized how suspicious we must look, with my bro and I in our work suits, so I pulled my hood back off my head so that it hung down from the back of my neck. Levi followed suit. My mind was racing and I blurted out the first thing to come into my head. "Exterminators! Um, yeah, we're exterminators. We got a call that you had a wicked bad infestation of termites?"

I was actually impressed by your quick thinking, pard! You might have even been able to pull it off if we weren't dressed like we were at the time. It was hilarious watching you try to look like an official pest control guy while dressed in your covert operations outfit...

Thanks, but it wouldn't have worked no matter what I looked like, because Nessa was having none of that. While Levi and I were trying to placate the receptionist, she totally ignored all the ruckus and started walking toward the front door.

That's when both us Rugg boys noticed the signage on the wall behind the front desk. There was the big 'T-V' logo that we had already seen splashed all over the place. But below that, it read 'TrashVantage: Taking Out Your Garbage Since 1999'."

"Oh boy," I said. "TrashVantage.'

"Yup. TrashVantage," Levi said. "Oh boy."

The fellow at the front desk kept getting redder and redder in the face. "I'm the office manager here!" He was practically shouting. "I didn't call for exterminators, you two young fools! And you, you there, girl," he hollered after Nessa, "you pay attention when I'm speaking to you!"

Nessa had her hand on the door, about to step outside, but stopped so suddenly it was almost like someone had splashed a cup of icy water over her head. She turned on her heel and glared at the receptionist. "Are *you*. Addressin' *me*?"

He flinched, but then plowed on. "Yes. Yes! You will explain yourself at once!"

Sure as shootin', that dude did NOT know who he was dealing with! Am I right or am I right, buddy?

You are right as rain, oh sibling of mine!

Nessa slowly, calmly walked back to the reception desk and leaned in, with her face about two inches away from Mr. Overeager. "*Girl? Pay attention? Explain myself?*" Nessa spat the words at him. His red face suddenly turned a pasty, eggshell white. He was starting to understand that he had made a bad, bad mistake.

"I have one bit of advice for you, my obnoxious wee friend." Nessa's voice was very low, but crystal-clear, and cold, cold, cold. So cold, it even made both of us Rugg brothers shiver. "Update your résumé and start lookin' for a new job. I have a feeling that upper management no longer has need of your services." Then she looked at me and my bro and said in her normal, sweet voice, "An' let's go, boyos."

We followed her out the front doors. The pasty-faced dude just gulped and sat back down at his desk.

Henry had the limo parked out front with the engine running, and he was holding the door open for Nessa. She started to climb in when I yelled, "Wait!" She turned to look at the two of us.

"Nessa, come on, give me the code. Please. Let me get it transmitted to the girls, and then on the ride back, we need to have a serious talk about what is going on here."

Levi backed me up. "Yeah, Nessa. Until we transmit that code, we can't consider this stage of the operation to be completed."

A look of pity crossed her face, and I just knew that couldn't be good news. "Oh, Levi. Noah. Don't you get it? There *is* no master code. The girls of Team Rugged Stuff *can nae* get into the power room vault, it's just not possible."

I must've sounded incredibly stupid as I stood there and said, "What? Wait. What?"

But I wasn't the only one. Levi was right close behind me with, "Wait. What? Wait."

"Come on, boys. Get in the limo and I'll explain everything to you as we drive back to the city."

Levi held his ground. "I think I'll stay right here and take the abbreviated version, thank you very much." (Way to go, Bro!)

I said, "Ditto."

Nessa sighed. "Alright. Here's the two-minute Reader's Digest version. Vault companies DO. NAE. HAVE. MASTER. CODES. It would absolutely defeat the purpose of havin' a vault, because no matter how tightly they held the information, someone would eventually break in and steal it. Someone would hack in, get the code, and bypass the vault. Just exactly like we planned on doing. Every master criminal in the world would have the same plan. It would make having a vault be an exercise in futility."

"Soooooo..." I interrupted, "if they don't have a master code, why did you propose this plan as our way to get into the vault? Why did you suggest breaking in and stealing this apparently non-existent code?"

Another big sigh on her part. "Because there was absolutely nothin' that could be done to help your cousins.

There's certainly no way that Rae and Danae can get into the power room vault at Null Corp, and no way that we can help them to get in. If they are going to stop that conference, they are goin' to have to find some other way to do it. And I wish them the very best of luck on that, I really do. Now won't you at least get into the car?"

Levi's stubborn streak was showing. "Nope. Not right now. Until you finish explaining yourself, I'm not moving one gol-durn step."

She rolled her eyes, but kept talking. "So. There's no way they can shut off the power. And in all honesty, that means that there is probably no way that they can stop the press announcement. Colin is just too clever, too devious to leave himself open in that way. That means the odds are, he's goin' to hold his press conference, and he's goin' to get credit for the OtherWorld."

I felt a scowl crawl across my face. "I don't agree with you. But for the sake of trying to understand what's happening, what has that all got to do with this wild goose chase? Why did you drag us out here to New Jersey, when we could have been helping the girls hack into his security controls? I mean, since you say there is no possible way to get into the actual vault to shut down the Null Corp power?"

Yet another sigh from Nessa. I was getting kind of sick of those sighs, to tell the truth. "If Colin is goin' to win, if he is goin' to claim the OtherWorld research, then there is no profit in trying to stop him. It's like beating your head against a wall: It gains you nothing, and it doesn't affect the wall in the slightest. No, if we accept that he is going to win, then I—or we—need to devote our efforts elsewhere. We need not pointlessly attempt to *prevent* his victory, but we need to work to make his victory less sweet than he thinks it will be."

Levi spoke up. "But don't you see?! We *do* have to prevent his victory! Otherwise all of Rachel and Danae's research will be for nothing, and he'll get all the credit for it!"

"You're right. Their research will be for nothing and Colin will get all the credit for it. However, even if he takes the credit and controls the OtherWorld, I can do something to make it so that he will NOT profit from the discovery nearly as much as he thinks he will." She shrugged. "And to tell the truth, hinderin' my brother is more important to me than helpin' your cousins."

Got to admit it, that's what the cousins warned us about. In almost exactly the same words, in fact.

I was getting lost in the mental convolutions. "What do you mean? If he makes the announcement, how will it not be as much of a victory for him as he thinks it will be?"

She explained it to me like I was five years old. "Do you remember when I told you that Colin has invested in a whole batch of waste-management companies? Do you remember when I said that he is planning to use the OtherWorld as a resource for no-cost garbage disposal?"

We nodded.

Nessa gestured toward the large TrashVantage sign on the front of the building behind us, the large sign that Levi and I hadn't seen earlier because we were on the floor of the car when we had driven past the front doors of the company.

Yup. Mystery solved as to why she put us under that blanket. It wasn't that she didn't want people to see US, it was that she didn't want US to see that we weren't really at the vault company HQ. I've got to admit it, pardner, you even tried to tell me that it felt as if we were being hornswoggled at the time, doggone it.

Nessa spelled it out for us. "Well, as you can see, *this* is not the TransVault company headquarters. *This* building houses the corporate offices of the TrashVantage company. And TrashVantage happens to be the number-one waste management business in the country. TrashVantage also happens to be the very first waste management business that Colin acquired when he started organizin' his take-over of the OtherWorld. Therefore, TrashVantage stands to see a profit of millions and millions of dollars when the OtherWorld technology is utilized by my brother as a quick, easy, and cheap way to dispose of garbage."

Levi and I looked at each other. We both said, "Oh." We both were beginning to see where Nessa was going with her story.

The way Noah reports it here, he makes it sound as if we said, "Oh." Calmly and matter-of-factly. In real life, it was more of a moaning sound, more like "Ohhhhhh," as in "Ohhhhhh, nooooooo..."

"I couldn't get into their system remotely," she continued, "so the two of you helped me get access to their mainframe computers, and I hijacked the money flow. It will still look, from the outside and on paper, as if the profits will go to my brother. But in reality, that sudden influx of cash that TrashVantage will see as a result of the 'OtherWorld Garbage Chute,' those millions of dollars will be funneled into *my* own organization." She smiled at us, a brilliant and warm and sweet smile, "See? We can't beat Colin in this situation, but we can hurt him in his wallet! The two of you and me! We made a great team! Now come on, get in the limo and we'll head back to the city." Henry was still holding the door open, and she turned to climb in.

But me and my brother, we both looked glum. Levi isn't joking when he says it was like 'Oooh, noooo.'

"Nessa." She stopped and turned to look at me. "I like you. I really do." Now it was my turn to sigh. "But you used us. You lied to us and told us that we were helping our cousins, when in reality, you had it set up so that we were really only helping you."

"Not just that, we are also hurtin' Colin—" she started to protest.

Levi cut her off. "And worse, you made Rae and Danae think they had a chance to shut down the power supply at the Null Corp building. It wasn't just that you brought us on a wild goose chase, but you sent them on one, too. You made them waste time on a strategy that you *knew* couldn't work. Maybe one of the backup plans will work as a feasible option. Or maybe one of them *would* have worked if the girls had enough time to figure them out, time that now maybe they don't have because *you* held up a non-existent 'master code' as a viable option for Plan A."

"Levi! Noah!" Nessa put on her best 'let's-be-reasonable' voice. "I feel really bad for your cousins. Truly and honestly. I like them, they are real researchers, and you know that I consider that to be high praise. If they controlled the OtherWorld tech, I'm sure they would be able to discover some great stuff. But we have to face facts. Colin out-maneuvered them this time. It stinks and it isn't fair. Believe me, I know. I've been in the exact same situation with him. But we've got to be realistic about what we can do to get back at him, and right now, helpin' Rae and Danae isn't the most efficient use of our time and resources. My way is the *only* way, and I hope that you'll come to understand that." She got in the limo and scooted over, giving room for us to climb in. "Now, come on."

Glumly, we shook our heads in the negative.

"No? What do you mean, 'No'?!" Maybe you've caught on by this point, Nessa doesn't take rejection well.

Levi waved her on in a 'go-away' motion. "You mosey on back to the city. We'll talk to you later."

"Yeah, we'll catch up with you after we help Team Rugged Stuff shut down that press conference and keep control of the OtherWorld. So long."

Nessa sputtered "Oh, you boys!" and stamped her foot on the car floor, then slammed the door shut. While her driver got in the front seat and settled himself behind the steering wheel, she lowered her window. "An' when you're through bein' mad at me and when you understand why I had to do it this way, give me a call and I'll send Henry back to pick you up."

As the long black car rolled out of sight, my bro and I looked at one another.

"What now, Levi? It's a looong hike back to NYC."

"You got that right, Noah. It may be that we end up regretting our choice not to catch a ride with her."

"Yeah." I kicked a pebble across the parking lot. "But I'm just too angry and disappointed with her to be able to sit there in the same car as her."

"Ditto." Levi pulled his black sleeve back from his wrist to access his smart watch. "I guess I'll signal the cousins and tell them that Plan A is a no-go. I hope they have more luck—*any* luck—with Plan B or Plan C."

Chapter 24

DANAE'S LOG 16: Behind Enemy Lines

Danae here again. Remember back in that chapter when I said that Rachel and I got a message from Levi and it made us both say "Dagnabbit"? Well, that shared exclamation was probably an understatement. In reality, when we got the message from our cousins that Plan A was not going to work, I felt like someone had punched me in the stomach. Levi's transmission didn't say why or how the scheme to obtain the vault's master code had failed. It was just a quick, one-line note: "Plan A is a no-go! Repeat, Plan A no-go. We'll be back when we can. More info later."

Rae looked physically ill about it, too. "Well. That's fairly devastatingly disappointing. That is to say, what a bummer. I guess I really thought, deep in my heart, this was going to work," she said. "I haven't given any serious thought to the other options that we have on the plate."

"Yeah. The same goes for me." But then I recalled how it was up to us to keep the OtherWorld world from becoming one big, giant garbage dump. I took a deep breath and tried to get rid of my depression. "Okay. Let's shake it off and get to work." Sis and I put our heads together and reviewed our next steps. First target; get to the security room. If we couldn't achieve our goal there, then we would move on to the second target and try to get to Colin's office.

We were going to need to move from where we were in the basement of the Null Corp building, up to the second floor. That's where the security ops center was located. That was our Plan B. If that didn't work, then we needed to get up to the seventh floor, where Colin's office was, for the last-ditch effort, Plan C. It only took about a minute to check the copy of the building blueprints on my tablet and find the stairway up to the ground floor. The power vault was located in the basement at the southwest corner of the building; all we had to do was follow a long hallway to the northwest corner and we came across the stairwell. With any luck, we'd be able to take the stairs all the way up to the security center on the second floor. And if we couldn't get into the security center, then we could take the stairs on up to the seventh floor for our Plan C.

This, however, was a bad-luck day for the Rugg sisters. We got to the stairs okay and trudged up the one flight to ground level, where we came to another door. I opened it and we went through to a concrete room that contained two more doors; one leading to the lobby and one leading to the stairway up to the other floors. But when I tried to open the door to the up staircase, it was locked! No way to get from Floor One to Floor Two by way of the stairs. And when I turned back to the door we had just come through,

I was shocked to find that it was locked, too. "What the heck?" I sputtered. "Why would Colin have stairs and then make it so that nobody can use them?"

Rae pondered a moment. I could tell she was running her own mental search on the subject, so I kept quiet for a minute. Then she finally seemed to have found what she was looking for in those brain files of hers. "This is an emergency stairwell."

"Okay. So?"

"It is not intended for people to use in order to get from one floor to another...It is only intended for people to use in order to get out of the building if there is some crisis and they need to avoid the elevators."

"Okay. So?"

"Okay, so that's it. It works like a funnel, directing all traffic toward the ground floor, where we are right now. From the basement, you can get UP to the ground floor. But without a key, you can't get DOWN to the basement from the ground floor." She illustrated her point by tapping the locked door *behind* us. "From any higher floor, you can get DOWN to the ground floor. But again, if you don't have a key, you can't get from the ground floor UP to any higher floor." She tapped the locked door *in front* of us. "A person could use the stairs in order to travel from a particular floor to a *lower* floor, but wouldn't be able to return the same way to the *higher* floor, not once the door closes and locks. Get it?"

Yeah. I got it. I also got that we were going to have to find another way to get up to the security center on Floor Two. "Okay, Rachel. I guess that means it's the elevators for us."

My sister nodded. "But there's something else. You know, D, up until now, we've been using stealth. We've been counting on not being detected at all. But I think that for the next stage of the operation, we are going to have to take a page out of Colin's own book and employ some camouflage. We're definitely going to encounter other people, whether in the lobby or elevator or the security center, there's just no way to avoid it. So we are going to have to do something to make them believe that we belong here, that we're not who we really are; we need to make them think we are NOT Team Rugged Stuff here to foil the plans of their boss and employer, but that we are someone else entirely."

She had a point, so I put my brains to work on it. "Hmmm. Yeah, could be that you're right, R. What are you thinking? Do a little bit of cosplaying as dewy-eyed middle-school students?" Sis and I both look younger than we really are. (When the subject comes up about how old we look, Rae likes to quote an old detective show from television and say, "It's a blessing... and a curse." *That's* a surprise, right? My sister quoting from a television show?) The thing is, she's right about it; when you look so young, it can be hard to get people to take you seriously. On the other hand, appearing to be younger than you are can really be helpful when you're trying to fly under the radar and not draw too much attention. People absolutely *love* to ignore and underestimate young kids. "How about it, Rae? Maybe we go with the old 'school-newspaper reporter' bit?"

She grinned. She loves that role.

We tucked all of our tech gear into our bags and pulled out pens and notebooks instead. We put on our best air of 'oh, don't mind us, we're just a couple of kids, no threat here, no need to pay attention to us...' and we each took a deep breath. I let Rae lead the way; she pushed the door to the lobby open and we slipped out and into the big airy space. Now to get to the elevator, get to the second floor and get into the security room, all the while just looking as if we were a couple of local school kids.

The first part of it went fine. There were a lot of people bustling around the front lobby and at the little café/coffee shop off to the side and no one even seemed to notice us. The elevators were set into the wall in the middle of the western side of the building, just past the front desk. We walked over, acting as if we knew just what we were doing and just where we were going. Rae pushed the 'Up' button at the elevator bank and slick as a whistle, the doors opened and an elevator took us up to Floor Two, where we stepped out and paused in the hallway to get our bearings.

I pulled out my tablet again and accessed the building schematics files to see how to get to the security room. "Okay, fingers crossed that most of the staff will be busy getting ready for the press conference and they won't be paying much attention at the security center," I muttered.

But remember how I said the Rugg girls were batting a thousand in the area of bad luck? Well, we hadn't seen the worst of it yet, because when we turned the corner to the hallway that my map showed as our target destination, there was a big, surly-looking security guard standing outside the doorway. She looked as if she had probably been a professional boxer or had a career as an MMA fighter before coming to work for Null Corp. So we just kept on walking; we didn't look at either the guard or the door, and tried to be inconspicuous. Even so, I could *feel* her staring at us as we went past and turned another corner. Once we were out of sight, we stopped for a 'what-now?' conversation.

"Shoot!" I grumbled, "I was afraid of that! The blueprint can only tell us the physical layout of the building, but it can't tell us where people and security personnel might be posted. It's not like my empathy-helmet and the Bright-Eyes! We won't know about actual live guards—like that big bruiser back there—until we practically run into them."

"Yeah," my sis agreed, "I wish it was only the door that we had to deal with, and not live security personnel." Then she smiled. "But here's where we put our undercover roles to the test! Just follow my lead." She turned back the way we had just come and marched back down the hall to where the security guard stood.

"Excuse me? Ma'am, excuse me?" Rae had her notepad in one hand, a pen in the other, and a seriously earnest and sappy look on her face as she stared up at the guard. I did my best to mimic her stance.

"Yeah? Whaddya want?" The security guard growled down at us.

I could feel the nervous sweat spring up on my forehead, despite the building's climate control. This woman didn't seem very inclined to help out a couple of visiting student reporters. But Rae just plowed on ahead like a professional actress.

"Ma'am, is this the Security Center? You see, my friend and I are reporters from the school newspaper, and Colly— Oh, tee-hee, I guess I should call him Mr. Null—well, Mr. Null said that we could do a story on his company's operations, because it's so, like, advanced and state of the art and stuff, y'know? And we checked in, like, at the main lobby, and we're s'posed to go on up to the Security Center, 'cuz that's what we're doing our story on, huh? But we got lost, right? So if this is, like, the right place, we'll just go in and do our reporter stuff, okay?" Wow, she was playing her role right up to the hilt. Other than the giggly stuff, she sounded as if she might be channeling what our cousin Izzy might have sounded like when she was in middle school. But the problem was, the guard wasn't buying what Rachel was selling.

"You checked in at the lobby, huh?" Her gravelly voice matched her no-nonsense appearance.

"Oh, yes ma'am!" Sincere, simpering and sappy.

"Then where's yer visitor badges?"

Rae and I glanced at each other. Uh-oh. Rae gulped. "Oh. Our, um, visitor badges?"

"That's right, kiddo. Ain't nobody supposed to be wandering around the building without either a staff badge or a visitor badge." By way of example, she pointed to her own badge that was clipped onto her belt at her hip.

Rae patted her pockets as if searching for her errant badge. I copied her. Finally, my sister shrugged her shoulders. "Gosh, I don't know? I'm sure I, like, most def *had* my badge, but now I can't find it. But pleeeeease, lady, can't you let us in? We're gonna flunk for sure if we don't write this article! Please?"

The guard looked skeptical. "Hmmmm. I dunno about this. Hold on for just a sec." She unclipped her badge (it said 'Nancy' on it and had her picture) and waved it over a sensor set into the doorframe. There was a 'click' and the door popped open. Nancy stuck her head through the doorway and called into the room. "Hey Frank, step out here for a minute for me, willya?" She clipped her badge back onto her belt as another guard stepped forward from the gloomy interior. His bulk filled up the doorway and as he fiddled with his own staff badge that was clipped onto his own belt, we could see blinking lights and controls in the dim room behind him. I could feel myself grinding my teeth at the thought of being so close, but so far away, from our goal. The door sitting there wide open but with the two of them blocking it, there was no way to get in.

The big galoot called Frank blinked in the relative brightness of the hallway and grumbled, "Yeah, what is it, Nance?"

"Anybody say anything to you about some student reporters showing up today to do a story about the security center?"

"Naw." He considered. "But then again, they don't never tell us nothing about what's going on. Irregardless, I still can't let 'em in without the proper authorization."

"Yeah, that's what I thought." She turned back to address us. "Too bad for you, I guess yer gonna flunk. Now you be good little kids and take a hike, huh? Go on now, scram."

Rae huffed herself up and shot back, "We're NOT little kids!" in such a way that she sounded *exactly* as if she was, indeed, a little kid throwing a tantrum. I wasn't sure exactly what her plan was, but I decided to play along. She kept it up and she was making quite a fuss. "We're not, we're not! We're not little kids! What do you think, that we're in grade school? That me and my friend hang out after school and play patty cake?"

Aha! *Now* I knew what she had in mind! It all became clear, just as soon as I heard the code word 'pattycake'! So I piped up with my two-cents' worth. "Yeah! We don't play pattycake! That's for babies."

The guards both rolled their eyes, and Nancy started to get red in the face. It was obvious that these two really, really didn't feel like dealing with a big scene right now.

Rae paused, and acted like she was thinking things over. "Well, I guess pattycake isn't *just* for babies." Looking up at Frank and Nancy, she asked, "Did you guys ever watch those old movies with Bob Hope and Bing Crosby and Dorothy Lamour? The movies that were called 'The Road Pictures'?"

Nancy just looked confused, but Frank's eyes lit up with recognition. "Hey! Hey, yeah! I remember those movies!" He pondered for a moment. "But those are *old*! Like, black-and-white old. What's a little kid like you know about some old movies like that?"

And I thought, *Well, he's not wrong. If it weren't for Rae's hobby, I sure as heck wouldn't know a Road Picture from a hole in the ground...*

My sis didn't answer him directly, but instead grinned and kept talking about the films. "And remember, Bob and Bing, they would always play pattycake?" She turned to me. "And then they would turn around and punch the bad guys and then make their getaway! Remember how it went? How they just *belted* them?"

Frank laughed out loud and even Nancy grinned a little bit at the thought of someone getting hit in the face.

But with that last bit, Rae had made the final part of her plan clear to me, and I knew what I had to do. I made a big show out of tucking my walking stick under my arm and turned to face Rae with my palms up and facing her. Standing right in front of both of the big guards, I announced, "Yeah! Pattycake, pattycake, baker's man..."

We started chanting the nursery rhyme in unison and exchanging hand pats. "...bake me a cake... as fast... as you... CAN!" In the Road Picture movies that Rae was talking about, when Bob Hope and Bing Crosby got to the word 'can,' that's when they would turn and sock it to the bad guys. But instead of us turning to punch Nancy and Frank (because, come on, they had about three feet and a couple hundred pounds of advantage over us! It would have seriously been kind of pointless, right?), on the word '*can*,' Rae gave me an extra-forceful hand pat, pushing me toward the two guards. I acted as if my stiff leg gave out on me and as a result, I stumbled against Nancy and then Frank. It was quite a performance, me dropping my walking stick and flailing my arms and hands around. I would have fallen to the floor if they hadn't reflexively grabbed me and held me up until I regained my balance.

"Oh gosh, Danae! I'm so sorry! Are you okay?" Rae had such a look of concern on her face, I almost busted out laughing. She is a great actress!

But instead of laughing, I put a tremble in my voice and managed to sound very shaken up. "I... I think so." I turned and looked up at the two guards. "Thank you for catching me."

They both scowled. Frank's good cheer over remembering some old movies where people got punched had disappeared and he said to me, "Yeah, whatever." Then he glared at Nancy and growled, "Get ridda' them," before turning, walking through the open doorway and back into the security center, and slamming the door behind him.

Nancy looked disgusted. "See, what happens when kids fool around? Someone could get hurt. And that someone is you." She folded her arms and puffed herself up, looking down on us. "Well, you heard him... get outta here. And don't let me catch you around here again!"

I grabbed my walking stick and we scurried down the hall and around the corner to the elevators, where Nancy couldn't see the grin on Rae's face or hear her chuckle, "Oh, we'll definitely do our best to see that you *don't* catch us!"

Chapter 25

DANAE'S LOG 17: Onward and Upward

We took the elevator back down to the first floor and grabbed a table at the little café that was set just off to the side of the main lobby. We sat down and put our heads together over a shared milkshake and took stock of the situation. "Plan A, the vault master code, that plan is now obsolete and defunct," Rae said.

"And Plan B, getting into the security center as student reporters, that one crashed and burned," I noted. "Not gonna happen, not with one big guard outside in the hall and her counterpart actually hanging out in the room itself."

"That leaves Plan C, infiltrating Colin's private office and initiating a security lockdown from there. And unless I miss my mark, it was the 'crashing and burning' of Plan B that may have provided us the resources to make Plan C work out for us." Rae looked at me questioningly with her eye-brows raised.

I made out like I didn't know what she was talking about. "Huh? What could you possibly have in mind?" I asked in my most innocent of voices.

Rae laughed. She knows me too well. "Oh, come on! I set you up perfectly, so if you didn't take advantage of the situation, you are really losing your touch!"

I laughed, too. And I held up the pair of security badges I had lifted from Nancy and Frank's belts when I had fallen against them in the hallway. "Oh, you mean *these* resources!"

"Bingo!" She crowed. "I never doubted you! But then again, it *has* been quite a while since we've used that old gag."

"No, you really *did* set it up perfectly, it was easy-peasy, especially after you gave that signal for me to look at their belts," I reassured her. "The only way it could have gone better is if they had actually handed us their badges them-selves! Now, if we can get ourselves up to the seventh floor, these security badges SHOULD gain us access to Colin's of-fice, and Colin SHOULD be down in the conference center getting ready for his press conference and so we SHOULD be able to complete Plan C and initiate a security lock-down on the building." But then I started to get worried again. "That's an awful lot of 'shoulds' that we are counting on, Sis."

"Agreed." Rae also looked concerned. "But everything else we've tried has failed. We are down to our last chance, and this is it, no matter how many 'shoulds' it's going to take."

I handed Frank's badge to her and stared at Nancy's as I turned it over in my hand. On the back of each security badge was the big red zero symbol—a circle with a slash marked through it. The Null Corp logo. On the other side, each had an employee photo. In this case, it looked as if they were actual and literal police-station mug shots of the two security goons. "I wonder how long it will take for them to realize these are missing?"

"I don't know, it's a pretty sure bet that they won't report the loss right away. They will hope that they just dropped them someplace, or set them aside and forgot where they left them, because if they have to tell their bosses that they lost their badges, they are going to look like real chumps. And with any luck at all, it will never even occur to them that *we* had anything to do with it. I don't think they're the kind of people to ever imagine that a couple of *kids* like us could ever put one over on them like that." Rae checked her watch. "But I think we'd better get a move on, before they finally give up and report that their badges are missing and we lose this advantage."

As we pushed away from the table and headed back to the lobby, I mumbled, "Pattycake, pattycake..."

Rae replied, "...baker's man. Let's get up to Colin's office and stop his press conference, as fast as we can."

Once inside the elevator again, I wasn't surprised to notice that the buttons only went up to Floor Five...according to the blueprints, this set of elevators could take us up to the fifth floor, and then we would need to transfer to a different one (the "Executive Elevator," Nessa called the one that went up to the sixth, seventh, eighth and ninth floors) in order to go any higher in the building. And finally some good news, we wouldn't have to go past Nancy in order to get to the other elevator.

When the button labeled '5' lit up and the elevator doors opened, it was just a generic looking hallway with a row of office doors. Rae gestured down a long hall leading toward the east side of the building and I spotted the door to the other elevator. We walked toward it, just like we belonged here, even though no one was in the hallway to question our presence here. On the wall beside this new elevator door was just one button, an *UP* arrow that glowed green when my sister reached out and pushed it.

Things finally came together in my mind. "Aha. I understand what's going on here. Colin has one elevator for all of the floors where people from the general public might have business. And then another elevator to access the levels where he does most of his work. He doesn't want just any riff-raff off the street to be able to walk in on him."

"Yeah, that's the impression I got from Nessa." The door slid open and Rae walked in, with me on her heels. After the door closed, she punched the button marked '7' but nothing happened. "Okay, D. What am I missing here?"

I scrunched up my face and concentrated. That's when I noticed a slim card-swipe groove on the side of the control panel. "Aha! Maybe our new 'resources' are even more useful than we thought!" I ran Nancy's badge through the groove and the '7' button lit up, but in a scary red tint rather than a nice friendly green. I turned to my sister and shrugged. "Well, that was my bright idea, but I don't know if it got us any further along."

Rae snapped her fingers. "Yes, it did!" She glanced at the ceiling, then she swiped Frank's badge and we were rewarded with a green light. I could feel the elevator begin to move.

"How did you do that?" I asked her. "What did you do there?"

She grinned. "It was just a guess, but it seems to have panned out, and I wouldn't have thought of it if you hadn't noticed the card-swipe slot. Once you got the control panel to react, I noticed that there is a thermal scanner set into the top of the elevator. Then I remembered how Frank the guard said that *everyone* had to have a badge, even visitors. So then I considered how paranoid Colin is—remember how he's got the emergency stairs set up so that no one without a key can use them to go *up* to a higher floor?—and postulated that he would have more than just the obvious security measures in place in order to get to the higher levels in the building. The security on this elevator is designed to make sure that *no one* gets above the fifth floor without one of those badges. It uses an infrared sensor to check how many bodies are inside the elevator and it won't engage until that many badges have been swiped into the control panel. It's a pretty clever process, actually."

"Hmmmm," I considered, as we watched the glowing numbers chart our progress up to our target floor. "Makes me glad I happened to snatch both of those badges. I had actually thought it might be a bit of overkill to take them from both of the guards."

"Yeah, I wondered that at the time, as well. But good thing you did get them both, otherwise we would be stuck on the fifth floor and Plan C would be dead in the water." The elevator made a cheerful '*ding*' as the seventh floor lit up. "As it is, we're full steam ahead!"

As the door slid open, we didn't know what to expect. The building blueprints showed a large foyer, but whether it would be staffed by more guards, or a secretary, or some other Null Corp staffers, we couldn't tell yet. As it turns out, there was nobody in the seventh floor lobby at all. Nobody, zilch, zero people. To be honest, it wasn't even much of a lobby; it was more of a wide-open space with a number of official looking doors and a big hall leading to the southwest corner of the building. (Yup. By some strange quirk of architecture, our new target was located directly above our original target, eight floors above the power vault in the basement.) At the end of that hall were a pair of large wooden doors (hand-polished teak, by the looks of them), beyond which was the inner sanctum of the Null empire. I noticed something and pointed it out to Rachel; There wasn't even a security-badge swipe unit on the wall or the door frame. I guess Colin felt that outsiders would never be allowed to penetrate this far into the building unless accompanied by his security staff, AND that his security staff would never dare to become the target of his wrath by entering his office without first being summoned there by him. I was glad we hadn't known this beforehand... if we had, then we wouldn't have swiped the badges, and if we hadn't swiped the badges, the elevator wouldn't have brought us up here. I felt as if perhaps our luck was getting better, after all! Another hallway led away from the elevators in the opposite direction, toward what the blueprints had identified as a laboratory and a communications center and some other rooms.

We approached Colin's office and stood there, staring at the entrance. Rae finally spoke up. "Well Danae, this is it. Behind these doors is our last chance to keep Colin from turning the BrightEyes' homeworld into a garbage dump. I've got my fingers crossed that we find what we need in there."

I let out a deep breath. "Yup. Knock on wood for even MORE good luck," I gently tapped the teak with my knuckles. I guess both of us were showing our superstitious streak. Then I turned the brass knob.

Even though I only opened the door about three inches, gently easing it ajar so that I could peek into the dimness of the room beyond, it still gave an ominous creak. The finger-crossing and the knocking on wood must've done some good, though, because the sound wasn't loud enough to be noticed by the person sitting at a big desk on the other side of the room with his back to us. The inside of the office was dimly lit, but I could just make out his silhouette as he hunt-and-pecked away at a computer keyboard. I gave Rae a hand signal to warn her that we weren't alone. This was something we hadn't considered, but how perfect would it be if we could slip right in and grab Colin?! He wouldn't be able to give a press conference if he was tied up and shoved into a corner someplace! I opened the door a little bit more, just enough for us to squeeze through without making any noise, and we started creeping across the darkened room in order to get the drop on our old enemy. I just hoped we could get right up close and one of us grab him from each side before he noticed us.

But when we got close enough to get a good look at the occupant of the office, we forgot all about being stealthy. It wasn't Colin sitting at the desk, but it was someone else who we certainly recognized!

"Mike!" Rae and I both gasped in unison.

Our head of security jumped up from the chair in which he had been sitting. Startled, he whirled around to face us, and when he saw who had called his name, his eyes bulged out and he let loose with a big gasp of his own.

Both of us sisters scampered over and wrapped him up in a big hug.

Rae: "You managed to get free!"

Danae: "We were so worried about you!"

Mike: "What do you—Oh, I mean, uh, yes, I managed to get free? I mean, yes, I managed to get free!"

We disengaged from the group hug and stepped back to look at our friend. With him working on Colin's computer, I could only imagine that maybe he was one step ahead of us in our plan to shut down the press conference!

Leaning against the desk to steady himself (he must have been awfully surprised to see us here!), Mike continued, "And just as I expected, you also managed to get free. I, urm, told my captors that something so basic as a locked room would never keep you two out of action for very long!" He raised his eyebrows quizzically. "But, ah, I was led to believe that Null's troops had warned of dire consequences to me, their hostage, should you move against him?"

"Yeah, he threatened to do some pretty bad stuff to you if we didn't back off," I agreed, "but we knew that you wouldn't want that to stop us!"

Rae joined in, "Yes, we knew that if you felt as if your well-being had been used as leverage against us, no matter what kind of tortures they claimed they would inflict on you, you just would never forgive yourself!"

"Oh. Oh, right. Indeed," Mike replied. But he must have still been recovering from the shock of seeing us here, because he didn't sound very sure about it.

"But how did you manage to escape from Colin's agents?" Rae asked.

Mike shook his head as if to clear his mind (probably trying to get rid of thoughts about those tortures that Colin had threatened). "Oh, you know. A little of the old razzle-dazzle, a jab here and an uppercut there. My captors let their guard down and, ah, ultimately paid the price for it."

Typical Mike. He liked to keep his cards close to his vest and not give out any info that he didn't have to. He was always very precise, except when he didn't want to be, and then, he was precise about being imprecise!

I looked at the computer on the desk, trying to figure out where the security override controls might be in order for us to complete our mission. "Well, however you accomplished it, I'm glad to see you! And you must have had the same idea that we did about how to stop Colin's press conference!"

Rae leaned over and tried to get a look at what our operations manager had been working on at the computer. "Yeah, Mike! You even beat us to Colin's office! That's what this place is, right? Colin's private office?"

"An' indeed it is." Rae and I both jumped in surprise when a voice—a voice that wasn't Mike's voice—answered from a dim corner of the room off to our right. This new voice was soft. It was calm. And it had a slight Irish accent. Lights suddenly clicked on from overhead, filling the office with a bright glare that revealed another door slightly ajar, a door we hadn't noticed before (it was on the blueprints, but our attention had been focused on getting into the office), with a well-dressed young man standing in front of it.

Colin Null closed that door behind him and stepped into the room toward the three of us.

Chapter 26

DANAE'S LOG 18:
Friends and
Enemies

"Well, well, well, an' what have we here? It looks as if Team Sluffed Gruff just can't help but put themselves into whatever trap happens to be available, hmmm?" That insufferable punk grinned smugly at us. The audacity of this guy! We outnumbered him three to one, yet he was just as calm as anything!

"Hello, *Colin*." My big sis spoke so coldly that you could almost see her breath in the room, just like on a freezing winter morning at Lake Tahoe. And she managed to get a worldful of disgust into the way she said his name. "You're looking well. And here, I would have thought that you'd appear much more worn down and tired, what with all the effort you've been putting into staying one step *behind* us and our research."

"Yes, hail and well met, Colin!" I grinned back at him, and I made sure that my smile showed even more teeth than his did. I tried to imagine that I was a shark and he was a tasty little minnow. "As far as traps go, I think you're looking at this all backwards. We came here looking for your override controls to the building and to stop your press conference. But now we can go one step better! We can put a stop to everything by just putting *you* under wraps."

Believe it or not, he just stood there and chuckled at me. "Oh, dear little naïve and deluded Danae. An' how in the world do you ever think that you might be able to—what was the colloquialism that you employed?—'put me under wraps'?"

"Well, I was hoping to find you here in your office all on your own so that Rae and I could maybe beat you unconscious, dump you in a laundry cart and wheel you off to some abandoned warehouse someplace. Then we would keep pounding on you, not just to get the information out of you about how you infiltrated our research, but also just for the fun of it." It was a very enjoyable mental image.

Rae joined in, "But now, our position of superior resources has suddenly become exponentially enhanced. And by that, I mean we've got our head of security here to back us up." She gestured toward Mike, "and he's forgotten more about field interrogation than most people could ever learn!"

But I didn't like the look on Colin's face. He still looked just too calm. I knew that Colin *had* to have researched all about Mike's background, his experience in the British Secret Service. The thought of being questioned by someone like Mike should have made the Irish boy very, very nervous. Instead, he just stood there smiling. In an effort to shake him up, I snarled at him, "Smirk all you like, but I don't think you stand a whisper of a chance against Michael..."

"Ah! An' here's what's funny," Colin replied calmly. "I was just about to say the same thing to you." Then he spoke directly to Mike. "You there. Take these two and stow them away someplace secure until after I'm done with the press conference."

Neither Rae nor I really understood what was going on. Rae glanced past our operations director, looking to see if perhaps one of Colin's guards had managed to sneak into the room somewhere behind us. So we were both of us shocked beyond belief when Mike reached out and grabbed our shirt collars, one in each hand, and sighed. "Sorry girls. You'll, urm, need to come with me now."

I screeched. *"WHAT?!"* Yup, literally screeched as I struggled, unsuccessfully, to break free from him.

Rae was, of course, more in control of herself, but I could hear both anger and confusion in her voice. "Mike? What is all of this about?"

He didn't answer. The face of our longtime friend was absolutely stoic and emotionless.

Colin, however, was a different story. "Ha ha ha! Don't you get it, girls? Are you really and truly so blinded by your loyalty to this two-bit opportunist who ran your security operations?" Chuckling, he gestured at Mike. "In reality, Mr. Kane here is one of the best employees that Null Corp ever hired!" But then the laughing tapered off and he frowned. "Our best employee, that is, up until the past few days. He *did* do a good job of lurin' you into the trap that was designed to keep you caught in the OtherWorld until after the press conference, I will admit that. But ever since then, it's been one big fat blunder after another." Colin waggled his finger at Mike in a 'tsk-tsk-tsk' gesture. "An' I'm particularly talking about the way he panicked when the two of you managed to get out of the OtherWorld and showed back up at your laboratory! He would have been *much* more useful to me if he had stayed right where he was, right there in the heart of your organization. But instead, what does he do? Stages a mock kidnappin' and runs cryin' to me here in New York like a wee stupid baby, that's what."

I thought about it for a minute. *But there was that note that was left behind.* So I said exactly what was on my mind, "But there was that note that was left behind..."

Colin snorted as my voice trailed off. "I don't even know what any note might have said. As I told you, he panicked and then tried to make it look as if my men had captured him. In short, he lost his nerve; he thought that you two would discover that he was my mole in your facility, an' he didn't want to face up to it."

"Arrrrrgh!" Rae groaned in frustration, as much at herself as at our situation. "I knew the tone and content of that note didn't sound authentic! I should have followed my instincts on that!"

"Yes." Colin was very pleased with himself. "Yes, apparently you should have."

I was still having a hard time believing everything that was happening. I looked over my shoulder and up into the face of the man who had taught me so much, the man I had trusted like an uncle. "Why, Mike? Why'd you do it?"

He didn't answer, he just looked sad and glum and miserable. But count on Colin to put in his two-cent's worth. "Oh, an' is it that you want to know why good old prim an' proper an' strict an' straight-arrow Mr. Kane would betray his beloved employers, the people who have treated him like family?"

I hate to admit it, but I could hardly have worded it better myself.

"Well, let me elucidate you!" Colin crowed. "Perhaps if your laboratories were not situated in Nevada, a state famous for its gambling casinos, you might not be in this situation. But our friend, Mr. Kane, has the unfortunate habit of making some very unwise bets. I'm afraid he ran up quite a deficit in downtown Reno, and some of my paid informants alerted me to the situation. It was then such a simple matter for me to arrange to purchase his debts from the gaming resorts and—ta-dah!— instant Null Corp employee!"

Neither Rae nor I could believe it. "Mike! Is this true?" Rae demanded.

No reply from our old and former friend, other than a deepening in the furrows between his eyebrows.

I mean, we knew he liked to play roulette and blackjack and all that sort of thing. It was part of his James-Bond-esque persona, the suave British government agent and all that. But we had no idea that he could have gotten into so much debt that he would sell us down the river to our arch-enemy!

And speaking of our arch-enemy, he started yammering again. "An' if you'll excuse me, *I* still have a press confer-ence for which to prepare." Colin shifted his attention from us to Mike. "Now then, you! Did you finish the preparations for the food and drinks in the conference center?"

Mike nodded and grumbled, "Yes, I was just checking on the status of the orders when the girls arrived."

Colin spoke to me and Rae again. "Nothin', and I mean *nothin'*, works better to influence the members of the press to report favorably about something than if you provide the journalists with plenty of refreshments! Keep them happy with enough champagne and caviar, and you've practically guaranteed a five-star review for yourself!"

He addressed Mike again, and his voice was laced with contempt and sarcasm. "*If* you think you can handle such a difficult task, I want you to see to it that these two are securely locked away. An' let me repeat that; SECURELY. LOCKED. AWAY. PERIOD. And oh, by the way, not that I don't trust your competence, but I've notified security to provide you with a couple of guards to ensure that the job is done correctly." Then he pretended to mull over the situation, hand in chin, eyes rolling toward the ceiling. "Oh, wait, no... it *is*, after all, *exactly* because I don't trust your competence. Once you've got that taken care of, meet me in the conference center to help me with the press gathering."

And now he turned his gaze to me and Rachel yet again and winked. "Aye, an' I hope you won't mind if I don't invite you along, but if you'll excuse me, I'm afraid I've a date to chat with the awful lot of reporters who are going to be coverin' *my* big announcement!"

Looking back at Mike, he snapped a final "Get it done!" and strode out of the room.

Mike pushed/dragged us out into the hallway, with no more effort than if we were a pair of unruly kindergarteners. We're both pretty well trained up on hand-to-hand combat, but Mike is the guy who had actually been our trainer, so we were definitely overmatched. Once he had us outside the office, we could see down the hall into the foyer where Colin stood at the elevator. The doors opened, and as he got on, the guards that he had sent for stepped off and started walking toward us. Rae and I looked at one another. "Well, I guess that figures," I groaned.

Rae nodded. Mike still had a tight grip on our shirt collars, but Big Sis managed to turn toward the guards far enough to greet them. "Hi Nancy. Hi Frank."

It was not a happy reunion.

Those two were more than a little upset with us Rugg sisters, let me tell you that. After they grabbed their security badges back from us, (they had had to borrow a couple of badges from their co-workers in order to ride the elevator up here to the seventh floor), they got into an argument with Mike about what to do with us until after the press conference.

Frank (grumpy): "And *I* say, just leave 'em here in the boss's office. Now that we've got our swipe cards back that they stole from us—" he paused to give us the stink eye, "—the elevators won't work for them, so they're stuck here on this floor anyways. They'll be locked up tight until you come back to get them after the big event. We'll stand guard outside, 'cuz I'm so mad at these two kids I don't even want to be in the same room with 'em."

Nancy (grunting): "Sounds good to me!"

Mike (aghast): "Good gracious, man, are you, ah, out of your mind?! No, no, and, uh, no! That's just what they want!" He gestured toward Colin's desk. "Their plan was to get in here and use Master Null's controls to shut down the whole building!" Then he shuddered. "Besides, this room is just not secure enough for my peace of mind. The doors are only made of wood, for heaven's sake, and I have personal knowledge that just within the past week, hmm, these two escaped from a sealed room barricaded with titanium doors!

I *demand* some good solid steel, at the very least, between them and myself! And you can't stand *outside* the door, you must be *in* the same room with them where you can keep an eye on them. That *still* won't be enough to make me entirely comfortable, but it will be better, hmmph, than keeping them in Master Null's office."

Nancy thought about it for a little bit. It appeared to be quite a struggle for her to fire up her brain cells. "Don't strain anything there," I snarked at her. I could tell that she wanted to give me a thump up the backside of my head, but she managed to control herself.

Finally, she came to a conclusion. "Well, if it's steel doors you want, most of the other rooms here on this floor have got some really thick steel doors."

"No, not the lab," Mike was very definite. "It has an adjoining door to Null's office. He just came into the office from the laboratory, not five minutes ago."

Frank spoke up, "Well, I know another room on this floor that only has the one door into the hallway. It's designed to be super strong and fireproof, because there's a lot of electrical equipment inside,"

This seemed to make Mike a little happier. "Now *that* sounds, hmph, just about right. Lead on, my good compatriots!"

Other than Mike keeping a tight grip on us, they had all been pretty much ignoring Rae and me, but I couldn't take it any more. "You'd better hope that we can't get out from that room, you traitor, you turncoat, you Benedict Arnold, you—" I yelled, while we both tried to shake loose (I even tried to take a swing at him with my walking stick), but Mike was just too experienced in hand-to-hand personnel restraint for us to get free. Frank and Nancy led the way down the hall, and Mike marched us along after them.

Down past the area with the elevator and a little ways into another hallway, we finally came to a big metal door, and Frank's description of it had been spot-on. It had to have been at least a three-ply steel alloy, with solid D-ring handles and a top-of-the-line locking mechanism. Nancy used her badge—the one that she had re-appropriated from us—to open it. The room inside revealed a media center of some sort, with screens and monitors filling the walls, and desks with control banks of switches and toggles and keyboards.

"A lot of electrical equipment, indeed," muttered Mike. "What is all of this? Why is no one here to operate this equipment?"

"It's the comm center," Nancy explained. "When the Null Corp teams are working out in the field, this is where the operations are managed, where they keep in touch with the agents. They've been awfully busy here the past month or so—I guess they had some sort of lab they were busting into out West—but they must've finished up with that mission, 'cuz it got pretty quiet. Lately, everyone's been prepping the conference center and no one's been using the communications room here for the past few days."

I caught my sister's eye and grimaced. *That's OUR lab she's talking about, R!*

Mike walked us to a corner on the far side of the room and scanned the interior of the space. "Ah, I see, I see. But there is no other entrance or exit to this room, is that correct?" he asked our guards.

"That's right. Just the one door," Frank grunted. His expression added the unspoken message of *Duh, that's what I already said.*

Mike finally released his grip on our collars and half-dropped, half-nudged us into a pair of swivel chairs, of which there were about a half-dozen scattered throughout the room. "Fine then. I remand these two to your, um, tender care. But I warn you: They possess an intelligence and cleverness to which the two of *you*," he looked down his nose at the security guards and sniffed, "could never aspire. They may try to manipulate you, or to trick you, but *do not* let them out of this room, nor out of your sight, until I return. Do I make myself clear?"

Nancy and Frank looked at each other and rolled their eyes, but replied to Mike in brisk military fashion, "Sir, yes sir!"

Mike strode to the door, but before he left he turned toward us. "Girls, I'm... so sorry."

"Apology NOT accepted!" I spat at him.

Rae spoke more calmly. "One last chance, Mike. Turn around, change course and help us stop this press conference." (I told you she's got a soft heart.) "But if you walk out that door, you have passed the point of no return. Is that what you really want?"

"There's...nothing to be gained by remaining on a sinking ship, I'm afraid. When all is said and done, Colin Null will be victorious and Team Rugged Stuff will have been torn asunder. I have to think about my own future. I have to look out for myself. That's...that's just the way it is." He shook his head sadly and exited the room, pulling the doors shut behind him.

Now we were alone with the pair of security guards who already had a pretty good reason to dislike us. Frank glared at us. "Now look, you two. I'm not very happy with you. In fact, I'm pretty doggone mad at both of you. I really don't want to have to hang out and babysit a couple of kids. I'd rather just stand guard out in the hall where I don't even have to look at your punk faces."

Nancy grunted an affirmative, then nodded and asked her partner, "You thinking what I'm thinking?"

"Yup." He thought about it. "That is, if we're both thinking the same thing." A real Brainiac, that Frank. He turned back to us. "So. There's two ways we can do this."

Was he serious? He had delivered this line with a straight face, so I just couldn't help myself. I raised my hand and said, "No, wait, let me guess! We can do this the *hard* way or we can do this the *easy* way?"

Believe it or not, smiles lit up the faces of both of our guards. They looked so happy, I didn't even have the heart to tell them that they were walking, talking clichés.

"Yeah, that's right!" said Frank. "So here's the easy way. If you two promise to us that you're going to stay here in this room and not try to escape, then me and Nancy will let you just hang out in here. We don't want to be stuck in here with you. I'll wrap this length of chain around the door handles out there and lock it with this padlock." Honest to goodness, he pulled about a meter's length of chain out of one of the cargo pockets of his military-style trousers. Even Nancy looked a little taken aback by this.

We stared at him in disbelief. "You, um, you just carry a chain around with you?" I asked.

"Well, duh. What does it look like?"

For once in my life, I was literally speechless. I mean, I just didn't know how to respond to this strange, strange fact. Finally, I said, "Um. Yeah. That's what it looks like."

Frank apparently thought he'd made his point, because then he continued his explanation. "So we'll lock it up and then me and Nancy will keep an eye on the door but we'll also be free to do our own stuff. Like maybe we can take turns running down to the main floor for that press conference and get a chance to grab some of that lobster and caviar and champagne that the boss is putting out for the reporters."

"Hmmmm." Rae looked thoughtful. "Okay, that's the easy way. What's the hard way?"

The big galoot frowned. "The hard way is exactly the same, except instead of the door handles, I wrap the chain and lock it around a couple of smarty-pants kids who don't know enough to take a good deal when it's offered to them. *Capiche?*"

I flung myself back in my swivel chair, rested my walking stick across the armrests like the safety bar on a roller coaster, and using my good leg, gave the chair a lazy spin. "We vote for the easy way."

Chapter 27

DANAE'S LOG 19:
Looks Like It's
Time for Plan D

"Yup, three-ply steel, just like the man said," I noted. After the guards confiscated our bags from us, stepped into the hall and closed the door behind them, we heard Frank wrapping the chains around the handles on the outside, then the click of the padlock. I tapped on the doors with the handle of my walking stick (those security guards were a couple of big jerks, but even *they* wouldn't take a cane away from a kid with a game leg) and the only response was the solid thunk of thick metal. "You know, Mike was right, we probably could have figured out a way to whittle our way through those wooden doors in Colin's office, but there's no way we're getting through these babies in time to stop the press conference."

Rae frowned. "Speaking of our former employee, Dr. Mike 'Traitor' Kane...I just can't believe it!" I've got to hand it to her, though, Rae didn't let it get her down. "Well, no use beating ourselves up about it now. Let's move forward and take a look at just what we've got on hand here." That's my sis, ever the optimist in life! She moved around the room, flipping every switch and lever and button that she could find into the 'ON' position. The screens lit up and gave off their electric blue glow, and she selected a feed showing a real-time stream of the conference center, from several different angles. The Null Corp Building meeting hall was a room the size of a small basketball stadium with rows of folding chairs set throughout, with a raised stage at one end where Colin would make his presentation. There was a long buffet table at the other end, loaded down with food and drink for the reporters. Two workers were puttering about on the stage, setting up AV equipment for the big event. I noticed a real-time timestamp in the upper left-hand corner of the screen and groaned. "Oh no! The conference starts in just about fifteen minutes, and we've struck out on Plans A, B *and* C! And failed even on my own personal plan that involved tying Colin up and locking him in a broom closet for the rest of the day..."

As if in response to my distress, the screen showed an image of Colin as he entered the conference center. He approached the stage, followed closely by our (former) head of security. I groaned again. "There he is, that fink! And Mike, too. Make it a pair of finks!" From all the hustle and bustle going on in that conference hall, it was evident that they were just seconds from opening the doors and letting the journalists all file in and take their seats.

Rae started chewing on her lower lip, a signal that her big brain was going into overdrive. "Okay, it looks as if we're down to the wire, Little Sis. We can't count on any help from the cousins, they're either stuck in New Jersey or currently *en route* back here to the big city. We're faced with only two options remaining." She held up her index finger. "Number One. The first option is to figure out some way to maybe revive Plan B or Plan C by making our way to the security center."

"Fat chance of that," I grumbled, staring at the monitor, "Look, the reporters are starting to file into the conference room already. Besides, we *did* promise Frank and Nancy that we would stay in this room and not try to escape. For what that's worth."

"That's true. So then there's Number Two." Rae poked another finger up to join the first one in a 'V' symbol. "We figure out some way to snatch victory from the jaws of defeat, right here and right now, with a Plan D!"

I laughed. Bitterly. "Not much chance of that, either, I'm afraid. Colin has got security coming out of his ears down there, more bruisers working the floor than I would ever imagine that he had on his payroll." I pointed to the screen. Our enemy was no longer anywhere in sight, and the reporters had begun to drift into the auditorium and settle in for the big show. "See, here's three goons flanking the stage. There's another pair on the main floor directly between the crowd and the podium. Another one at the main door. And that's not all, I can pick out another three or four mixing in with the crowd, pretending to be reporters and mingling among the invited journalists."

Rae laughed, but not a sour, sad little laugh like mine had been. She sounded actually and honestly amused. "Check it out, there at the food table. One of our captors is availing herself of the complimentary refreshments. That is, there's

Nancy grabbing a bunch of tiny quiches and stuffing them into a paper bag!"

I had to admit, that was pretty funny. Then another familiar face caught my eye. "Look there at the podium, that Null Corp employee who is plugging in the directional microphones and adjusting the smart spotlights. I know her, she's a hardware engineer who specializes in cutting-edge tech. She does a lot of freelancing, because she got fired from one of the big defense contractors for selling a bunch of secret new developments to a competitor. Corporate espionage, they call it."

My sister looked at me and pursed her lips. "Well, well, well, you don't say? Now *that* is interesting." She got a far-off look in her eyes, then shook her head and started messing with the control panel. "Sis, give me a hand. Let's see exactly what there is for us to work with here."

"Why? The only reason we were able to escape from the last locked room was because we had the BrightEyes to help us. But here and now, there are no special circuits for us to duplicate, and even if there were, there's no way for us to do it. Besides, there's no point in it because the doors are chained shut. Plus, we promised that we wouldn't." Despite my *kvetching*, I rolled my chair over to one of the control banks and started pushing buttons and flipping switches to see what would happen. "But okay. Let's see what we got. Anything in particular you want me to look for, or should I just play with knobs until something breaks?"

"Oh, if I'm right, and I usually am, the object of our exploration will become evident upon discovery. That is, you'll know what you're looking for when you find it."

"Sis, you are *so* weird." But the crazy thing was, I started getting the feeling that maybe she was right on the money.

The controls felt familiar, somehow. I decided it would be nice to zoom one of the camera views in a little bit for a closer view and I found the controls on the first try. I wanted to fire up the other monitors on the wall bank, and my fingers went to the proper toggle switches without any hesitation or error.

"How's it feel?" Rae asked me, with a knowing smile.

I shot her a puzzled scowl. "I'll tell you how it feels. It feels as if I've worked these controls before, but I think you already know that. What gives? What's going on in that super-sized brain of yours?"

Ignoring my question, she said, "Since you seem to be pretty much at ease with these controls, do me a favor, will you? Give me a super-close zoom-in on all of that audio-visual technology gear at the podium and the foot of the stage, huh?"

I made myself more comfortable, really settled in at the control panel, grabbed the pair of headphones sitting off to the side of the desk, plugged them into a jack on the board in front of me, put them on and got to work. I realized that the control panel was set up in a configuration that was very similar to my own gear back at the Team Rugged Stuff labs. "Okay," I mumbled to myself, "just about anyone who has worked with AV tech before could exercise some rudimentary control over the cameras with the analog gear, but the digital system might give me a lot more power over what we can see." I put my right hand on an ergonomic mouse/joystick and the left one on a big keyboard built into the panel and I felt...at home. It was as if the control system had been made for me. Tappity-tap-tap on the keyboard. It was comfortable and... familiar. "Booting, booting, boot— and I'm in! Okay, let's take this baby for a test drive." I dropped myself into the (figurative) current and went with the (digital) flow, pulling up a video feed from the conference room's security cams. I cut in really tight on the equipment Rae had asked for and threw them up on a split screen on one of the large side monitors so we could take a good look at it, while still keeping an eye on the stage and on the rest of the room.

My attention was on the control panel rather than the screens; I was *still* trying to figure out why it was all so comfortable. But Rae peered intently at the images I had pulled up and then gave another laugh. And this one wasn't just an amused laugh, it also had an aggressive, victorious undertone. "Ha-ha-HA! Hey, Danae! As our new friend Nessa," (at this, I made a 'ptui-ptui' sound as if I had just tasted something disgusting) "likes to say, *I* know something *you* don't know."

"Okay, even though you had to sink so low as to go and bring her into the conversation, I'll bite. What do you know that I don't know?"

"I know that Colin thinks very highly of your work in the field of audio-visual technology. Including your work in holography. He likes it so much that he stole your work from Team Rugged Stuff."

Oh, that? That was old news. "Ha, the joke's on you," I replied, "I already knew that. I knew that when I saw the AV gear that he used to project that little image of himself from the booby-trapped treasure chest over at the BrightEyes beach in the OtherWorld. Don't you remember?"

"Yes, yes," my sis retorted, still sounding very amused, "Well, then, let me go one step further. He likes your work so much that he stole it and IS USING IT IN HIS CONFERENCE ROOM EQUIPMENT RIGHT NOW AT THIS VERY MINUTE."

What? "I, um, hmmm. What?"

"Take a look for yourself."

I focused on the split screen and looked at the tech gear set up there. The casing was a little different, but when I saw the lenses and the input/output setup, I could see that Rae was exactly correct! That was *my* technology he was using in his AV equipment! "Argh! *That's* why everything seems so familiar! These controls don't just *feel* like they were made for me, they really *were made* for me! Or at least designed by me!" Yup, there may have been a few extra bells and a couple of additional whistles, but now I could recognize that this control panel was configured to fit with my very own system!

Rae looked smug as all get-out, but given this particular situation, I figured I could forgive her for that. "Affirmative! When you mentioned the fact about that woman down there who is working for Colin, the fact about her being a tech pirate, it got me to thinking and then everything just kind of fell into place."

"Huh, what do you know? And now that we found out about our ops director who was in reality a traitor in our midst, it's obvious how Colin was able to steal all our research and our tech and everything else. The pilfered info was sent to Null Corp, and Colin's team, including the tech pirate, who implemented it for him. I wonder just how long Mike has been feeding him all of the data from all of our files?"

"He's been helping Colin for quite a while, if all of this," Rae gestured to the equipment in the room, "is any indication. But now let me take my ideas even one step *further*." As if I could ever stop her once she got to brainstorming! "I know that whenever you write computer code, you put in a sort of a back door into the program, right? A secret password or process that can give you access into the heart of the software?"

"Yeah. And I'm not the only one who does it. Even though it's kind of frowned upon, it's a pretty standard practice throughout the industry." Whatever she was getting at, she'd better get there soon. Watching the video feed from the conference center, about half of the seats were filled and journalists were still coming into the room. This ship was about to set sail, this train was about to leave the station. But I'm afraid there's no stopping my sister when she's decided to follow a particular line of inquiry!

"And your AV equipment actually runs on *your* own proprietary software, right? Isn't that one of the upgrades that makes your equipment work so much better than tech gear that is designed and sold by the larger corporations?

"Well, yeah. Not only is all of the input digitally scrubbed when it comes into the equipment, but all of the control signals—like the volume, direction, even the on and off switches—are converted to digital input/output and run through a helper-program algorithm to make the physical components more responsive to the needs of the person controlling the equipment." (I guess I'm just as bad as Rae! Even though we were in a time crunch, I was willing to yammer on for hours about my work!)

And then it finally dawned on me. I finally understood what my sister was getting at. (Yeah, yeah, I'm sure it has already occurred to anyone reading this. I'll admit it, I was kind of slow on the uptake at the time. So sue me, I was under just a little bit of stress at the time!) "Hey!" I yelled. "Hey! That means that from *this* control panel, I can get in through my 'back door' and control the AV equipment down there!"

Rae grinned. "Yeah, Little Sister, that's kind of what I was thinking!"

"I could shut it all down! Completely blank out all of the gear! Maybe they'll have to postpone the conference!" I put on my radio-announcer voice. "Plan B comes from behind for a stunning photo finish!"

But to my surprise, Rae was shaking her head 'No' at me.

"Huh?" I asked. "We *don't* shut it down?"

Rae grinned even more. "Nope, Sis. Not Plan B. Plans A through C are history. We're moving on to Plan D."

That's my big sister. She's a puzzlement. "Okay, Rae. If shutting down the conference isn't your big idea, then just what exactly *is* the plan that you've got rattling around in your head? Plan D, if I remember correctly, is to 'snatch victory from the jaws of defeat,' right?"

Her voice got kind of dreamy. "Affirmative. If we cause the press conference to be cancelled, that just buys us some time, and we're faced with the same problem a little bit later. Colin could just set up another conference for next week, before we could get ourselves organized to counter him. That's not victory. Harken to me, my younger sibling, and let me describe to you our Plan Delta."

"OMG, you really *are* so weird! But tell me what's on your mind."

And so she did. It only took about two minutes, but all the while, more and more journalists were filing into the conference room, as we could see on the monitors. It got to the point where there were no more seats available for them, and the latecomers had to find places to stand at the back of the room near the food table. When Rae finished explaining her Plan D to me, she asked earnestly, "So? What do you think?"

I pondered. Hard. "It could work. It really could work! But it would all really depend on you. Do you think you are really prepared for something that difficult?"

That's when she got that mad, determined look on her face again. "Prepared or not, it's something that HAS to be done."

If this was going to work, we both had our jobs to do. Rae started doing some stretches and running through voice exercises while I turned my attention to the control panel in front of me and booted up every last piece of electrical gear in the room, from microphones and cameras to toggles and switches, from software to hardware and from soup to nuts.

Chapter 28

DANAE'S LOG 20:
Lights, Camera,
Action!

The conference room was full to the brim with people, and thanks to all of Null Corp's security and surveillance equipment, I had a perfect view of every*thing* and every*one*.

The whole show was running just a little bit late. It was about ten minutes after the time when the conference had been scheduled to begin when Mike—or should I say, *Mike-Fink*—climbed onto the stage and tapped the microphone, causing a squeal of feedback. From my master panel here in the comm room, I had hacked into all of the controls for the AV gear, so I moved a slider button on my console from its position at '*4*' all the way up to '*10*', intensifying the feedback into an ear-piercing screech that made everyone in the room wince. Go ahead and call me petty if you like, but I saw the chance to make Mike look stupid, and I took it!

Flustered, Mike started to speak into the microphone. I abruptly cut the sound, so no one could hear what he was saying. Then, as he raised his voice, I switched it back on, resulting in another attack on the crowd's eardrums. The room boomed with his voice saying, "GENTLEMEN AND—" Mike was so embarrassed that his ears turned red. But now that I had had my fun, I put all of the microphone settings back to normal, so that when he tried again, it came out just fine. "Ahem. Gentlemen and ladies of the press, it is my pleasure to introduce the head of Null Corporation, Mr. Colin Null. Please hold your applause until the end of his announcement; a question-and-answer session will follow the presentation."

Colin stepped up to the podium. Mike didn't get out of his way fast enough and ended up getting shouldered aside by his (new) boss. After a slight flash of annoyance, Colin put a big, faux-friendly grin on his face and spoke into the microphone. "Thank you! Thank you! Members of the fourth estate, thank you!" He paused, waiting for the crowd to clap, but they all looked kind of hesitant. I mean, Mike had just told them to please hold their applause, after all, so no one was quite sure what to do. A few of the reporters finally gave a few weak claps and then the room went quiet again. But I've got to hand it to Colin, he took it all in stride. He was dressed to impress, with an expensive Italian suit and his fresh-trimmed haircut and he looked sharp. Worse than that, he looked honest and friendly and believable. Moving right along, he began his pitch. "Friends, I promised you the story of the century, so without further delay, I give you—the OtherWorld!" (That thieving little slimeball didn't even bother to change the name that Rae and I had used for our discovery!)

Colin pushed a button on the digital control panel on his podium. I could see it all as it happened, because I had a digital, real-time, mirror-copy of his controls displayed on a small touch-screen monitor on the desk in front of me. The conference-room lights dimmed and a three-dimensional holographic representation of the Earth was projected above the crowd. It was a spectacular image, if I do say so myself... after all, it was my own design, and my new holo-tech just can't be beat!

But I could see that the globe was being projected just a tad too low in the air for the audience members who were sitting directly below it to get the full effect of the image. Ever so gently, I used my control toggle to budge the projection just a little bit higher, maybe five meters higher and closer to the auditorium-style ceiling. I didn't want anyone in the room to miss out on the show that was about to take place. On the video monitor that gave me a perfect view of Colin, I could see him look a little puzzled when the image moved, apparently all by itself, but he didn't worry about it for too long, because he had to continue his speech.

"Earth!" he announced grandly (as if anyone in the crowd of journalists wouldn't recognize the globe spinning in the air above them!) "Home to humanity! But as humanity's knowledge has grown, our world has grown smaller. Just as young chicks outgrow the nest, mankind has outgrown the planet. But young birds have only to spring up, out and away from their childhood home and spread their wings in order to fly off to explore a new world. Sadly, humanity has been trapped in this nest that we call home." All the while he was speaking, the holographic images were giving a really impressive show, with the camera angle seemingly swooping in from outer space, closer and closer to the planet's surface, finally to ground level and then a closeup to a bird's nest, showing a trio of bluebird chicks leaving the nest for the very first time. In the dim light, Colin was barely visible on the stage, enjoying the sound of his own voice and grinning at the effect that the graphics had on the crowd. He looked so pleased with the result that you'd think he had developed the projection technology himself!

"For far too long, man has been trapped at the bottom of a gravity well. We have attempted to escape, to explore beyond our nest, our home, our planet, but the costs have been too great." Images of early spacecraft, followed by footage of NASA's space shuttle and the International Space Station. "Even the shuttle program eventually came to an end, and today, it costs some $10,000 to put a pound of payload into orbit. With that kind of a price tag, only a 90-pound weaklin' can afford to go into space for much less than a cool million dollars!" There was a polite chuckle from the audience.

Since I had access to the program that he was using to project the holograms, I could see exactly what Colin was leading up to, but it was still a masterful feat of manipulation. He was winding up the reporters to make them think that he had developed some new sort of space travel, so that when he changed course and talked about the OtherWorld, the announcement would make even more of an impact, would be even more spectacular. Say what you will, our sworn enemy is quite a showman.

Annnnnd, here it came. "But what if someone were to discover *another* place, a *different* place, a place that doesn't exist out beyond our planet's atmosphere, but instead, just around the proverbial corner?"

The hologram swirled above the audience like paint on a gyroscope, then coalesced into a large, psychedelic question mark, pulsating in time with Colin's voice.

"And what if someone were to develop a technology that would allow us to access that place? Well, I'll tell you one thing, it wouldn't be easy, oh no. In fact, it's not likely that anyone other than the most adventurous, the most intelligent, the most darin' of today's researchers could accomplish it!" His voice swelled to a crescendo. "But what if that someone could create a portal to a...whole...new...world!?"

That was my cue! According to the speech that Colin had loaded into his teleprompter (and that I was following on my monitor), he would now pause, and the room would go dark. He would let the crowd mutter amongst themselves for about 20 seconds, then a spotlight would focus on him. If everything went according to his carefully choreographed plans, he was just about getting ready to say to the audience, "An' I'm here to tell you that that's exactly what I have done! I have created a portal to a new world!" Then the itinerary was about 15 minutes of him talking about how cool the OtherWorld is and how great he is for discovering it.

But all of that isn't important, because that's *not* how things went down. Like I said, his *whole new world* line was our cue. Now it was time for Team Rugged Stuff to jump into action!

With a quick crack of my knuckles and a quick tap of the keyboard—all made possible by my secret back door into the pirated software and hardware that was running the Null Corp communications network—I took control of the conference room audio-visual equipment. ALL of it. COMPLETE and FULL control. No more nudges or tweaks, no more little pranks. Nope. I exerted my mastery over

EVERYTHING...all of the tech in the press conference, along with the equipment here in the communications room. I felt like Mozart or Beethoven or Salieri or some other old-timey musician sitting down and running my fingers up and down the keys of a baby grand piano.

Colin's choreography? *Colin's* itinerary? Phooey on *that*. This had just become *my* show.

I killed the hologram, plunging the room into darkness, making some of the reporters gasp, just as Colin's script called for. So far, there was no way yet for our rival to realize that *his* plans no longer had any bearing on the event.

But that didn't last long. Because when I turned the spotlight on, it didn't highlight Colin. No, he was still standing there in the dark. Instead, it revealed my sis, Rachel Rugg, the elder partner of Team Rugged Stuff and the world's top young scientist adventurer. The audience saw her standing on the stage—off to the side of where Colin had positioned himself—and beaming a big old grin out to the crowd, smiling as if she had just won the lottery or something. She held a microphone in her hand and hollered into it, "Helloooooo, New York!" She looked just like the lead singer in a rock band about to start a concert in Madison Square Garden. I worked the slide button on my panel like a pro, keeping her greeting loud—but not too loud—adjusting the undertones, the bass and the treble so that her voice came out warm and beautiful and glorious. (There is so much more that goes into effective and persuasive communication than just the *words* you use... frequency and amplitude of the voice is a *huge* part of how well-received a verbal presentation is. I wrote a paper on it, you should read it sometime.) Then I killed the spotlight and brought the house lights up, so everyone could see Colin up there on the stage in addition to Rae.

Before he could even react, she quarter-turned in his direction, facing him and the audience together. "Colin Null, thank you *so* much for that wonderful introduction! How did you put it? 'The most adventurous, the most intelligent, the most daring of today's researchers'? Well, I'm much too modest to apply those labels to my sister and myself..." she turned to the crowd and winked, "but if that's how you want to describe us, I certainly won't argue with you!" That got a big laugh from the reporters.

All eyes were on Rae, but if anyone had happened to glance at Colin just then, they might have noticed the look of confusion, and then anger, that swept across his face before he regained his composure and plastered a sickly smile on his mug. Behind him, Mike Kane looked as if he were having a heart attack. For real. He even clutched at his chest. I made a pledge to myself that if he actually collapsed, I'd put an emergency call in for an ambulance, but otherwise, I needed to pay full attention to the presentation that was taking place.

Rae continued speaking to the audience, and I'm here to tell you, she had them eating out of her hand. "For anyone here in the group who doesn't know me, I'm Rachel Rugg, and together with my sister Danae, we are Team Rugged Stuff, and we are what you in the media have dubbed 'scientist adventurers.' And those of you who *do* know me, you'll remember that my sister and I have had quite the friendly rivalry with Colin Null and his Null Corporation over the years." There were some snorts of amusement from the reporters at the use of the word 'friendly'...they all knew very well that we couldn't stand each other! "That's why it's so very gratifying to have him introduce me as I present the latest research and tech development from the Rugg sisters." She turned a little further toward Colin and gave him a polite little golf clap, which was joined in on by the journalists. He responded with a tight facial expression that was more grimace than smile, and nodded weakly.

While Rachel continued speaking, I saw Colin finally get the big idea to cut her off by turning his microphone back on and taking control of the audio-visual gear from the panel on the podium. I laughed out loud as he tapped the buttons, and then when, getting no result, he started to pound on them. Without trying to draw attention from the reporters in the audience, he gestured for Mike to join him at the controls to try to get them to respond for him.

Rae went on, "In fact, in appreciation to Colin for making all of the arrangements for this press conference—for providing the space, inviting the media, and even for bringing in all the refreshments (make sure to try the caviar and champagne!), Team Rugged Stuff is happy to present him with a little thank-you gift." He gave another little half-hearted nod to her, but his attention was still on his dead control panel, where Mike was also unsuccessfully trying to get the controls to work. But with Rae's next words, she had ALL of his attention!

"One of our top employees, Dr. Michael Kane, has been working with Colin on this whole thing recently. So Team Rugged Stuff would like to formally announce that Dr. Kane will be joining Null Corp on a full-time and permanent basis. He is, as of this moment, completely and entirely Colin Null's responsibility from now and forever more." Her voice took on a certain, diamond-sharp edge. I'm sure some of the reporters must have noticed it, but they couldn't have had any clue about the reason why. On the stage, Rae turned her attention to the pair standing at the podium. "Colin, we hope that Mike proves to be every bit as loyal and helpful to you as he has been to us." They both turned beet red at this inside verbal jab. Ha! That's the way to stick it to 'em, Sis!

"And now, back to the question that Colin posed to you! What if, indeed, someone—well, let's not be coy, shall we? That is, what if *Team Rugged Stuff* could create a portal to *a whole new world*?" She favored the crowd with a warm grin. "And as I'm sure you've deduced by now—because let's face it, you all didn't get to be the top journalists in the field by virtue of *not* making intelligent deductions!—we can get rid of the qualifying phrase, *What if?* Let's leave those weak words behind, because Danae and I have accomplished it. It is no longer a question of *what if*. I stand before you right now to announce that we *have* developed a portal technology to another world, to a hitherto unknown location! Whether it is a doorway to a different dimension or it is a gate to a site located within our own time-and-space framework is yet unknown."

Then she raised her eyebrows and spoke in a hushed, conspiratorial voice, a stage whisper that made it seem as if she were letting the reporters in on a little secret that she was keeping from our Irish rival. "Although, unlike Colin, we on Team Rugged Stuff aren't quite ready to give up on space travel yet, thank you very much, and we look forward to great leaps in interplanetary exploration in the next few years, as well!"

The people in the crowd laughed as they frantically took notes.

"There's too much detail to go into right here and now. That's why I'd like to take this opportunity to invite each and every one of you to schedule an *individual* interview with my sister and myself. We'll meet with you wherever you like. Or we will host you out at our lab facilities at Tahoe. You will each get exclusive and personalized information tailored to be pertinent to you and your news organization's focus."

A collective gasp went up from the crowd. Most of the reporters had hoped to get a good sound bite or quote from the event. But the opportunity to get a full-blown interview about a whole new scientific discovery was a chance in a lifetime for most of these journalists. It would be one big pile of work for Rae and me to come through on this promise, but on the other hand, by discussing the whole project in such depth with each of them, it would prove beyond any doubt that *we* were responsible for the OtherWorld discovery and technology. Colin would *never* be able to come back and steal the credit for the OtherWorld from us after this!

Rachel wrapped up her presentation with, "We're counting on your coverage to help us introduce this new world—this OtherWorld—to *our* world, in a way that will be most beneficial for *both* worlds. To explore the OtherWorld in the spirit of preservation, rather than exploitation. Thank you for joining with us in this wonderful new discovery!" The journalists loved it. Rae was treating them as partners in the story, rather than as tools to be manipulated for her own goals. Who says nice guys have to finish last?!

"Colin has shared his invitation list with us," (Well, maybe he didn't exactly *share* it with us. It would have been more accurate to say that we had *obtained* a copy of the list, since I had hacked into the computer files and appropriated it!), "and the Team Rugged Stuff organization will be contacting each of you individually over the next few days in order to schedule your interviews. In the meantime, I think I can field a few quick questions." This was the part I was an itsy-bitsy worried about. Rae had been able to pull off her big act up until now, but actually inviting the reporters to interact with her was maybe pushing our luck, I thought.

But I guess in order to explain why I was concerned, I'll have to go back a bit and clue you in on just what was taking place, how Rae came to be addressing the crowd of journalists in the first place.

Right. So let me back up and remind you what I had going for me. Colin had pirated all of my tech for his own audio-visual gear. That means hardware and software. And I've already talked about how I used my back door to get in and take control of the software that in turn gave me control of the hardware. But let's take a *look* at that hardware. Colin had a hologram projector (*my* hologram projector!) set up in the conference room. And here in the control room, part of the gear included a camera and microphone, also all based on my own personal technological upgrades. See where I'm going here? Right? Right! All of the technology that Colin was using was really Team Rugged Stuff tech. And just a few days ago, I had pushed out an upgrade to that tech to allow for absolutely perfect, 360-degree hologram projection! AND I had programmed a fail-safe emergency secret entrance into the software that runs the hardware!

So I took control of the AV gear, here *and* there, and I mean *complete* control, including holographic *INPUT* and *OUTPUT*. Rae *looked* as if she was on the stage, but she was really just acting it out here in the AV room. I had a digital camera capture her image and scrub all the background out. Then I sent it down to the conference room holoprojector where it presented her image onto the stage. By watching the monitors very closely, she could adjust her movements and act as if she were really right there looking at Colin or the crowd and make it seem very realistic. Just like when a movie actor is filming in front of a green screen and reacting to stimulus that isn't really there. And just like how the final product from one of those big special-effects movies can look so real, that's what it was like with Rae and her performance.

And she had done a bang-up job! Sitting here watching her image on the stage, it was practically impossible to tell that it wasn't really her in the flesh and blood down there, even when I could see her out of the corner of my eye here in the control room. For someone who *didn't* know that that wasn't really her on the stage (meaning everyone who wasn't me or Rae), there's *no way* they could have known the reality behind the appearance, other than by actually going up to her and trying to touch her image.

But now she was going to actually verbally interact with audience members. Or more accurately, she was going to have to make her hologram look as if it were interacting with audience members. Rae was going to have to simulate eye contact and judge subtle movements in the crowd. I mean, I knew that she was good at this sort of stuff. I mean, *really* good. I just didn't know if she was *that* good.

"Are you sure about this, Sis?" I hissed as I shot her a questioning glance, whispering softly enough that the microphones wouldn't pick me up, "Remember, I've upgraded the hologram software for the *image*, but the AI algorithms aren't ready yet! The digital program won't be able to make your hologram react to its environment...in other words, you'll have to make it look like the 'you' down there is interacting with them even though the real 'you' is locked up here in the comm center!"

Rae took a deep breath, shot me a reassuring glance that said, *Don't worry...I've totally got this, D!*

And she did! I'm here to tell you that my sis absolutely rocked it like a boss.

As soon as she invited questions, dozens of hands shot up. Rae laughed. "Remember, these are going to be quick questions and short answers! I'm not going to go into much detail right now, because then you might never get to the drinks and desserts at the after party! In fact, it looks as if some of Colin's staffers have already gotten into the complimentary food and drink!" The Rae-on-stage gestured to the back of the room, and yup, it was obvious that someone (in fact, it was Nancy, our friendly neighborhood security guard, remember?) had put quite a dent in the refreshments. It was another stroke of brilliance on Rae's part, another way to absolutely solidify in everyone's minds that she was on stage, large and in charge and in the flesh. Not that it seemed that anyone had any doubts to begin with, but you know...just in case.

Rae turned her attention back to the reporters. "How about you, Mary, do you have one for me?" My holographic sis pointed to a science reporter from the National Geographic magazine with whom she had met and chatted a few times in the past.

Mary beamed. "Thanks, Rachel. I know you'll go into this more later on, but there's one subject that just can't wait. The first thing that scientists looked for on the Moon, on Mars, even on Comet 67P, was evidence of organic material. To put it bluntly, is there life on this brave new world you've discovered?"

It seemed that everyone in the room was holding their breath. Rae nodded. "There is definitely life. The initial OtherWorld point opened onto an island that exhibited tropical vegetation very similar to that found here on Earth. And I'll go you one further. There are multiple flora that produce fruits compatible with, and edible by, fauna from our own world here, our own Earth."

A collective gasp. The reporter spoke again quickly, before anyone else could steal the spotlight. "Vegetation? Okay, that's a starting point. But what about animal life there? What about, even, *sentient* life?'

The room went absolutely silent. Even Colin and Mike leaned forward to hear what Rae would say. She pursed her lips and spoke thoughtfully. "Mary, in all honesty, I'm not quite sure how to answer that. What I *will* say is that we *will* be including both cryptozoologists and cognitive scientists in our core exploratory team."

A collective yelp rose from the crowd. "That's a 'yes,' then?" Mary pushed for an answer.

Rae smiled. "We will be including cryptozoologists and cognitive scientists in our core exploratory team," Rae repeated and that's all she would say. "Next?"

I zoomed in on Colin's face. He looked absolutely stunned. *Sucker*, I thought. Unnoticed by the crowd, he finally gave up his efforts to regain control of the AV gear and then he stalked off the stage, pushing Mike ahead of him.

A hipster-looking guy with short hair, big glasses and about three-days worth of stubble on his face waved his hand to catch Rae's attention and she called on him. "Hey Bongo! Nice to see you here!" she said. You might not know it by looking at him, but this was the internet's most cutting-edge tech journalist. Then again, maybe that's exactly what you would expect him to look like.

"And it's nice to be seen!" he replied. "Now, you've talked a lot about Team Rugged Stuff and about your and your sister's discovery—but I don't see her here today. What is Danae up to while you're here pitching to us? Can we get her out here and have her give us her take, her viewpoint on all of this?"

Ha. No way *I* was going to try to pull off a remote, blind conversation! I shook my head an emphatic "No" before the final word was out of his mouth.

Sis took my none-too-subtle hint. "Oh, she's handling some of the technical aspects of the conference. In fact, without her expertise, you wouldn't see me up here talking to you about this." The real Rae in the communications room with me gave a quick glance over my way. The movement made it look as if the virtual Rae on the stage was making a quick scan of the crowd. "And I mean that quite literally!"

She must have felt that she had established beyond any doubt that she really was in the room, and that Team Rugged Stuff really had discovered the OtherWorld, because she raised her arms over her head and clapped her hands. "I'm afraid that's it for today, folks! Please feel free to make your way to the back of the room to eat, drink and be merry. Don't let the security folk eat it all, they don't really need any between-meal snacks. Take some food home for the dogs, the kids, the significant others—after all, Colin and Null Corp are footing the bill!"

Hologram Rae made for the back of the stage and once she reached the curtains, I cut the audio and video feed and gave Rae in-real-life the thumbs-up sign. Then we both collapsed—Rae on the floor, me in my chair—exhausted and exhilarated.

"Cut it! Print it! That's a wrap!" I yelled.

"Best performance of my life!" Rae yelled.

"What a field test for my AV gear! I told you it was state-of-the-art!"

"You did! And it is!"

"You were spot on! I could hardly believe you weren't really there!"

"Did you record it?! I want to make an animated GIF of Colin's reaction when he saw me on the stage and send it to him!"

"Yeah! And Mike, too! The possibilities for some hilarious memes are simply endless!"

I finally calmed down enough to wipe the sweat from my brow and the tears from my eyes. "I had one camera pretty much zoomed in on Colin the whole time. I recorded the whole thing and saved it into a file and I already emailed it to us! I'll swear that Colin never did tumble to the fact of how you could possibly be on the stage when you were supposed to be locked up here the whole time."

Rae had finally caught her breath, too. "Hmmmmm. Then that would mean..."

It struck me what she was talking about. "Oh. Whoops. You're right. Then Colin is..."

Both of us simultaneously. "...ON HIS WAY UP HERE RIGHT NOW!"

Chapter 29

DANAE'S LOG 21:
Just Us, and Justice

I spun back around to the control desk and managed to tap into the building's security surveillance feed, then used it to locate Colin and Mike. They were in the elevator, on their way up and heading our in our direction. And I was delighted to find that the security cams included audio, because their conversation was priceless.

SECURITY CAM TRANSCRIPT

Colin: An' how many times must you fail me before I understand how truly incompetent you are? 'Yes, Colin, the girls are locked up tight. No, Colin, there's no way they can get loose this time, yes, Colin, I'm absolutely sure of it.' Well, I'll tell you what, Mikey, me boyo, you Make. Me. Sick.

Mike: But they just *couldn't* have gotten loose! I have guards posted on them to make sure of it!

Colin: Oh, I see. You tell me that they *could nae* have escaped from your guards. An' because of that, they *did nae* escape from your guards. And I *did nae* see Rachel Rugg up there on the stage takin' credit for the OtherWorld project. And they *did nae* absolutely undo over a year's worth—to say nothing of millions of dollars' worth!—of plannin' and plottin' and schemin'. Thank you ever so much for explaining that to me. [pause] An *that* was sarcasm, just in case you are too incompetent to pick up on my tone of voice.

Mike: No, no, you'll see! When we get to the room where I have the guards holding them, you'll see! And as for the project, it's not too late, you can hold a new press conference, tell the reporters that Rachel was wrong, was mistaken, or that they stole *your* research, or—

Colin: Oh, grow up, Kane! It's done! The whole point of this dog-an'-pony show was to be the first to announce and to take credit. To the scientific community, that's all that matters... smart people can be just as dumb as everyone else, but that's just how things work. If I had established authorship of the research here and now, the Rugg girls would never have been able to sufficiently reclaim it. Or at least not in time to make any difference. But they pulled the old switcheroo on me. On ME! There is *no way* for me to repair that damage, the damage for which you are directly responsible!

END OF SECURITY CAM TRANSCRIPT

I gave my sis a high five. That's exactly what we wanted to hear!

The monitor showed the elevator doors opening and I switched my feed from the interior camera there to the exterior one in the foyer. Mike was wringing his hands and practically babbling. "No, no it just couldn't be. Come, come, follow me and I'll *show* you!" He didn't even care that Colin's big plan had failed, he just wanted to somehow prove that *he* wasn't the one who should get blamed for the failure. What a chump.

We watched on the monitor as the two of them came down the hall and approached Frank and Nancy standing there, right outside the doors to the very room in which we were locked. Mike looked startled to see them both there in the hall, instead of being inside the room and guarding us in person, but he didn't want to show any uncertainty in front of his bad-tempered new, official, employer.

"You there! The two of you!" Mike practically yelled at the guards, he was so frantic. I was loving it. "Tell me, did either of the two Rugg girls leave this room?"

Me and Rachel were both curious as to what their response would be. As far as they were concerned, they knew there was no way for us to get out other than through those doors, and at least one of them had stood watch on-site and in person for the entire time. We hadn't left the room through those doors. Therefore, as far as they were concerned, we hadn't left the room, period. (And they were right!) But from Mike's demeanor, they could tell that *something* had obviously gone sideways, so they decided to take the same strategy as Mike; namely, the old 'I-don't-know-what-happened-but-I-do-know-that-it-wasn't-MY-fault' routine.

"Did. They. Leave. This. Room?" Mike repeated.

Nancy and Frank both looked at him like he was crazy. Then they both turned and looked at the length of chain that was still securely wrapped around the handles of the locked doors. Then they looked at each other. Nancy finally replied. "Um, Mr. Kane? There ain't been nobody getting through *these* doors. They're, um, chained up pretty tight."

Mike narrowed his eyes and hissed in a low voice, hoping that Colin wouldn't hear it, "And just *why* are they 'chained up pretty tight'? I believe I gave you explicit orders to guard those two in person?"

Frank fielded this one. He put his hand to his chest as if aggrieved that anyone could possibly question their motives in not staying in the room with us. After brushing away a bunch of crumbs on the front of his uniform (so at least we know that Nancy shared some of those mini quiches with him!) he started his own little presentation. "Well, you see, you made it sound like those two girls are some kinda super spies or somethin'. So we wuz thinkin', maybe they might have some kind of knockout gas with 'em or something."

"Or maybe they might be able to *hyp-mo-tize* us, maybe," Nancy chimed in.

"Yeah, that!" Frank continued. "So we figured it'd be better to not let something like that happen, so we could make sure they couldn't get away. So we chained 'em in." Now he drew himself up with a saintly air. "After all, no one can hypmotize three feet of iron chain, now, can they?"

All in all, the two guards weren't terribly convincing about *why* they weren't in the room with us, but there wasn't much Mike could do about it. He was fuming, with his face all red. But his face didn't stay red for long. When he turned to speak to Colin again, the look on his boss's face made all the color drain away, and he looked as white as a sheet.

Colin spoke. He spoke in a voice that was low. Soft. Deadly. "*This* is where you locked the Rugg girls? Two of the most innovative and talented tech nerds in the world, and you thought it would be a good idea to lock them in a room full of..." He paused. Then screamed. "*...FULL OF COMMUNICATION TECHNOLOGY?*"

He was trembling with rage. It was a wonderful sight to see! Gradually, he calmed down just a bit and started mumbling to himself. "That might explain how they could control the lights and microphone, but...but not how Rachel could have gotten out of there and all the way down to the conference room. Because, as stupid as you all are, you're right, there is no other way out of the room, no other exit." Now he spoke to the guards. "You there. Heckle and Jeckle." (I don't know who or what Heckle and Jeckle are, but from the way Rae giggled at that, I had to assume it was some old obscure pop culture reference.) "You are absolutely, absolutely, *absolutely certain* that no one left this room?"

From the looks on Nancy and Frank's faces, they didn't quite get what the Heckle and Jeckle crack meant either. They looked at Colin. They looked at the chain. They looked at each other.

"Uh, Mr. Null?" The big woman spoke up. "My name is Nancy. And this here is Frank. Do you want us to go find those other guys you said, um, those Heckie and Jackie guys?"

"Uh, 'cuz we'll be happy to do that for you," Frank joined in. "But about the other part, it's just a stone-cold fact, there ain't been *nobody* get out through these doors."

Even though Colin was nearly six feet tall, he still had to crane his neck to glare up into Frank's eyes. Both of the guards loomed over him, but our Irish rival didn't even flinch. He just gave one simple order. "Prove it."

Nancy and Frank looked at Colin. They looked at the chain. They looked at each other. Frank stuck his key in the padlock and removed it and Nancy began to unwrap the chain from the doors.

"Oh crikey!" I squeaked and jumped to my feet. I had been so entranced with the show taking place on the screen that I totally forgot about our situation! They would be coming into the room in just a few seconds! Rae hustled around and worked to hide any evidence of our activities, while my fingers flew over the control panel to shut down everything and put all the gear back to how it had been when we were first locked in here. But even with the security feed audio of the hallway turned off, we could hear the metallic clinking of the chains being pulled off the door!

We hadn't given much thought about how to play it when confronted by Colin, so I figured I'd just see what Rae had in mind and then follow her lead. (When in doubt, do what Rachel does!) We heard the last of the chain links slip off the handle. The doors burst open and Colin stomped in, with Mike hovering behind him like a worried chicken. Frank and Nancy brought up the rear.

As Colin opened his mouth to speak, Rae took the initiative and interrupted him in mid-breath. "Well, well, well! It's about time!"

This stopped Colin cold in his tracks. "Wait. What? Huh?" All of his indignant rage hissed out of him like a deflating balloon. Phhhhhhhhtt.

"I said, It's. About. Time. We've been cooling our heels here in this room for quite long enough. It's about time you unlocked the door and let us out. We've got places to go, things to do and people to meet."

I piped up. "And *I've* got to visit the ladies' room!"

Colin sputtered. "But... you... I..." It was an event nearly unprecedented in recent history; Colin Null had been rendered speechless! And the best thing was that he *still* didn't know how—or even *if*—we had gotten Rae onto that stage in order to steal his thunder out from underneath him.

Rae held her hand out to Frank in a no-nonsense gesture. Without a word, he handed over both of our bags that he had taken from us before locking us in the communications room. Rae marched herself out the door with me close on her heels, and I made sure to put a little flourish into each movement of my walking stick. The two guards just let us stride on by. I think there was a little hint of amusement lurking in their eyes at the way their ornery little boss was so flummoxed by the two of us, who I'm sure they still thought of as being little kids. Down the hall and into the elevator, and as the doors slid shut behind us, we could hear the sound of Colin yelling at Mike, "*Your* fault! All your fault!"

Rae turned to me with a wry look on her face. "So much for our dramatic exit...I forgot we can't use the executive elevator without the security badges that the guards took away from us!"

"Whoops, me too!" But I had the solution in mind. "To the stairwell!" Our earlier failures were now coming in handy and we had all the information that we needed in order to get out of this place.

"Oh right!" Rae nearly yelled in relief. "Like a funnel...everything flows toward the ground floor!" We double-timed it down the back hallway, Rae jogging and me hop-skipping (because of my leg), until we located the doorway to the stairs. Then it was a simple matter of making our way down to the ground floor, then through the lobby and onto the street, where we hailed a taxi back to our hotel.

Chapter 30

DANAE'S LOG 22:
Cut it, Print it,
That's a Wrap!

We had only been back in our hotel suite for about fifteen minutes—the adrenaline rush hadn't even faded yet—when there was a knock on the door. "Do you think Colin changed his mind and sent Frank and Nancy after us?" Rae pondered.

I shook my head. "Naw, if that was the case, they probably would have just busted the door down instead of knocking. I wonder if it could be Mike, though." I glanced through the peephole and got a fish-eye view of our unexpected guests. Happily, it wasn't anyone from the Null organization, but instead, some faces I was much more delighted to see; it was our cousins, Noah and Levi. I opened the door to let them in, but before they could take even one step, a terrible stench wafted in. I could practically see a green haze of noxious gasses floating around them, it was that eye-wateringly bad.

I held my nose and closed the door behind them while Rae made a big show of pretending to gag. "What is *that* all about? Do you guys want to visit the powder room to freshen up? And where's Nessa? Is she with you, or couldn't she stand to be around Messieurs PePe and Pierre LePew?" You could tell how giddy she was about our recent victory by the way she was razzing the guys.

Noah spoke up first in a dejected tone. "In reverse order, Nessa's not with us, and we don't know where she is. Probably back at her apartment. In the grand scheme of things, she's actually more of a stinker than we are, so *we* ditched *her*, instead of the other way around."

"Oh ho!" I exclaimed, "The Irish cutie-pie falls out of favor with the Rugg twins? Sounds like a story that I want to hear! And I won't even say I told you so!" Pause. "Well, I won't say it more than three or four times, anyway."

"And yes, please, the washroom would be much appreciated," said Levi, "And then we'll tell you the whole story, and more. But first, you both seem awfully chipper...can we assume that Plan B was successful?"

"Nope. But Plan D was!" Rae beamed, "and we'll tell you all about it. But first, *please* go and clean up!"

#

"...so as soon as Nessa vamoosed, I sent you the message. I didn't want to worry you—and plus, the info wouldn't help you any—so I didn't go into all the business about Nessa's ulterior motives. I just wanted to warn you as soon as I could that we weren't going to be of any help, and that Plan

A was a bust." Levi was stretched out on the sofa, giving us the background on their day, and smelling of scrubbed-clean lavender.

Noah was at the mini-fridge, freshly showered and water still dripping from the ends of his long hair, rummaging for something to eat. He finally gave up and grabbed an apple from the fruit basket on the table. "We just couldn't stand to be around her after what she did. But that left us to hoof it back from New Jersey on our own. As it turned out, the only other vehicles going in or out of that property were trash collection trucks, so we snuck a ride in the back of one that was heading this way. And here we are. Hence the um...delicate odor...that we acquired along the way."

#

The next morning, Rae and I caught a flight back home to the Reno-Tahoe International Airport. We rode in actual seats in the passenger cabin, this time, thank goodness. Izzy picked us up at the terminal and then it was just a quick drive out to the ol' homestead and back to our new fuzzy, furry, friendly little pals. Our older cousin had taken great care of them, and one of the BrightEyes even seemed to have adopted her as its own special friend. It was Crackly, one of the two remaining electricity-type BrightEyes. (Remember, Poppy had morphed into a forest-and-creek flavor...I couldn't *wait* to look into that development!) Izzy had decided to change the critter's name and had taken to calling her new buddy 'Ellie'...short for 'Electricity!'

"I hate to leave, but I've got to get back home for a bit," Izzy said, while nuzzling her little buddy up against her cheek. The ambient energy from her BrightEyes friend made loose strands of hair stand up from static electricity, and I had to laugh at the sight.

"Don't worry, you can come back and visit any time!" Rae assured her.

I gave my cousin a hug. "And just give me some time to make sure these little guys can adapt okay to our world, and then maybe they can even come down and visit you out there in California some time." I had hated being away from Phoebe while I was out in New York, and I understood how hard it would be for Izzy to have to leave Ellie here with us. And since all of the preliminary evidence from our arboretum was that the BrightEyes were going to fit right in just fine here on our world—or here in our dimension, or whatever—I was fairly confident that we'd be able to let them out of Tahoe quarantine before too long.

#

A few days later, Noah and Levi showed up on our door-step. They had stayed behind in the Big Apple—New York City—for a while in order to keep an eye on both of the Null siblings, but from what I could tell, both Colin and Nessa had decided that 'out of sight, out of mind' would be a good strategy for the time being.

"...although, that's just on the surface," I muttered. The four of us were sitting around on the arboretum deck, eating pizza and playing with the whole flock of BrightEyes. "Because Colin still has all the data that he stole from us. With all of that technological information, all the nitty-gritty specs, it won't take him long to build his own portal and to gain access to some other location in the OtherWorld. We managed to retain our public claim to the research, but that won't stop him from exploiting the discovery in some less-public-more-underhanded way."

Levi cleared his throat. "Uh-hum. I, uh, actually don't think that will be a problem. At least not for the immediate future." The rest of us all stared at him. He blushed, looked sheepish and ran his hair through his crewcut.

"What gives, Bro? Are you privy to information that the rest of us don't have? And if so, just *what* is that said something and *how* do you know that said something?"

"Well…" Levi all of a sudden seemed very interested in the fingernails of one of his hands, while he rubbed the back of his neck with the other hand. "You see, it's like this. Nessa—"

"Nessa!?" I squawked.

Rae shushed me and said, "Wait, let him finish." But she didn't look overjoyed, either.

Levi continued, "Yeah, well, Nessa felt really bad about the way she behaved and all. So when she heard about how Danae had taken control of the audio-visual tech that Colin had actually stolen from Team Rugged Stuff, it gave her an idea, see?"

He looked at us, his incredulous audience, for encouragement to continue his tale. Seeing none, he cringed, cleared his throat again, and continued. "It gave her this idea to launch a seek-and-destroy virus into the Null Corp Computer system. It's some kind of an anti-information software program that her team developed, and she keyed it into the Team Rugged Stuff code signature in his computers. It's kind of like if you do a 'Find-and-Replace' command in a text document on a word processor, but instead of finding and changing a particular word, this program finds all of the code and info that originally came from *your* computers, the Team Rugged Stuff computers, and changes it into gibberish."

Noah: "She can do that?"

Rae: "I believe she *can* do that, the question is, *will* she do that?"

Me: "YOU TOLD HER ABOUT MY BACKDOOR INTO THE AV SOFTWARE!?"

"Yeah. Yeah. And yeah," he answered. "First off, she's really smart. Secondly, she really did feel bad about taking us on a wild-goose chase, and she wanted to make it up to us, to do something to show us how much she regrets not being straight with us. And thirdly, well, yeah, sorry about that, Danae. But she didn't seem shocked. In fact, she said she would have been surprised if you *hadn't* built a secret way into your own code, because you are just so good of a programmer."

"Hmmm," I replied. "Okay, then." They say flattery will get you nowhere, but I'm here to tell you that it works on me.

"Wait. A. Minute. Levi." Rae frowned. "Just exactly *when* did reformed and regretful Nessa Null tell you all of this?"

A couple of minutes earlier, I would have bet that Levi couldn't get any more embarrassed than he already was. But the next few seconds proved that I would have been wrong. "Ah. Well. Um."

"WAIT. A. MINUTE. LEVI!" Noah shouted, sounding scandalized. "You—you—you kept your burger date with her, didn't you!?"

"Ah. Well. Um. Yeah. She texted me with a message that she had something important to tell me, and you know, I was getting pretty hungry, and well, come on Noah, it was a date with *Nessa*..."

Noah looked outraged. Then he seemed to think about it. Finally, he just shrugged. "Fair enough. I would probably have kept that date, too."

"NOAH!" Rae and I both shouted with disgust. I rolled my eyes and said to Rae, "You know, Big Sis, not a day goes by that I'm not thankful that I'm not a boy."

"You've got *that* right," she replied. "But getting back to the subject at hand, I guess it *would* be nice to think that her virus really did wipe our info from Colin's system. If it's true. I mean, she *has* lied to us before."

I agreed. Replying to Rae's comment—but looking at the cousins just to make sure they got the point—I said, "Hmmm, yes. Yes, she *has* lied to us before. And when was that? Let's see, oh yes, it was... JUST THREE DAYS AGO!"

"So, fellows." Rae gave them a stern look. "How can we know that this isn't just some new fib from your *femme fatale*?" The 'fellows' didn't seem to have an answer; they just looked at one another and shrugged again.

But then, as if on cue, Rae's phone beeped, with Mike Kane's name showing up on the caller identification screen. "I can't believe I'm doing this, but I wonder what in the world he has to say!" Rae punched the answer button and put him on speaker phone. "Well hello, Mike. We all, that is, my sister and our cousins and I, were just sitting around chatting about what a fine, upstanding, dependable kind of guy you *aren't*."

A worried voice came from the phone speaker. "Rachel? Danae? It's, it's me, Michael. Mike Kane..."

"Hello, Mike-Fink!" I called from across the deck. "If you're calling to ask for a reference for your résumé, you can forget about it!"

"No, no, it's not that." He sounded so stressed out that our jibes didn't even seem to register to him. "It's just that—I don't know how you did it, really, ah, really very clever of you, but now that you've managed to erase the data pertaining to the OtherWorld project from Colin Null's computer system, he's convinced that I had something to do with it. He's really, ah, really very furious with me, especially after the fiasco with the press conference." He gulped, and his mouth sounded very dry indeed. "I know that I can't expect any, well, favors from you," ("You think?" I grumbled, and Rae shushed me yet again.) "but in light of all of the years that I worked for you and your, um, family, would you just do me the tiny favor of letting Null know that it was *you* who wiped the data? Could you just let him know that it was, ahem, *you* and *not me*?" His plea ended with a desperate sounding whine. "For...for old time's sake?"

Oh. Oh! This was just *too* good! I called out to him, "Aha, Mike, how about that!? But you've got it all wrong! It was—"... I was going to say, "It was Nessa," but I cut it off short, because Rae was waving her hands at me in a big, 'No, no, no, shut up!' gesture. I stopped talking and let her address him.

"Mike. I will swear to you here and now that neither Danae nor myself, nor Noah nor Levi, took any action to wipe any data in Colin's system. That is the honest truth. Telling you this truth is the last and only favor that I will grant in memory of all our years together and all you did for us before you became a traitor. In other words, you're on your own from here on out." And she pressed the disconnect button.

Levi grinned like a big goofball. "Well, there you have it! Proof that Nessa was being honest about the virus that she put into Colin's computer system after all!"

Rae scowled toward him. "Yeah, I guess so. But don't expect us to send her a thank-you card or anything. I'll probably end up forgiving her for her double-cross. Someday. But not today."

"Not today and not for a long time to come," I added.

"Yeah, yeah, she understands that. She even said she thought there would need to be a cooling-off period." Levi started sounding a little bit like his normal self. "But she also said to tell you that her virus only erases the data in the system. Now that he knows about the OtherWorld and now that he knows about the portal technology and because he has records of what kind of gear and equipment the project used, he'll be working to replicate the info on his own. Anything he develops from scratch won't have the Team Rugged Stuff meta-data and tag-markers embedded in the code, and so the virus won't attack it. She said to tell you that she figures he can have your research completely duplicated in about 12-18 months. That's a year, or year and a half, tops."

I did some quick calculations in my head, thinking about what all had gone into the project. "That...sounds about right. If I had the general outline, but not the actual data, I could probably reconstruct the files in about a year."

Rae got that serious look on her face again. "That means we have that much time to figure out a way to save and protect the OtherWorld. We had better get busy and make use of it!"

DANAE'S LOG: Epilogue (Tune in Next Time)

It was a few months later that I received an encrypted email from Nessa, addressed to me and Rae. I was tempted to delete it without opening it, but curiosity got the better of me.

The message was simple and it came with an MP4 file attached.

"What do you think, R? Do I open the file, or is it a trick for her to plant a virus into our system?"

Rae grimaced. "I hate to say it, D, but I think that if she wanted to insert some malevolent program into our computers, there's nothing we could do that would stop her. Might as well open the video file and find out what it is that she thinks we should see."

I transferred my screen onto the large smartboard in the wall of our office and clicked the 'play' icon. From what I could tell, we were looking at the inside of another lab. In the center of the room were two squarish platforms set side by side, with what looked like a metal mushroom on one side and a computer station on the other. I glanced at my sis. "Uh oh."

She glanced back at me. "Yup. Uh oh. That looks suspiciously similar to our OtherWorld platform."

The video played and nothing happened for a few seconds. Then a big ball of blinding white light popped into sight on the platform. When it disappeared, it left in its place a lone figure in a environment suit, holding a carpet bag in one hand. The figure used his free hand to remove his helmet...me and my sis both groaned.

Me: "Awwwwgh."

Rae: "Ghwwwwa."

You probably already guessed it, the person standing there was none other than Colin Null himself. Dropping his helmet to the floor, he hopped off the platform and walked to one of the long lab tables. Setting the satchel flat on the surface in front of him, he unclicked the clasps and opened it up. The look on his face was one of greed and anticipation.

Almost immediately, three BrightEyes floated out of the bag and began to float lazily around our enemy's head and shoulders.

Rae reached her hand down to my keyboard and hit the 'pause' button. "Danae? Are you seeing what I'm seeing?"

"Yeah, Rachel. But... something seems to be a little... off... or am I imagining it?"

"No, you're not imagining it. Those aren't the BrightEyes we know and love."

I tapped on the keyboard and zoomed in on the three creatures floating around Colin. Instead of bright, vibrant colors, their skin/hide/fur and tails seemed to be more of a matte texture, almost as if they were absorbing the light and colors in the room, soaking it up and giving nothing back. But that wasn't the worst of it. "Rachel! Those *eyes*!"

"I know." Her reply was hushed. Worried.

Our BrightEyes companions all had friendly eyes that shone and glowed with bright cheery colors. (Hence the name, right?) But the BrightEyes that we saw on the screen, the BrightEyes that had apparently befriended Colin, their eyes were black, black, black. They looked as if they were windows into the heart of a black hole, someplace where no light or warmth could ever exist.

I pressed the 'play' button again, and we watched as the three hovering creatures settled on Colin's shoulders, two on one side and one on the other. "Ah, my wee little beasties," Colin cooed to them, "you are just the beginning of my revenge on Team Rugged Stuff. You are just the beginning of the downfall and demise of their hopes and dreams." He cocked his head, as if he liked the sound of that phrase. "Demise. Yes."

Colin plucked one of them from his shoulder, held it up to his face and stared into its cold, black eyes. "Demise. Or as you shall now be known... DimEyes!"

With that, the tape faded to black.

Acknowledgements

So much goes into a book like this one and there are so many people to thank.

Let's begin with a shout-out to all my friends and family on the Flathead Reservation and around Northwest Montana. A big thank-you to the town library and the school libraries in the community of St. Ignatius (or Mission, as it's often called by those of us in this neck of the woods). Although the libraries are consolidated now, it was a different story back in the day, and I'm also grateful to my school teachers who used to let me take time off from class to walk into town to use the public library. Sincere thanks to Naomi Billedeaux, who served as Salish Language Consultant for the book; any problems with the Salish included here are strictly due to errors on my part.

And let's continue with the debt of gratitude owed friends and family on the Jewish side of things, from Israel to New York, from New England to Tahoe, and all the places in between. Thanks also to the members of the Sunday Writing Group formed by the Jewish Book Council as an offshoot of the 2023 Jewish Writers' Conference and to the online Jewish Science Fiction and Fantasy Writers group.

Any problems with the Yiddish presented in this book are entirely errors on the part of the author.

A nod of appreciation to the Fleischmann Planetarium and Science Center at UNR in Reno, Nevada. Without the Widmanstätten-pattern meteorite on display there, Team Rugged Stuff might never have developed their portal to the OtherWorld.

Enormous thanks to the fantastic and legendary Prentis Rollins. Go visit his site at prentisrollinsart.com right now!

Thank you to all the Rugg family who provided the ideas and inspiration for the OtherWorld. (And who let me borrow their name for the story!)

Finally, sincere and heartfelt thanks to the folks at Tree-Lion Press. They encouraged me, they supported me, and they allowed me to write the book that I wanted to read.

-S.R., July 2024-

About the Author

Sage Rooker enjoys coding and tech and puns and the wilderness and the city and breaking barriers and breaking stereotypes and gaming and running and cooking and drawing and writing and cats and dogs and horses and dragons and ice cream. Lots and lots of ice cream.

www.ingramcontent.com/pod-product-compliance
Lightning Source LLC
Chambersburg PA
CBHW031139160726

47991CB00004B/1490